I0552126

THE HANDS OF THYME

H. D. HUDDLE

This is a work of fiction. Names, characters, places, and incidents are products of the author's imagination or are used fictitiously and are not to be construed as real. Any resemblance to actual events, locations, organizations, or persons, living or dead, is entirely coincidental.

World Castle Publishing, LLC
Pensacola, Florida
Copyright © H. D. Huddle 2018
Paperback ISBN: 9781949812015
eBook ISBN: 9781949812022
First Edition World Castle Publishing, LLC, October 15, 2018
http://www.worldcastlepublishing.com
Licensing Notes
Cover: Karen Fuller
Editor: Maxine Bringenberg

Table of Contents

CHAPTER 1

Slow and steady footsteps echoed eerily down a long, white corridor. The sound of a ticking clock seemed to thunder like a heartbeat from somewhere up ahead in the darkness. A woman, terrified but curious, walked slowly through the empty hall, unable to see much past her own two feet in the dim lighting. Doors to rooms that lined the walls to her left and right were dark as well, with no signs of life beyond them. Her voice cried out to see if anyone else was around, though the molasses-thick silence that returned confirmed her suspicion that no one was there. At the far end of the hallway came the audible click as a light switched on, but the sound was empty and hollow. It was an overhead lamp, swinging back and forth slowly from the ceiling. No one could be seen, but someone had to have pulled the string to the switch; lights did not turn themselves on. Ahead of her another light, further up from the first one, switched on and light now sliced through the darkness like a razor, revealing what appeared to be a hospital ward.

"Hello? Please, is…is anyone there? M-my name is Margaret. Hello?" her voice called out shakily. No reply, only the slight squeaking as the overhead lamp swung in the empty void ahead of her. As the light slowed, the squeaking noise lessened, leaving the hallway once more in a dreadful silence, except for the ticking sound coming from a clock.

As she stood looking around the place, it occurred to Margaret that she had no idea how she'd even gotten here, or where here was. A mild sense of panic began to swell within her gut—could she be dreaming this? No, she was sure she was very much awake and perfectly aware of the events happening around her. Yes, but what day was it? What was the current time? She could not seem to remember. There was the clock that hung on the dingy white wall in front of her, but it appeared to be stopped, which told her nothing. But why, then, did she distinctly hear the sound of time ticking? There had to be another time piece around out of sight.

Intently she watched through the dim light for signs of anyone moving around, though almost everything now was motionless, including her own shadow. As Margaret continued to peer through the darkness, she noticed a young woman, appearing out of thin air, standing at the end of the hallway on the far side of the nurses' station. She wore a white hospital gown, no shoes, and remained silent, head hung down so Margaret could not see her face. Margaret dared not step closer, but as she stood and stared, the young girl began to walk slowly down the hallway underneath the swinging lights, though no footsteps echoed within the deserted ward.

"Who are you? Is anyone else here with you? Are you a patient here?" Margaret asked, curious but nervous.

No voice responded to answer her questions. The figure of the young woman continued to shuffle quietly down the hallway, keeping her head down. Strands of long, golden hair flowed downward, hiding her face away from Margaret's view. Though it was such a grim, sterile place, the young woman's hair glowed richly with an unearthly hue and warmth; the angelic look of this young girl was so very out of place and unsettling. Margaret considered approaching, but found she was unable to move forward.

As the girl walked on, the sound of splintering glass and metal scraping became audible to Margaret, and crimson streaks remained on the floor where the young woman had just stepped. There upon the hospital floor, broken medicine vials and syringes cracked as the weight of the young female crushed the broken glass beneath her bare feet. Needles from the syringes punctured the flesh of the girl's naked feet, drawing forth fat, perfect droplets of scarlet blood.

"No! Stop! Get away from there! Can't you feel your feet? They're being cut and jabbed by those dangerous things! Please, come away from there!" Margaret called out, a tone of urgency leaking outward with every word.

The young girl ignored the emergent request and continued her path beneath the suspended lights. A strong sense in Margaret's gut told her that she was somehow supposed to catch the attention of this young woman, and she tried once again to call out. In her moment of awkward emotion, she stepped forward, her arms outstretched, physically trying to extend her plea to the hospital-gowned girl.

"I promise, I won't hurt you! But you're injured…please stop, I may be able to help you!" Margaret called out into the darkness. The young girl stopped this time, directly underneath one of the lights hanging from the ceiling. She remained motionless, head down and hair still hiding her face. Margaret could see that she was a mere child. Pale skin was visible where the white hospital gown did not cover. Margaret placed the child at around ten years of age, but could not quite see enough of the girl's face to know for sure. Stunned by the girl's unexpected compliance, Margaret was momentarily taken aback and studied the girl with curious eyes.

"What's your name? Can I help somehow?" Margaret called, not taking her eyes from the girl. As Margaret looked her over, she felt a great sense of sympathy for her. How terrible it must be for a patient to be so young, and furthermore to be in an eerie place like this, Margaret thought to herself.

The young, nameless girl sucked in a breath and raised her head slowly. She paused, taking yet another breath before turning her head. Under the dim light shining down from above like a glow from heaven, the young girl smiled as she began to look towards Margaret, revealing pallid features that remained beautiful and innocent for the moment. As the girl continued to smile at Margaret, clear, blue eyes blinked and held a curiosity that Margaret knew all too well.

But the serene, innocent child-like expression was quickly replaced by terror. Suddenly, from behind Margaret, the sound of wheels creaking began at the end of the hall where she'd just come from. As she turned her head to look behind her she saw nothing, though she thought perhaps an orderly was wheeling someone in a chair into the ward. The thought that this could be a chance to ask someone where she was occurred. The sound of panic drenched the breath caught in the chest of the golden-haired young girl, making Margaret switch her attention back to her.

"What is the matter? Is there someone else here? I-I don't see anything," Margaret said, trying to figure out what caused the look of horror to cross the young girl's face.

"He's coming...," the young girl whispered before she released her breath. She continued to look past her, peering at something that Margaret could not see.

Margaret's head snapped back toward the sound of the creaking, but she still failed to see anything. The young girl began to sob, and Margaret looked in her direction; she felt caught between watching through the dim lighting for an unseen force and running to the aid of a frightened child. As the young girl sobbed quietly, Margaret noticed her clear, salty tears began to change. From red-rimmed azure eyes streamed dark red streaks of bloody tears that stained the white flesh of the girl's face. Startled, Margaret jumped, and the image of the child in the white hospital gown simply blinked out of sight. Margaret's eyes darted quickly about the hospital ward, but the young girl was simply no longer there. Everything was clean, and no broken glass or bloody footprints dotted the floor underneath the hanging lights.

Again, the sound of wheels creaking met her weary ears, and reminded Margaret of the blonde-haired patient's words. A dreary sense of loneliness met her probing eyes as she searched for the source of the sound. A sudden cold chill washed over her from nowhere, and a shadow cast out around the corner at the far end of the hallway behind her as an empty gurney turned toward her. Slowly the metal hospital cot wheeled down the hallway toward the woman, but no one was pushing it from behind. The creaking sound grew louder and louder as the skinny hospital bed rolled ominously closer. Ripples of fear flowed in waves over her body as a deep sensation of dread accompanied the mysterious gurney. As more and more lights switched on overhead, forming a line down the center of the hallway, more light was shed on her surroundings, though they remained somewhat grim, the bulbs themselves dirty with the ash of days long past.

"Come on, quit kidding around! Is somebody in here?!" she called out, her voice squeaking in a raspy prelude to panic. At first nothing met her anxious question, but after a few seconds a tired, heavy sigh sounded from the direction of the nurses' station. "H-hello? Please, can you tell me what this place is?" asked Margaret, walking quickly to the desk, but she found it deserted.

Though no one appeared in front of her, a weary voice moaned a single word response.

"Purgatory."

The voice was ethereal and hollow, and resonated from all

about the hospital ward. Through the distortion of the voice, she could not tell whether it had been that of a man or woman, though a detail of that sort would not matter much in a time or place like this.

"W-why would you say that?!" Margaret asked, astonished as she frantically looked around for the source of the voice. As she spun around, she noticed the gurney was no longer empty. A suspicious, body-shaped form covered in a white shroud now lay upon the unstable stretcher. A hand flew up over her mouth to muffle the scream that was crawling from her spastic lungs up into her throat. Startled, Margaret took a step back, and though she could feel her legs go through the motions of stepping backwards, instead found her body moving forward toward the gurney.

"No, no, no! I do not want to see! I don't want to know!" she muttered, shaking her head. But her body betrayed her, and she watched in sheer horror as her hand reached out to touch the pressed fabric. The very moment her fingers made contact with the white linen cloth that covered the body, a spot of dark fluid began to soak through the fresh, white sheet. The body began to hemorrhage from beneath, the blood stain quickly turning from a small spot on the stark white cloth to being completely blood-soaked. The sound of liquid dripping onto the tile floor echoed in the emptiness of the deserted hallway in a thick, sickening fluid spatter.

Finally, her relentless curiosity to uncover what lay beneath that bloody, white veil took over, and she reached out with slender but nervous fingers. Her body and hands quaked with fear as her ivory flesh touched the blood-soaked sheet. Shaking almost violently now with anxious apprehension, she ripped the cloth back, partially revealing the corpse underneath. Finding the face of the cadaver in an advanced state of decay, Margaret did not recognize the person lying before her. The withered, leathery gray-brown skin had shrunken so tightly against the skull, it distorted the shape of the eyes, pushed the nose flat over empty nostrils, and left the lips cracked and curled inward, partially covering time-yellowed teeth. This could not possibly be even a remote shadow of what they had been in life. The grayish-brown discoloration of the body's skin gave the corpse a very unnatural appearance. Margaret tried to look past the decay, but found nothing else besides a few handfuls of yellow-white locks of scraggly hair that had begun to fall from the rotted flesh of the scalp.

The longer Margaret remained hovered around the body, the more noticeable an overwhelming stench became, and it grew stronger with every second that ticked by. The dead body began to swell before her very eyes, and as she pulled the sheet down further to reveal the torso, the source of the horrific odor became evident. Rolls of drooping flesh hung motionless from across both sides of the stomach, which had ruptured. Intestinal contents had spilled upward, filling the abdomen with a mix of gases and inky fluids that were attempting to leak out.

As the unspeakable stench escaped from inside portions of the corpse that remained exposed, the threat of vomiting grew immensely from deep within Margaret's stomach. Her brain was unable to process much more, and she closed her eyes for a moment to try and push back the thousand gruesome thoughts that stabbed at her mind like tiny swords of fear.

When she opened her eyes once more, she found herself sitting in a darkened room at a round, stone table with three other people. Quiet whispers rose up the moment her arrival was noticed. Multiple voices spoke at once, though she could not discern what was being said as the voices spoke over each other. Margaret's head began to spin; thus far the events that had transpired made her feel dizzy. She stared at the dark table, trying to figure out exactly what was going on. In this sleepy realm nothing made sense to her, and even though she tried to focus, the idea of making sense of these things seemed impossible. Perhaps she was not meant to figure things out just yet. As her eyes adjusted to the darkness, she became aware of another chair that was empty. An inexplicable sensation emanated from it; pulsing with energy, the chair was actively awaiting the arrival of another. She looked around, surveying her surroundings, but she failed to see anything more in the shadows.

The table appeared to be made of a dark, polished stone that felt cold under her warm, sweaty palms, and it sent a shiver down her spine. But as she focused on those present with her, she knew this chill was from something more ghoulish than just the cold stone. A mysterious sense of unbridled curiosity tainted her blood stream, sending mixed emotions of fascination and absolute terror coursing through her like hot electricity. Those present were her mother, great-grandmother, and great-great grandmother. Under normal circumstances, this would have been a welcomed gathering, but the truth haunted her even as she sat among them. It was quite the misfortune that those matriarchs, who represented many years' worth of her family history, should all surround her, as she was the only one currently left among the living. Fantastic, unbelievable, and terrifying, a thought struck Margaret's mind—what if sitting at this table meant death was on the way for her as well, or perhaps that her death had already occurred?

Margaret's mind lingered on this possibility a moment as she considered how much death had always been a part of her life as she'd watched family members die off throughout the years. But she found her blood running as cold as it did with her very first encounter with viewing a deceased relative. Everything around her felt so strange, so impossible, and her mind could not settle on a realistic explanation. This was no mere encounter with a restless spirit roaming the halls of a lonely house, or wandering about the thick gray dreariness of a cemetery; Margaret's spirit was filled with a frigid sense of doom that made her feel a weight in her body, crushing like a ton of bricks upon her chest. As she pondered why she'd been brought here before this table, the whispering voices continued; an intense sensation that the room was going to fall away from underneath her feet washed over her. An impending sense of despair spread through Margaret's body, making her insides shiver from the death-like cold. The whispering voices of her deceased family members quieted down, giving pause for her to reply. A moment of eerie silence bounced off unseen walls and back to Margaret's uneasy ears; her breath was so shallow, she was not sure if she was even breathing. She tried hard to figure out what was going on around her. Slowly, her curiosity replaced the anxiety that stirred within her guts like a swirl of serpents writhing about, and she attempted to speak.

The three late family members appeared as they would in their graves. The death-faces they wore matched the length of time each had been deceased. Discovering that Margaret could hear them, a blur of whispers rose up from the "living" corpses once again, each overlapping the other and making it impossible to decipher what was being said, or by whom.

"Wait! I can't—I can't understand you. What are you saying? What do you mean?" Margaret said, panic setting in again as a tremendous sensation of grief and dread washed over her. Though the corpses were right across from her, their voices seemed so distant and woeful that she felt an unspeakable pity for them. She tried closing her eyes, tried blocking out the horror, tried to imagine each corpse being restored in her mind to her former living self. This proved difficult, as the memory of each person was based largely upon photographs she'd seen as a child.

Another heartbeat passed, and it became clear that time itself had slowed down, allowing her mind to focus in an unnatural way. Though the sound of voices seemed to be real enough,

Margaret could see no mouths moving. Their communication was on a psychic level rather than a physical one, but Margaret hadn't the slightest clue how to respond. She desperately wanted to better understand the psychic abilities that drifted throughout her mind but could not seem to grasp how they had come to be within her in the first place. No matter how deeply rooted her affinity for the occult life, there were many things still unanswered. As her shattered mind pondered the depths of the dark wonders around her, three distinct voices became clear and spoke individually. Collectively, the three voices rapidly asked a multitude of questions, but because she was able to focus, she began to discern one from another, answering each question nearly as quickly as it had been asked.

Why am I dead? the first mother asked in a thin ethereal voice.

How long have I been dead? the voices of all three mothers asked in a mournful tone.

Are you dead? the questions continued from the third mother.

When did you die? the first mother questioned, her voice fading in and out.

Why did you come here? Did you come here to join us? the second mother asked; the voice was of Margaret's mother, Mary.

Where am I? the third mother asked. Due to the decay her expression held a look of confusion, having not expected to exist again, let alone as a rotting specter.

"Yes! You are dead...all of you! Why are you all here? I always wanted to meet you...to talk to you. Eva, you have been dead seventy years now. Mary — my mother Mary — why did you leave me? You have been dead thirty-eight years. Ruth, you have been dead twenty-eight years. I want to see you, to know you as you were...but this isn't right! We should not be here together like this. I — I'm not dead. I'm not dead...right?" Margaret said, nearing a level of frustration that was as odd to experience as the sights in front of her. But exactly who was it that had crossed into the other's world? Were the three dead mothers in her realm, or was she in theirs?

Where are we? the three mothers asked as one, their voices suddenly coming together in a loud, ethereal, bone-chilling tone.

"Purgatory." Margaret answered based on the answer she'd been given moments earlier, though her voice now sounded ethereal and distant; she felt it belonged to someone else.

She felt large, heavy wet drops fall upon her head, and as she raised her eyes everything went black again. Her mind had wandered into a state of fogginess, and the frightened woman realized she now stood in an eerie cemetery, darkened by nightfall. The feeling of cold stone under her warm palms that had only moments before been caused by a table was now caused by a black granite grave marker; the icy sensation was enough to help release her from the grogginess. She stood in a small interment lot in the side yard of a rural country church, and though it was vaguely familiar, she was sure she had never been there before. Rain poured in torrents down over her as a thunderstorm raged.

Blinking as drops of the water trickled over her eyes like tears from the sky, the woman peered through the solid darkness to reveal a name upon the headstone. Margaret felt a dizzy sensation begin to whirl around at the back of her skull. She was quite familiar with this feeling, and knew it to be what she called her "third eye opening." This sensation at the back of her head always tended to supersede reality anytime she felt it, and she had learned over the years to stop what she was doing and pay attention to it. She was used to listening to her gut about certain things, though she could not explain where this extra sense came from; yet another reason for her interest in the occult. Even though Margaret knew what was happening to her at that instant, she also knew bad news was on the way, and her premonition with the grave marker and the cemetery was about to become truth.

Margaret stood at the grave stone, trying to focus through

the hollow darkness so she could read the name carved in the granite.

Lucille.

A telephone began to ring in the distance, and at first, she ignored the sound. Was this the name of a person who was going to die or who was already dead? What was the second name on the tombstone? Margaret tried hard to focus and read the next letters etched in the stone.

Ord….

The sound of the telephone grew louder and closer and, startled, she awoke to the sound of her telephone ringing in the house. Sometimes she wished they did not have a telephone, but since the telephone company had made it available some four years before in 1907, it was nice to be able to speak to out of touch relatives long distance. She blearily got out of bed, the last remains of that deep sleep sensation lingering as she fumbled to put on her housecoat and staggered out the bedroom door. After such an intense dream, she thought it best to investigate even though the phone had stopped ringing. As she shuffled wearily toward the kitchen, she couldn't help but notice that rain was still pouring outside like it had for the last week there in Missouri.

As she rounded the corner and stepped into the kitchen, she was met by her husband, Henry. He turned towards her slowly as he hung up the phone, looking at his wife with fallen eyes and a furrowed brow.

"Henry…what is it? You look like somebody just died," she commented, noticing his pallor.

"Margaret…." He only called her that when he something very serious had happened.

"Aunt Lucille…" Margaret sobbed breathlessly; the dream having given her the knowledge of what had happened.

***

"Yes…she died this morning. How did you—?" Henry

stopped his question. Did it really matter how she knew? "The funeral is in a few days," Henry explained, embracing his wife. He knew how much her Aunt Ordiki meant to her, and could see that Margaret was utterly distraught. "Go pack—I'll make arrangements to get you down to Louisiana."

CHAPTER 2

A terrible thunderstorm rocked the rural area around New Orleans. Harsh winds blew, howling like a dark creature longing to escape from some unearthly tomb. The gusts shuddered across the grounds of an old plantation, shaking the very foundation of the Ordiki Estate, while wicked purple lightning crackled across the sky like tiny forks of pure evil lashing out from some unseen hell.

Lucille Ordiki had been the widow of a locally famous cotton plantation owner and had inherited a great deal of wealth over the many years the plantation was in operation. Inside the overly lavish Ordiki house, which stood three stories high and was just as starkly white as the day it was built, family members and close friends of Lucille gathered, their faces grim with the toll of weariness. Of course, when sitting up with the dead, such looks were bound to arise in even the most steadfast of hosts. Soft voices wrapped in dark clothing whispered stories of days gone by, and while some remembered good naturedly, others cried, in heavy grieving for their loss.

Summertime in the deep, humid south bore an ungodly steamy atmosphere, permeated with mystery in the swamps of New Orleans. While unfortunate times had fallen upon the

Ordiki Estate, dark eyes waded through the sea of greedy family members, watching for the one who deserved everything.

It was during this particular gathering to mourn and celebrate the memory of the last member of the Ordiki name that Mr. Arnold Flatts, butler of the house and family friend, thought it best to unveil the strange and enchanting heirloom, as per the late Mrs. Ordiki's wishes. Though he did not wish to do so openly, because he knew giving away anything in a house full of gold-diggers would cause a stir, he had a limited time to pass along the treasure before his time at the Ordiki Estate would end. Mr. Flatts did not want any part of the bickering that he was sure would inevitably take place among the many assorted guests in the house overnight; he simply wanted to finish his task and walk away unnoticed.

As Mr. Flatts made his way through the house he tried to bypass as many guests as possible, though he had to cross some main portions of the house to do so. Having to take a detour from one of the larger sitting rooms, he decided to cross the outer bounds of the family room. It was unfortunate that nearly every inch of the great plantation house seemed to be filled with money-grubbing descendants—the family room alone harbored two plush sofas, each wide enough to seat at least five people. Their rich brown coloring blended well with the additional pieces of real wood furniture that had been placed there by Lucille herself decades ago. The scent of fresh linen from the newly pressed drapes and furniture polish wafted about the air.

As he passed through, Mr. Flatts was saddened by the thought of leaving all of these sights and scents that he'd known for so long behind. In the large family room just off the main staircase in the east wing, Mr. Flatts gracefully weaved his way through the mob of dark-dressed acquaintances toward the attached miniature greenhouse. The rich maple stains on the wooden base of an emerald velvet-cushioned ottoman complemented the shelves and picture frames which dotted the walls inside the family room. Each shelf contained some collectible animal or knickknack that Lucille had been given as gifts throughout her life, and it was truly heartbreaking that empty spaces were already being noticed before the wake was even over with. Portraits of Lucille's long deceased kinfolk graced the company that visited with wry smiles and hardened eyes that peered hauntingly out in varying shades of sepia. As people mingled and wandered about in grief, the portraits of people from days long ago also cast a mournful stare in Lucille's direction, though none among the living noticed. The other rooms in the house were furnished in nearly this same fashion, as the Ordiki family, while very wealthy, had wished to maintain their passion for a more humbled look. Mr. Flatts had not witnessed much change in the furnishings of the home in his time of servitude and had grown accustomed to a less ritzy display than some of the other wealthy families felt the need to flaunt.

As the butler crossed this crowded room, he was finally successful in reaching the door to the "flower shack," as he called it. Once inside the door, a natural freshness awaited his senses as he stepped out of the house and into the indoor-outdoor area. Lush green plants thrived as they would in the middle of a jungle forest, while brilliant exotic flowers in pots lined the many, many rows built to contain them. Colors splashed out like the paints used on an abstract portrait. The scent of fresh, rich earth drifted about the air, though at the time of a wake, the smell could easily remind one of a newly-dug grave. Here, tea roses in various hues of burgundy, red, and pink spiraled around wide, white cement posts that guarded the entrance to the greenhouse area. Chrysanthemums, petunias, and carnations bloomed fully in many colors among the variety of green ferns and foliage that shared the space in this many-windowed room. The aroma of the flowers should have been quite pleasing as the light scents

20

floated about the arboretum, but again only the thought of peace lilies lining the altar by an open casket came to mind.

Earlier in the evening Mr. Flatts, who had been Miss Ordiki's faithful servant and butler for as long as he could remember, had spotted Margaret chatting with second and third cousins near this inside garden area. He could never forget her; long brown hair that reached to her waist, chestnut eyes flecked with deep amber, and fair skin untainted by freckles or any unsightly blemishes. She had always worn braids that were tied with light colored ribbons as a child, and it was strange to see her all grown up and her hair styled like a true turn-of-the-century woman. Margaret had spent many seemingly endless summers with her aunt, as her mother had died when she was only three, following a sudden and as of yet undefined illness. Her father was unable to afford — both monetarily and mentally — to take proper care of her throughout the entire year, and so Aunt Ordiki had stepped in and offered her the necessary shelter and a more wholesome family life, which a young child deserved. And while Mr. Flatts had spent a great deal of time looking after the girl, it was a sad day when it came time for Margaret to leave for the last time; he remembered it must have been around 1886, or perhaps even the following summer.

Voices of the past echoed throughout the walls of the great house, and Mr. Flatts felt a nagging pang of sorrow knowing that all he'd come to know and love was at an end. He had worked for Ordiki for years, and now that she had passed on, he would likely have to find work elsewhere for another, hopefully kind family. He had hoped that if the estate did not remain in the family, someone new would purchase the property and continue the Ordiki's tradition, including keeping him on as household help, though he'd heard whispers throughout the great house that suggested otherwise. He tried quite hard not to think about it, but he feared what his future could hold. He did not know any other kind of work and had no other skills. But he supposed he would do better to think about it only when or if it became necessary to do so.

Mr. Flatts carried the item under a fine linen cloth, as not to attract any unwanted attention. Lord only knew how difficult a challenge he would have to explain why no other family member was receiving anything special. Once the package was delivered to the new owner, he hadn't a care what came of it. For a very long time Mr. Flatts had loathed knowing of the heirloom's existence. He felt something so extraordinary should not be held in the hands of a mere mortal — but then again, who was he to be judgmental? After all, it was only while in his possession that he needed to be careful with it.

A small group of southern belles quietly fluttered their antebellum-style petticoats away in a whoosh of expensive, colored satin fabrics as Mr. Flatts approached. Though it had been decided that slavery was no longer acceptable and freedom for all had been proclaimed, his kind was still not treated equally or with much dignity. He could feel their unkind stares like pricks of electrical static at the back of his neck even as they walked away, but he had to pretend like he had not noticed, though he could clearly hear their statements.

"It's a shame, the uproar and letting someone like him have rights…." One voice didn't bother to whisper.

"And you know what's worse is that blasted 'holiday' they celebrate…what's it called? June, something?" another voice said loudly, trying to make sure Mr. Flatts could hear.

"Oh yes, that *Juneteenth*-thing. I wonder who ever came up with that silly idea. Celebratin' the end of owning your house staff. Why, it's outrageous, the idea!"

"Well, it's nice to see decent folk taking charge nowadays. I haven't seen many of the large celebrations like we did a decade ago. Seems to me like it's fizzling out for them colored folks. And

I couldn't be happier about it myself," another voice chimed in.

"The next thing you know, one of them'll be runnin' for president. Just you watch!" one of the women sneered.

Mr. Flatts allowed the harsh words to simply roll off his back, for he knew better times were in store for people of his color. He turned his dark face away from the unkind words that dripped from the mouths of the overdressed ninnies. He tried to focus on better thoughts, like his life on Lucille's plantation and the memories that came along for the ride. Servitude in the hands of the Ordiki family had been his only livelihood, and likewise had been for his father before him. Ms. Ordiki, while a good and stern woman to the face of society, had often consulted Mr. Flatts for advice on certain things that were better left alone and forgotten except in some hoodoo witch's lair.

But none the wiser were the deceased's closest family and kin, except for Margaret. And it was not until this night, when death finally came calling for Lucille Ordiki and left things in an uproar, and that same *loving* family and kin began battling for rights to the estate, that certain truths would surface, and a new chapter of the bloodline would begin.

Mr. Arnold Flatts, heirloom securely and discreetly in tote, strolled up and greeted Margaret in the most hospitable fashion, with her eliciting no ill will toward him, as had been the way since he'd known Margaret. A slender woman in her late thirties, Margaret stood in a state of serene contemplation that contrasted with the turmoil during such a time of grief, peering out into the greenhouse, feeling nostalgic as she connected with ghosts from the past. The butler gently caught her distracted attention, but at the very moment he did so, a large clap of thunder erupted; the sound boiled across the face of the angry, gray sky above. Margaret jumped, spilling some of the tea from the cup she held onto her light blue Victorian blouse.

"Oh my! What a mess! Im'a so sorry, Miss Maggie," Mr.

Flatts said to her, genuinely apologetic. He had not intended to startle the lady, merely to break the spell that mesmerized her so he could talk to her.

"Ah, Arnie!" Margaret exclaimed softly. She'd always called him "Arnie," and had never known him by anything different. "You scared the daylights out of me!" Margaret said with a light laugh.

"Forgive me…. Im'a fool," Mr. Flatts suggested, taking the linen and handing it to Margaret so she could dab at the spilled tea. He'd momentarily forgotten it concealed the heirloom.

"Why Arnie, what on earth is that?" Her honey-tinged brown eyes grew wide with curiosity.

In his dark hands Mr. Flatts held a small jewelry chest. A tiny, fragile-looking padlock guarded entrance to the diminutive cherry wood box. Tarnished brass adornments affixed to the wood really gave the box an antique look of mystery and intrigue, and Mr. Flatts held it as gingerly as he would hold the universe in his gentle, work-calloused hands, which trembled slightly. But he attributed it to age — Arnie had not been a young man for decades.

Margaret stared at it a moment, as if dozens of possibilities of the contents ran through her head. Mr. Flatts had always known Margaret to be quite the curious one, interested since early in her life in things that were not widely accepted in society. One more reason she'd gotten along so well with her aunt, he suspected. Margaret had spent many an hour reading the rare and banned books on the occult that were contained in the Ordiki private collection.

The enchanting summers she'd spent running barefoot as a carefree child on the plantation, and the adventures she'd had just on the two hundred acres of land surrounding the great, white house, came flooding back to Mr. Flatts, though he dared not start up that conversation. God only knew how long such a conversation would last between them.

He wanted to deliver the chest to the new owner and free his fearful hands of it for good. In only a moment's pause, as Mr. Flatts watched Margaret study the box inquisitively as a baby would do with something it had never seen before, he realized he was still holding onto it. Margaret was saying that she was sure she had never seen this jewelry chest before, even after having spent so much time in her aunt's house.

"Miss Maggie...dis here be for you. Miss Lucille has held dis chest for you since before you were born," Arnie said, though he had no proof whether or not it was actually true. He'd only said what Lucille had instructed him to say, and he felt obligated to respect her last wishes.

***

With his strange words, Margaret looked at the servant, a touch of sympathy gracing her soul. Now with her Aunt Lucille gone, what would become of Mr. Flatts?

"What do you mean by *before* I was born?" Margaret could not help but ask, though she knew that Mr. Flatts would not know, and she had not really intended for him to answer.

"Well, now, Miss Maggie...dat dere be a story dat, really, only your aunt could explain. Sorry, but it be too late for dat. Unless...." Arnie left off, both further intriguing Margaret as to what he could possibly have meant, and leaving a momentary pause of awkward silence, though he never went back to finish what he was going to say.

"Is there a key to the padlock? Or shall I have to pick it open with one of my hair pins?" Margaret said with a laugh upon closer inspection of the delicate lock.

"Im'a fool. Here...." Mr. Flatts withdrew a tiny brass key on a polished silver chain he wore around his neck. The high, starched collar of his white uniform shirt had hidden the chain conveniently from sight.

25

Mr. Flatts slipped the chain easily up over his silver-haloed head and dangled it out before Margaret. As she reached for it, he pulled it back just out of her reach and looked at her with lines of worry furrowing his brow.

Margaret cocked her head to one side and looked at Mr. Flatts with wonder. He looked at the key, to the chest, then to Margaret. He shook his head and sighed heavily before saying what he wanted, carefully choosing his words.

"What you find, ain' nobody business—just *yours*. Dere be some of de help here dat might point you in th' right direction. If you need help to solve de puzzle within, seek out Madamé Hanté. She be a very special lady...and so are you," Mr. Flatts finally said with a strange pitch to his voice. If Margaret did not know any better, she would say it was the sound of something unsettling boiling its way out of his very soul and out his windpipe.

With that, Mr. Flatts handed her the key and spun gracefully on his heel to walk away. Before she could start to ask any questions, he took the opportunity to disappear into the darker corners of the house as Margaret took a brief moment to remember one of the housekeepers speaking of a rumored swamp witch when she was a kid and wondered if that same housekeeper was possibly still employed there. By the time Margaret snapped out of her moment of intrigue, Mr. Flatts had already disappeared within the mob of grievers. His black butler uniform blended in well with the ebony apparel of those present, and Margaret never managed to locate him the rest of the night.

As the disquieting storm rumbled on outside, Margaret attempted to slip away to one of the corner bedrooms in the west wing of the estate. She had hoped that no one would notice her missing for a little while, as that would certainly strike up a rumor that she was trying to abandon her Aunt Lucille on the night of her wake—or worse yet, conspire in a dark corner of the house to take more than might be bequeathed to her. Margaret made sure no one was looking as she slipped through the door separating the two halves of the large house, closing the door as quietly as possible behind her. She slowly made her way up the wide, spiral staircase, and she was relieved and grateful that even as old as the house was, its upkeep had been perfect. No boards creaked under her cautious steps, and Margaret made it upstairs without incident.

When she reached the top of the stairs, a large, arched window faced the western edge of the acreage. It had been custom designed and lavishly bore the family crest. A large deep, blue-colored shield served as the background of the crest. The foreground was the image of a lowly court jester bowing before royalty with a rose in his hand. To the left of the two figures in the crest was a dove rising out of the flame of a candle. The pieces surrounding the pictures were a mix of brilliant yellow and orange, complementing the azure of the shield. At the very bottom of the window was a small brass plate that was inscribed, In memory of Eva. Margaret sighed softly, wondering what a kind and inspiring person her grandmother must have been to have such a beautiful dedication made to her. Words etched in black glass read, Love before Wealth; quite the breathtaking site to behold. At this weary hour, however, it appeared a bit grim, and the images turned somehow gothic when brilliant flashes of lightning from the storm flickered behind them from beyond the confines of the window.

The long, open hallway spread out before Margaret was lit only by two small electric wall lamps. The entire house was lit one way or another to keep the place as warm and inviting as possible while the family was present, though most of these rooms had not seen occupants in quite some time. The hollow feeling of loneliness pervaded the empty, dim hallway, and Margaret could almost sense some other worldly presence there with her. Laughing to herself, she shook off the strange feeling that followed her as she had made her way past the family portraits hanging on the walls down this upstairs hall. With the feeling of being watched, the eyes of the portraits seemed to move, following Margaret as she walked to her old room with the chest. A creepy sensation tingled down her spine — one that a big old house like this might conjure under the right circumstances.

With a large clap of thunder, the house shook, and the lights threatened to go out, leaving only the option of candles to light the way. Margaret had passed through this same hall earlier in the day when she'd arrived and had chosen a room to stay in for the duration of her visit. It was only natural for her to choose her old room, left pretty much the way she remembered it from years past. Belongings she'd all but forgotten about remained in that room, waiting for the day Margaret would rediscover them. Besides a bit more dust than in those earlier days the room was unchanged. The same thick emerald green drapes hung heavily across the large window of the room. Light pink roses edged in gold still dotted the walls in the room, though portions of the wall paper had begun to lose the grip of the adhesive and puffed outward as it threatened to let go of its hold on the plaster. A large canopy bed, far bigger than any child would ever have required, sat in the same place against the far wall, but centered. A large bureau and mirror set were positioned in the back corner; the condition of the English oak was excellent for the antiques they were.

The light green lace shroud that created the canopy over the bed was still gently tied to either post of the bed with pink ribbons that contrasted with the green color. The ribbons looked quite aged, and had most likely been there a long while before Margaret had ever come to stay there as a child. Ragged toys lay atop the foot of the bed, but Margaret had long since given up that sort of play. A child's brush and comb set lay neatly to one side of the mirror, untouched for ages. Margaret thought it would be quite a nostalgic treat to take them back home with her and pass them on to her children. Margaret had breathed in some of the memories of the room previously in the day, but now she wanted to focus on the heirloom she'd been handed.

Almost as if holding a bomb, Margaret sat down very carefully on the edge of the bed, her hands trembling slightly as she held onto the box. Margaret took the tiny key and slid it gently into the padlock. With a barely audible click the lock popped open and hung freely, waiting for her to remove it. She found herself extraordinarily anxious to open the chest, and yet wary. Why had Mr. Flatts seemed so hesitant about giving away the key to it? And who was Madamé Hanté? Why had Mr. Flatts run off like he did once he'd given her the key? All of this was strange to Margaret, but her curiosity was overpowering, and she was determined to find answers.

Ignoring the angry thunderstorm outside, Margaret placed her hands on either side of the lid to the small chest. In its entirety, the chest could not have been more than six inches across, six inches wide, and six inches deep. The lid curved high, giving more room inside the chest than one would think.

Two bronze faces adorned either side of the lock's loop; one was the face of a woman, the other, the face of a man. The wood of the chest was dulled by time, but in decent condition for as old as the box appeared to be. Margaret slowly lifted the edge of the lid. At first it resisted, not unlike something that had not been opened in quite a while. It was at the same moment that a loud knock thundered upon the door to her room.

Margaret jumped, uncharacteristically engulfed in the moment. Thinking quickly, she frantically grabbed a pillow and shoved the box underneath it; it was deeply disappointing she had not had the chance to open it up. The door creaked open and the familiar face of a cousin appeared around it. With suspicious eyes, the cousin wondered aloud why Margaret was not downstairs with everybody else.

"Well *there* you are! Mah goodness, whatever are you doin' up here?" the overly eccentric southern accent of Susannah pierced the quiet of the room. Margaret instantly missed the serenity that was now broken. Margaret looked quickly up at the slightly older woman, trying to think of a reason as fast as she could; she hated being put on the spot. She was relieved when an idea hit her right away, and she smiled to herself in her mind.

"Oh, not to worry! I was just on my way back down. I just came up to grab my camera. I saved up for it when it first came out back around 1907. It'd be nice to have a few last photos. And with the whole family gathered…well, that's just a once in a lifetime opportunity!" Margaret said, hating the fact she had to come off so phony.

Susannah smiled broadly, her flawless teeth shining white against painted ruby lips. Brilliant gold locks hung in droves along her porcelain face, but somehow her perfect everything seemed phony, which matched her personality quite well.

"Of course! Well, come on down then! We're going to serve some coffee and pie. It's hard ta keep awake durin' these things, I *do* declare!" Susannah said, her tone of voice suspiciously quite warm and inviting.

Margaret figured she would just play along and keep everyone happy until it was time for her to leave for home. She had never really gotten along with some of the other members of the family, but rather had tried to remain neutral all these years. With an inside roll of her eyes, Margaret smiled the best she could, wishing she'd had just a few more minutes alone. Nevertheless, things were going to happen the way they were, and there was nothing she could do about it. Margaret grabbed up the camera and headed down the stairs with Susannah. It was going to be a very long night.

***

The oak grandfather clock downstairs in the great room struck three a.m. Eyes were tear-swollen, red, and looking mighty weary, but the sound of sobs had long since come to an end. For the most part, the family members and friends had settled into groups in various corners and shadows of the great room as the storm continued to rage incessantly outside. Torrents of rain poured down directly from the heavens, also mourning the loss of the lady of the house. Had Lucille been alive, she would have been worrying right now about the rose trellis outside by the flower bed; but dear Lucille was laying in her pine box as still as the grip of death would allow, posed as though sleeping peacefully. Earlier in the evening, some of the female relatives had gotten together and used various shades of a makeup case to paint a false appearance of life on the drying flesh of their deceased loved one. The family had wanted a certain look for the general public at her funeral, and had worked on into the evening to ensure they achieved it. Because the fate of the Ordiki Estate was in the balance, everyone wanted to put forth their best façade in the hopes of snatching up some of the fortune for themselves. The closest cousins and friends had marveled at their own work, which one could be sure would be their conversation starter tomorrow at the funeral; a morbid idea. Margaret only shuddered, sickened by the lack of proper respect for the dead, and pretty much stayed away from the larger groups.

When the groups had broken down as fatigue began to take hold, those who'd really cared for Lucille had their chance to say their quiet goodbyes. They knew once the official funeral began the next day, their chance would fade to nothing as those only after undue pity, attention, and their share of the estate took the spotlight unjustly from Lucille. Margaret, so as not to attract any more unwanted attention, made good on her statement about taking family photos. As she mingled her way through the various family members, she could not help but notice Susannah

31

looking her way a couple of different times. She moved from group to group politely asking for a photograph, careful to save film for final pictures of Lucille. Though Margaret had spent a good portion of her younger life living the old-fashioned ways of the south, she had always been mortified by the photos of the dead that people tended to want for a reason she could never seem to grasp. She was appalled by the thought that her final memory of her loved one would be such a dismal one, but kept this opinion to herself since she knew some of the older family members would definitely want a copy.

Many times in Margaret's childhood, when she had spent carefree days running around on her aunt's plantation, photo albums had been brought out to relive old memories and tell stories of the past. Among the many stiff, cardboard backed photographs, images in shades of off-white and brown were displayed consisting of the living posed with those who had recently passed away; a tradition known as memento mori, and a tradition she frowned upon. Margaret remembered well the sometimes, open-eyed stares of the deceased, and shudders trickled down her spine. Some of the photographs were poorly staged, and if examined closely, the wires and stands used to pose the bodies could clearly be seen. The ones she had the hardest time gazing upon were also the ones that fascinated her the most. Among the various post mortem pictures were photographs of children who had gone from this world. The looks upon some of the faces brought the sting of tears to her eyes; the effect was the same as it had been for the sensitive child she once was.

The evening drifted by and those thoughts brewed ever more intensely in the forefront of her mind. No matter what Margaret chose to keep her mind from swimming in thoughts of the inevitable, she found her mind returning to the dreaded moment repeatedly.

She did her best to stay away from Lucille until she could

no longer put it off. She was down to three pictures of the eight photographs, standard for the 116 size roll of film. As she held the camera in her trembling hands, she nervously rubbed her fingers over the imitation leather that covered the wooden body of the camera. Using extra money earned by sewing quilts, she'd bought it new in June of 1907 when the camera was first released, and had practiced using the reversible reflecting finder to focus and take clear pictures. Now here it was, almost exactly four years later, and the camera that had allowed Margaret the joy of some great memories was about to betray her by capturing one of the most horrifying moments in her life. She felt a knot begin in her stomach as she turned away from the gathered friends and family and faced the pine box upon the long banquet table at the opposite end of the great room. As a couple of people, including Susannah, noticed Margaret cross the room, audible sighs of envy floated about; their hunger to be the one in the spotlight at such a large gathering could not be disguised. Phrases such as "I wish I'd thought of that"' and "Oh, remind me to ask Margaret for a copy of the pictures" circulated about the crowd of mourners. Behind her Margaret heard the comments, but knew she was being watched now and had to go through with this. She kicked herself, wondering why she couldn't just accept this tradition as everyone had, but in her superstitious heart she knew something was not quite right about it.

As she neared Lucille's plain pine box bed, she swallowed down the lump of nervousness forming in her throat. To see such a kind, warm-hearted, and caring woman reduced to spending her final rest in such a cold, unfeeling way was an injustice in itself. As she stepped closer and closer, Margaret wondered if she was going to be able to pull this off after all. From nowhere Margaret found her heart racing so fast she felt it was going to beat right out of her chest. As she raised the camera and focused in on Lucille's corpse, Margaret's breath caught in her chest and she felt lightheaded. Around her the already quiet room went deafeningly still. Flashes of Lucille sitting straight up in her coffin and begging her not to take the photographs flickered before Margaret's nervous eyes.

The room began to grow a deep crimson color, and the sound of a heavy heartbeat thundered in her ears out of nowhere. A bright light flickering like a strobe light began to toy with Margaret's vision. Photograph one was captured forever on film, and as Margaret snapped the second of the three photos, she noticed that Lucille's eyes looked like they were twitching, like during REM sleep. Margaret gasped and peered at her deceased aunt closer through the camera. Frightened but intrigued, she quickly snapped the third photograph, and at that moment an icy cold breeze began to blow through the great room. Margaret wondered if someone had opened a door or window, but she knew better and shivered in the bitter cold of death's presence.

Without warning the image of the jewelry chest with the two brass faced adornments came to her mind. The faces were alive and screeched like a banshee announcing death. The woman's face was contorted mid-scream and her eyes were brimming with terror, while the man's face enjoyed the thrill of the terror of the fires of hell. Margaret looked back, searching for someone to help her, but the family members sat frozen in place. Not only were they completely oblivious that anything was happening around them, but they had been stopped cold—halted in the moments leading up to Margaret's vision. Upon closer inspection of the currently inanimate family members, Margaret found their eyes to be devoid of any emotion or life—they may as well have been dead themselves. Margaret shuddered, wondering why this was happening to her. At first, she thought she was being punished for taking photographs of the deceased, but if that were true, why would the images from the chest come to her frazzled mind?

Margaret looked back at Lucille, and to her shock found

a dark, shadowy being hunched over the body. The thing, whatever it was, looked particularly interested in Lucille's black opal necklace. It held the silver chain between wispy fingers, and Margaret found herself worrying that if the creature could hold onto a solid object, the creature must be solid as well, despite its obvious smoky appearance. It wasn't until the being turned its horrific, eyeless face to her that she felt the intense feeling of dread emanating from it. The terrible stench of decay wafted through the entire room, nearly choking Margaret. Her ears began to ache, and the sound of the screeching increased to a deafening level within her head.

In the midst of the chaos that filled the room now, Margaret noticed the creature was not able to remove the charm from the old woman's body, and that a separate entity was now hovering about the deceased's right side. The dark shadow creature generated a feeling of trepidation so powerful that tears welled in Margaret's eyes. She pictured it as she would picture the figure of death itself—cold, dark, hollow, and quite frightening. The second being, however, was also semi-transparent, but otherwise the complete opposite. A brilliant blue-white light flowed all around a humanoid figure, though distinct features were not apparent. Among the smell of death, a warm freshness wafted throughout, the two scents intermixed as awkwardly as the two beings clashed. With new, however unknown, intentions, the shadow turned its attention to Margaret rather than toward the presence of the lighter apparition. No words leaked outward from the rotting mouth of the dark one, but a message somehow made its way into Margaret's mind. Though the faceless shadow had no eyes with which to stare, she felt the blank darkness peering directly into her soul.

"Take it," the voice beckoned.

Margaret at first could not comprehend what was happening. The middle-aged housewife began to feel a great wave of nausea swell within her gullet, overwhelming at first, but tolerable as the wraith's command began to grow into an intense demand.

"*TAKE IT!*" the voice commanded with an urgent hiss.

In a nearly trance-like state now, Margaret felt deeply compelled to step forward with the intent to remove the black opal from Lucille's corpse. In all the years Margaret had lived with her aunt she'd never seen the black opal, nor could she figure any reason anyone on Earth would be so interested in the costume piece, let alone a monster.

Across the room the other entity, now taking on a more distinct human form, sent forth a feeling of great urgency that Margaret should not make an attempt to further approach the body of the deceased. This lighter presence was in complete contrast to the black shadow. Certain details were not visible, but Margaret could now tell the form was supposed to be female. The shape was growing ever more detailed, but remained illuminated with the mysterious bluish-white light. The increasing scent of flowers and rain blossomed forth upon a warm wind that floated like the breeze off a tropical waterfall. Margaret realized the two creatures were of opposing forces, and the dark one cringed as the other's presence grew stronger.

Torn between taking the charm and keeping clear of the other lighter being, the dark shadow abandoned its interest in the opal and focused its attention solely on Margaret. Now sure that whatever this dark being was knew what it was doing, Margaret's body welled up with a paralyzing fear. Panic gripped her in a way she had never felt before, despite thoughts still tumbling around in her mind to listen to the demands of the shadow. Though aware the other entity obviously served the good side, the evil that was aimed toward her was quite overpowering, and she was fearful of the sensation of weakness she'd felt just moments ago when she'd taken a step closer to Lucille's body.

In an attempt to force the darkness away, Margaret tried

to think the most pure, righteous thoughts she could, but the mere sight of the shadow had her somehow entranced. As the scene within her mind grew more and more grim, she noticed a whirlwind begin to form in the center of the room about her, and surprisingly found herself nearly abandoning all she'd ever known to be consumed by the vortex. It was almost as if something about the wraith was familiar to her, but she did not understand why. To her horror—and strangely, her delight—the corners of her full and sultry pink lips turned upward in an unnatural grin. As the strong, ebony wind swirled about, loose items from all about the place were drawn toward the center of the growing cyclone. The dark cone spun before her as all of the chaos that had brewed within her mind had manifested itself as a physical object. Margaret looked back at the other grievers in the hopes there were other witnesses to the supernatural phenomenon happening in the great room, but found them motionless—all animation remained suspended. The feeling of something scratched at her neck, her nervous fingers reaching, startled, to swat away whatever it was. Shaking, her fingertips felt a deep nausea, discovering she now wore the black opal around her neck. Nearing hysteria, Margaret tried to think of how she could put a stop to whatever this was, but her overwhelmed mind could not organize any thoughts and she came up with nothing. For the moment, her mind had gone completely blank.

The shadow rushed toward her and stopped, hovering just inches from her face. Margaret could feel the creature's rancid breath upon her skin as it blew back the stray hairs around her face; the light stroke of the fine hairs across her bare flesh heightened the insatiable sense of delight as goosebumps boiled their way out of the fine white alabaster it rubbed against. She caught its gaze and looked at it straight where the eyes should have been, but were not.

The death face stared right through her, seeking to steal

her soul as well, but the lighter being charged at the shadow, sending it spinning across the room. It stopped right at the edge of the cyclone that now spun out of control in the center of the great room. Before the shadow of death could make its way back toward Margaret, the lighter half rushed toward it so fast it was just a bluish-white blur to Margaret. As it passed by the scent of the rain and flowers grew stronger, and Margaret was blasted by a gust of warm air that snapped her out of the strange trance she'd fallen into. Margaret shook off the harrowing sensation that had begun to feel like guilt from deep within the pit of her stomach. She shook her head, the thought of doing so intending to shake off the intensity of what was happening around her; without surprise, it had no effect. The blue blur of the angelic being flung itself at the dark shadow and pushed it into the core of the cyclone. The fiend shrieked in defeat, and the cyclone ceased as the figures of both entities disappeared.

In the same instance, Margaret found herself posed over Lucille's body, and the camera read that she had just clicked the last of the three photos. Margaret dropped the camera and sank to her knees, sobbing. The others in the great room resumed their normal activities, some of them rose from their seats and rushed to Margaret's side, while others simply gasped and stared first at the camera as it bounced off the floor, then up at the shattered woman.

"Oh mah goodness! Poor thing. Sorrow finally got the best of her!" Susannah exclaimed through her dramatically heavy southern accent.

The few that had come to Margaret's aid fanned her flushed face as they tried to get her to calm down. Between diminishing heavy sobs and the fading feelings of dread and terror, her heartbeat began to return to normal. A thought occurred to her, and Margaret knew she could never tell anyone about what she had just experienced, especially in a room full of fanatically religious and superstitious relatives; it just wouldn't go over well. Only her Aunt Lucille would have understood. But unfortunately, it was her aunt that lay the silent victim of mortality.

Margaret sat crumpled on the floor as a cousin — somewhere down the family line — hugged her and smoothed back her hair; her thoughts kept flashing back to what had just happened. She rested, trying to maintain slower breathing and keep herself under control. Luckily under the circumstances, no one could blame Margaret for her collapse, though the reason was only assumed by those present, and they did not question her odd behavior.

As Margaret began to recover from her brush with the supernatural, she saw Miriam floating about in the crowd as she gathered up the dirtied dishes from around the great room. Miriam was a second-generation housekeeper who mainly worked in the kitchen area. She had become quite accustomed to keeping up with large amounts of housework in Lucille's years of entertaining the droves of socialites that always came around. Margaret's intentions were set upon asking the housekeeper to impart what she knew of the local legend, if the woman had any information at all.

Miriam was happy to take a moment of her time to assist Margaret when the younger woman flagged her down. Miriam knew Margaret harbored a genuine sorrow for Lucille's loss, and did not bat an eye with helping her when asked if she knew where she could find Madamé Hanté. The housekeeper had heard rumors of the swamp witch's location, and pointed her in the direction of Flat Top Mountain, the focal point of more than one local fable. Margaret thanked Miriam for her help, and planned to leave before first light.

It was a good hour and a half later before Margaret had fully recovered and sat quietly drinking a cup of hot herbal tea as the family and friends returned to their cliques and low whispers. A few of the much older family members and the handful of young children had long since retired to their rooms or slumbered gently in their mothers' arms. The house was much quieter at this late hour, though thunder continued to rumble in the distance and lightning flashed less frequently as the storm passed along and faded away into the night. As Margaret enjoyed a bit of quiet at the table by herself, she became aware of young eyes upon her. One of the shyer cousins had been watching her from across the room with a look that said she wanted to approach Margaret about something and had spent her time gathering up the courage to do so.

Caroline, an immature twenty-two-year-old, had watched Margaret take pictures of Lucille. The young woman, with her long red braids and shimmering green eyes, slowly made her way to the table and had a seat across from Margaret.

"You took pictures of Aunt Lucy. When are you 'specting you might have 'em ready to look at?" Caroline asked in a low voice.

"Oh, it might be a week or so. I won't have the time nor the money to get the film back while I'm here. Your kin just moved, didn't they?" Margaret asked the younger woman, changing the subject. She didn't really feel much like talking about those dreadful pictures, especially after what had happened.

"Why yes. Um…I know it might be awkward, but if I gave you a little bit of money, would you mail me a copy of the pictures? My momma would like to have them, but I know ya'll don't get along so good. I've never had a problem with ya…," Caroline began, but her voice trailed off as she looked down at the table.

Margaret looked at the young woman. She knew what her home life was like and knew she would never stand a chance to escape to her own life as long as her mother and father lived. She placed a gentle hand on Caroline's and gave it a soft pat.

"Oh honey, of course. You don't have to be shy around me.

It's not your fault certain things have happened. Your parents just live in a different world than I do. They always have and always will. But that doesn't mean that you and I can't get along…does it?" Margaret's soft brown eyes looked into her green ones.

"Momma doesn't really even want me talkin' to ya, but she also knows it won't be long before I try and leave home. I think she's easin' up on me a bit 'cause one day I'm gonna get out of there!" Caroline said, her eyes misting over.

At that particular moment Margaret felt very sorry for the poor girl. "Ah, don't worry yourself. If there's something out of life that you want…well, you have to go for it. If your kin can't respect the choices you make, then they have deeper issues they need to work out with themselves. I know women don't have equal rights and say in things right now, but trust me child, it's going to change. Here before long, before your very eyes, things will be very different. Then you can show the world what you're made of, and you won't have to be afraid anymore," Margaret said, giving Caroline some encouraging words that she knew the girl would never get from home.

"Oh, you're so smart! Well, I'll give you our new address. Some of the old neighbors got together with my father and uncle and built a new house for us. There were too many things wrong with the other one, and…well, you know my mother. Anyway, I'll try and check the mail every day. Maybe we could write more often," Caroline offered, looking around to make sure her mother wasn't listening in.

"I'd like that," Margaret said as she located a paper napkin. Caroline withdrew an automatic pencil from the holder sitting on the table. Margaret smiled as the girl scratched out the address.

From behind her left shoulder, Margaret heard a woman clear her throat in a condescending tone. Caroline's head snapped up and she looked to see her mother glaring at her from a few feet away.

"Oh, I've talked to you too long! Momma wants me to go. Sorry!" Caroline said in a hoarse whisper. Margaret only nodded in understanding. What else could she do? This was not the appropriate time, nor the place, to stir up a family feud.

By the very early morning hours most of the house guests had dissipated and surrendered to the need for sleep. Very few had actually maintained the ability to stay awake and stand watch over their precious deceased. Margaret went through spells of drowsiness, but these moments had been interrupted repeatedly as others used Margaret for conversations for the purpose of staying awake when coffee was no longer having an effect. Though the remainder of the night did not present another opportunity for Margaret to look at the chest, the events of the evening had drained Margaret's energy, and exhaustion left her in such a way that she was just too tired to care. Since Margaret knew where to go looking for the fabled swamp priestess, her goal was to get as early a start away from the house as possible. Though the morning was sure to meet a sullen and weary Margaret, it was also sure to bring along with it an eerie intrigue as the Midwestern woman entered a world she could only imagine at this point.

CHAPTER 3

The harsh rays of morning burst too soon through the great room's large east window. To the bleary eyed it would have seemed that the light itself was attempting to break the glass. Some dozing family members woke up with the arrival of morning, and the bright rays only aggravated others. The few who had managed to stay awake the whole night through were proud to say they had done so, but they still had the entire funeral procession to get through before they could finally rest. Caroline was one of the first awake, and had wanted to find Margaret before her mother rose so they could talk some more, but she was nowhere to be found. When asked, Susannah had mentioned seeing Margaret heading toward the gardens outside, making no effort to hide her indifference. All Susannah knew was that "you'd have to be an idiot to go traipsing about in the yard after such a horrible rain storm" — in *her* opinion, anyway. Caroline thanked her and searched the large outdoor garden area but found no trace of Margaret.

***

Before many had risen within the large home, Margaret's driver had picked her up early and taken her to a secluded place near one of the swampier areas about ten miles away. Margaret thought about what her husband Henry would say about this but felt it important enough to go anyway. He had never been fond of Margaret's never-ending sense of curiosity, but he also knew she could be as free-spirited as a wild stallion. Besides, how could she possibly ignore the nagging sense of intrigue that had always plagued her?

As the 1908 automobile chugged along up the winding hill to the creepy house at the top, Margaret could feel all sorts of wild eyes upon her. She worried about alligators attacking out of the swamp; though she was riding in a motorized carriage, she knew those carnivorous reptiles could be quite vicious. And who knew what else was lurking about the home of a swamp witch? Margaret remembered Lucille speaking about the local hoodoo priestess many years ago during the visit of a friend as they sipped mint juleps in the tea room. For as timeless as the woman sounded in her aunt's stories, she figured the woman must be dead by now. The fable was told, Margaret recalled, as a threat for the local children who misbehaved, for if they were misbehaving children, their punishment would be a visit to the witch. A visit, according to the children, from which you never returned, though no one knew of any one case of a child really found to be missing in the town's history. Other variations of the story included the dismal promise that if a naughty child were brought before the swamp hag for misbehaving, she would take the child for her own and turn it into one of her voodoo dolls. With grim threats like these, parents were sure that their children would be scared straight. And for the most part, it held true.

As the driver guided the automobile along the path toward the house, Margaret had to marvel at the jungle-like appearance of the vegetation. How different things looked from a small rural town to the swamp just ten miles away. She would never find such diversity in her home in Missouri—save for the weather, perhaps. The driver looked about with nervous eyes. As she rode along in the back seat, Margaret held the chest in her lap and fought the urge to peer inside. She didn't want to upset or inadvertently intrigue the driver—she just wanted to get to Madamé Hanté and see what secrets were behind the mysterious chest.

At the top of the hill the land began to level out. It was no wonder that locally this area was referred to as Flat Top Mountain. The driver, whom Margaret swore could have been Arnold Flatts' brother, brought the automobile to a stop a few feet away from the house. The cabin was hand-built; its rounded log planks bowed outward in some places where time had taken its toll. Rain from the previous night's storm had soaked the timber used to build the cabin, which added to the ominous appearance, as its nearly black color added to the feeling of unease that already surrounded it. Several tall oak trees dotted the tree line around the yard; Spanish moss hung in lazy clumps from many of the higher branches.

The driveway made a horse-shoe shape off the road, making it easy to pull the motor car around. The drive itself was a mix of sand, dirt, and broken shells, and did not look inviting to bare feet. Here and there a bit of emerald-blue clover popped up from beneath the sandy mix, adding out of place green specks among the dappled shades of grey, white, and brown. While the sun shone brightly, the partial canopy of trees that covered the driveway allowed splashes of yellow to peek through as the light made its way down past the leaves. The intricate, lacey patterns swayed and shifted upon the ground with every wisp of air that blew past the tree branches.

Margaret wondered whether or not the cloudless day would last and prepared for her short jaunt to the cabin's door. She had invited the driver to join her, but he insisted quite sternly that he needed to stay by the car. Margaret noticed that he seemed to be rattled but passed it off as her imagination and turned toward the house. The driver found himself awaiting Margaret's return. Margaret had placed the chest into a large handbag she'd brought along and slung it casually over her shoulder as she walked. She wanted a pure response to the coffer, not one that may be preconceived if Madamé Hanté saw the thing before she was ready to reveal it.

Misshapen stones lay firmly planted upon the ground, creating a pathway of sorts which led leisurely toward the log cabin's porch. Each stone had a symbol painted upon it; some ritualistic meaning to them, most likely. Dozens of tiny, gray clay pots lined each side of the stone walkway, containing what appeared to be an array of herbs. As Margaret passed by them, the aroma of peppermint, rosemary, parsley, and basil met her tense nostrils. This small sign of life seemed surprisingly comforting against the otherwise intimidating surroundings.

Upon arrival on the porch, Margaret's steps sounded off underneath her with a rather annoying creak that would give the sound of fingernails on a chalkboard an unusual welcome. Margaret inspected the place for a doorbell or knocker but found no such thing. Wind chimes made of animal bone clacked against one another in the light breeze that blew through the swamp. As she raised a fist to knock upon the door, it opened gently, and a freakishly tall man stood just inside.

"Madamé Hanté will see you now."

His voice was deep, intimidating, and heavily accented; it hinted that he might have hailed from some exotic island, but Margaret swallowed her fear. She wondered if the swamp witch actually knew she was there, or if this was the typical greeting drilled into the servant's repertoire of skills. The man who'd answered the door opened it wider and invited Margaret in with a sweep of his hand. As Margaret stepped through the threshold, the door closed on its own accord with a mild slam, making Margaret jump even though she was expecting it to close. As the man led her deeper into the house's living room, she was immediately intrigued with the mystery about the place.

The lighting inside the quaint house was quite dim for such a bright morning, despite wide open curtains on all of the windows in the room. The thick royal blue curtains draped the windows, their velvet appearance soft against the darkness of the interior. Many white and red candles kept the room gently lit, but despite the warm invitation of the glow from the candles, other strange items present on shelves about the house kept a feeling of comfort from presiding within. On the wall farthest from her hung what Margaret could only discern to be shrunken heads; the sight sent tingles of shock eerily down her quivering spine. As she looked over at the heads, she could swear she heard moaning coming from the mouths of the mummified horrors, though the mouths had been sewn shut ages ago. An array of animals sat upon various mounts and shelves adjacent to the shrunken heads, and Margaret guessed the process of stuffing animals would prove to be somewhat the same as shrinking a head. She imagined the leathery skin stretched out over the structure to make up the animals' bodies, and found herself having that strange inner feeling just as she had back at Lucille's house when she saw the shadowy phantom.

The tall man disappeared through a hand-made beaded doorway, and Margaret listened to the clicking of the beads as they swung from the disturbance. Slowly the strings of beads grew still again and the clicking stopped, and she snapped out of the trance she'd slipped into. No sounds were present in the house, and though Margaret knew the tall man had just walked into another room, she could hear no footsteps or other indications of movement. Unsure how long this visit would take, Margaret took a glance at the large open room where she stood. Locked cabinets lined the walls practically all the way around the room, though small windows gave a bit of insight as to what the cabinets might contain. Shelves of rare and out of print books, some quite old looking and bound in cracking leather, lined the rest of the wall where breaks in the cabinets left empty spaces. The titles of the books fascinated Margaret, and she tried to quickly memorize a few of them so she could later find a copy to read.

A glass case stood against one of the corners, short enough to fit underneath a section of the cabinets that hung along the wall. Upon closer inspection, Margaret discovered this case housed what appeared to be voodoo dolls, or so she guessed. Tiny dolls with locks of real hair and colored glass eyes sat in an eerie array of different positions within the case. Some were male, some female, but all were made of burlap and wrapped together with string. Hastily and poorly made, Margaret had no doubt that these little dolls were very useful tools to the practiced witch. But perhaps these dolls were not simply cloth dolls sewn sloppily together, Margaret thought. Maybe, just maybe, this was what happened to the so-called missing children from the town. Had the swamp witch the power or motive to do such a thing? An accusation of this nature would not be something one would simply blurt out. To prove such a horrifying story would take some investigation and time. Margaret shuddered at the ghoulish thought and tried to push it completely from her mind but found it difficult as the eyes looked out from the glass cage that contained them as the soulless creatures they were. Margaret wondered just how the forces that supposedly drove magic through the world could be channeled by such a plain looking artifact.

As Margaret peered back at the dolls through the transparency that separated them, a weary voice that sounded strangely ethereal called out behind her. With a jump, Margaret spun to face Madamé Hanté. The old woman smiled, crinkling the corners of her noticeably aged eyes.

"*C'est les cheveux et leurs yeux,*" the old woman crowed in French.

Margaret's eyes widened; she was sure she was making a huge mistake. She hadn't expected to visit a woman who practiced witchcraft when she'd left her home in Missouri, let alone a strange woman who didn't even speak the same language. The tall man had reappeared and translated what the swamp hag said with a deep throaty laugh.

"She says it is the hair and their eyes," he said, taking a bodyguard-like stance behind the old woman. "What makes them eerie, that is." His thick, dark-skinned arms crossed over a broad chest that moved in rhythm to his breathing.

Margaret could feel blood begin to rush toward her ears as her pulse grew more rapid. Nerves had always had strange effects on her in awkward moments like this, and always left her mouth dry and her wondering what to say next. Margaret looked at the dolls, then back at Madamé Hanté. The old woman smiled wider, increasing the crinkled edges of her worn out eyes.

"*Les poupées, vous vous demandiez, non?*" the old hag asked. Margaret was growing quickly wary of the French.

"I'm sorry, I do not speak French," Margaret said, looking away from the old woman.

The tall man laughed again, his folded arms bouncing on his chest with each guffaw. "Then how do you know it is French she speaks?" The man eyed her suspiciously with the raise of an eyebrow.

"Well, sir, I know the *sound* of French—I just never learned to speak it." She tried to keep her temper steady, but the tall man's statement was uncalled for, and she thought it rude of him to mock her.

"*Ah, vous avez aporté le coffre,*" Madamé Hanté commented, eyeing the large bag slung over Margaret's shoulder. The old woman pointed to Margaret then touched her own shoulder. Margaret reached up and touched the strap of the bag and nodded her head. She didn't need translation to know what the old woman had said.

"She said you brought the chest," the tall man said, though he knew it was unnecessary.

"Well, if you know the chest is in my bag here, then you must know what is inside, right?" Margaret asked, hopeful.

The tall man looked at Margaret a moment before turning to look at Madamé Hanté in confusion. "She does not know?" the tall man asked the witch in disbelief.

Madamé Hanté waved him off. She only cackled before speaking again to Margaret. "*Ce soit le commencement des Gémeaux, naturellement!*" the old witch explained, astounded that Margaret did not already know anything about the chest.

"She says it is the beginning of Gemini, of course," the tall man said in almost a jeering tone.

Madamé Hanté looked at the tall man and frowned. He had obviously overstepped some silent boundary with his mistress. His smile faded, and his gaze dropped to the floor.

Upon mention of the name "Gemini," the candles within the front room flickered, each seeming to be blown on by an invisible source; no wind had entered the room, and yet the flames of the burning red and white candles danced with an unseen force.

From the kitchen of the house sounded the whistle of a pot on the stove. The tall man turned to take a step toward the beaded doorway, but the hoodoo woman threw up a hand to stop him. She picked up her layers of skirts and disappeared in a scurry to tend to the whistling pot. In moments the woman returned with the steaming pot in hand and carried it to a small oval table just behind Margaret. Upon the table was an assortment of small urn-like jars containing various dried herbs and ingredients, while a well-used mortar and pestle sat on the opposite side. Margaret imagined this was how an alchemist's laboratory would have looked in the days of castles and dragons. Madamé Hanté took some of the dark purple leaves out of one of the small jars and ground it up before tapping the pulverized ingredient lightly into one of the clay cups also sitting on the table. The old witch poured the steaming hot water over the leaves and stirred it with a silver spoon three times before taking a sniff of the concoction. Margaret watched the old woman's brew being created right before her eyes and was fascinated that there were hints of ritualistic meaning in the way the witch had done certain things. Satisfied with her creation, the old woman handed Margaret the cup, and the younger woman hesitated a moment before taking the potion gingerly from the old hag's hand.

"*Boire ceci…*," the witch invited, raising a hand to her mouth holding an invisible cup. Margaret recognized the cue to begin drinking the purple-leaf tea but was uncomfortable with the idea.

"She says drink this," the tall man instructed, nodding at the cup in Margaret's hand.

"Wh-what *is* this?" Margaret asked, leery.

"*Thé de l'arrangement,*" Madamé Hanté continued, looking at the younger woman.

"Tea of understanding," the tall man clarified for Margaret, who eyed it a moment longer before raising the cup slowly to her dry lips.

Before she even had the chance to smell the tea the enchantment seemed to take its hold, and Margaret found herself gulping the lavender-tinted liquid, attempting to quell a voracious thirst. Despite the boiling hot temperature Margaret found the tea quite pleasing and found herself swallowing down the strange brew without hesitation. But in seconds the entire room was spinning and the images of the magical artifacts all around seemed to be closing in on her. Feeling her heartbeat pounding in her ears, Margaret quickly set the cup upon the table with trembling hands before she dropped it. She looked around and spotted an over-sized couch to her left. With one hand holding her head, she made her way across to the cushions of the soft, brown sofa and sat down hard; all of the energy had simply left her body at that moment. Leaning back, an immense sensation of heat began to burn within her insides, along with a static electric tingling from head to toe that was so intense it bordered on being painful. The whole ordeal lasted only a few seconds, but it seemed like an eternity to Margaret as her anxious body tried to figure out what was going on.

"How be it dat you feel?" Madamé Hanté asked, looking at the young woman, patting her on the shoulder.

"Like I've been drugged," she answered without hesitation.

"Well, in a way, chile, you have," the witch answered with a smile.

Though she was being pleasant at this moment, something about the mystic seemed somehow sinister. Margaret blamed the tea. As the clay cup sat upon the table, the table began to quake ever so slightly. Both Margaret and the witch looked at it with silent questions. The silver spoon that lay motionless upon the small end table now quivered with an unseen vibration. But just as quickly as the table had begun to shake, it stopped, and the table was quiet once more.

"What in de name of de lunar goddess was dat?" Madamé Hanté asked, the brief phenomenon puzzling her. The hoodoo woman gazed at the table, half expecting to see something more. But as it remained silent, she simply shrugged and looked at the middle-aged housewife with an unsettling grin.

"Wait…you—you speak English now?" Margaret asked, sitting up and looking at the old woman with queries in her eyes as she realized she could understand the old woman.

"Oh my, you be a slow one, no?" the old woman laughed.

Margaret slapped a hand to her cheek as she realized it must have been the effect of the tea. "Oh God…the tea. I-I don't think I should've—" Margaret was interrupted by the witch.

"Oh no, don't you be sayin' dat now. How else ol' Madamé

Hanté to tell you de story of Gemini?" she chided; her accent painted her words heavily.

"Fine. Just tell me, how long before the effect of the tea wears off? I'm not sure I am entirely comfortable with...." Margaret asked, her brow etched with worry.

The old hag smiled broadly. "Ah, you worry for nothin'. De tea last as long as you need, no? Dere no side effects dat you need concern yourself with."

The hag's answer was cryptic and didn't make Margaret feel any better. Margaret looked around and noticed the tall man had disappeared. As she silently wondered where he'd gone, Madamé Hanté shook her head and nodded toward the stairs.

"He has chores. Dis story is not meant for him. Only your bloodline. You be ready for answers. You be ready to listen, no?" she asked. The old witch paused a moment before continuing. "You ever hear of de nephilim?" she asked.

"No, can't say I have. What is it?" Margaret asked, curious.

"De nephilim is de seed of de fallen angels, chile. Dey choose human female mates to create dere offspring. Not so much dese days as in de biblical times, but dey happen. Like you," Madamé Hanté explained.

Margaret jumped to her feet, her hands out in front of her attempting to push back the words the witch had just spoken. "No! Things like that aren't—" Margaret began, mortified by what the hag was suggesting.

"Dey do, chile. Dey do. An' your family is de proof. Long ago in your family history, for whatever de reason, your bloodline was chosen as a breeding ground for dese half-beings. I always thought dis tied somehow to de whole Gemini ting, but I don' know why. I only know dat I tink you be one. Come now, chile, and sit down. Standing up like dat ain't gonna make tings change," Madamé Hanté tried to explain.

Slowly, Margaret sat back down. "Okay, so say I can get past the half-angel theory; what has this got to do with me? Why all the mystery?" Margaret asked, feeling her sense of intrigue with the occult being put on trial, perhaps as a test for just how much she was willing to believe in.

"Would you be willin' to completely believe in all dis if you could hold it in your hands? If you could make de legend behind your bloodline become a physical object?" Madamé Hanté proposed.

"I would be more willing to believe. So are you talking about *this*?" Margaret said as she removed the bag from her shoulder. The cherry wood strong box appeared just as unusual as the first time she looked at it.

"My, it has been a long time since I be seein' dat box," the old woman said, placing a hand over her heart; she seemed shocked to see it again after so very long.

"You have actually *seen* this box before?" Margaret asked, stunned.

"From Eva Ruth, to Ruth Agatha, to Agatha Mary, to Mary Margaret—until her demise and your aunt Lucille took possession, waiting for you to come along. I have spoken to dem all. And now here you are at last, sitting where dey sat," Madamé Hanté confirmed, shaking her head.

"But-but that would make the chest over a hundred years old! That would make you...." Margaret stopped, unable to process the possibility she was about to suggest. The witch just smiled but said nothing. "What the hell is the deal with this thing anyway? I'm not sure I would trust my jewelry to go in that thing." Margaret looked the intricate clasp on the box over. She was so very anxious to open it, and yet terrified to do so.

Madamé Hanté laughed, the crow's feet around her eyes deepening. "My chile, dis be a summoning box, no? It not be for no gems and such."

As the two women spoke, the rays of sunshine disappeared

through the window and the sky began to cloud over. The wind picked up and rattled the bone wind chimes that hung just outside on the porch. Inside the house the flames on the candles disappeared, shrinking down until they snuffed themselves out, bowing humbly before some unseen sovereign.

The great room became bathed in a yellow-orange light that surrounded the area of the ceiling above Margaret and the witch. The housewife felt she should have been terrified out of her mind, but blamed her new inhibition on the tea, which seemed to keep most all ordinary feelings, like fear, at bay. The pair of women settled into a trance-like state as events began to unfurl above their heads and envelop the room. Images explaining a supernatural story as it had been played out over a thousand years began to form and whirl about them. Celestial images of a star-bound universe swirled in misty clouds above them, and all other things in the present time ceased to matter.

"Before time there existed the two founding beings of the universe—Legna, the good mother of light and peace, and Nomed, the father of darkness and chaos," Madamé Hanté began as the image shifted. Like a projection upon the wall, images began to dance in flickers of supernatural shades. Shapes jumped off the wall into the very air in front of them, incorporating the shadows that lurked in various areas of the room where Margaret and the swamp witch sat. As the withered old woman continued with the story, Margaret felt her head begin to spin and a crippling sense of vertigo washed over her body.

"The pair ruled the universal balance between good and evil. Their children are the angels and demons that populate Heaven and Hell. This is true, except for Gemini. This one child, being of two half-souls, is both, and yet each twin possesses their own separate entity. Together as Gemini, the combined half angel, half demon, holds all the power of the universe; however, it is not allowed to break up the natural direction of the power. It must be decided equally between the two as a whole to use the power for good, or for evil. It absolutely will never be both. Nor can the decision be reversed once made." Madamé Hanté told the story well, as years of repeated tellings had burned the details into her memory.

Though Margaret fought hard to focus on the voodoo priestess's words, a whirlwind in her head pulled her with a great force of distraction. As the images changed with the story, Margaret found herself feeling nauseated from the dizzying display in front of her. As it grew in intensity, she felt bile rise up at the back of her throat and swallowed hard, forcing back the vile liquid.

"Legna's half begat Sky—named for the never-ending goodness and peace. Locks of gold and sapphire eyes represent the fairness and innocence of the light. While Nomed's half begat Thyme—named as a cleverly guised version of 'time' to symbolize a constant, unchanging threat against all living creatures. Charcoal locks encircle the brow of Thyme, representing the darkness of Hell. Emerald eyes sparkle devilishly, like the sins of envy and jealousy." As the images floated above and around Margaret and the hag, the depictions continued to change to match the part of the legend Madamé Hanté was speaking about. Strange, ghostly faces appeared within the unknown universe, mingling together with everything Margaret knew to be real.

The faces in the vision morphed from what the human eyes viewing them perceived to be Legna and Nomed, first into something that no other word besides "angelic" could describe. But while entranced by the great beauty of a flawless female figure surrounded in a bluish-white light, they were also mortified by the demonic black chaos of Thyme's appearance. Unsure if these visions were actual images of the celestial beings themselves or merely the display of what their minds thought each half of Gemini should look like, Margaret tried to maintain some level of awareness to remember what she was viewing for future reference. Margaret fought hard to listen to Madamé Hanté as she continued with the details of the legend, despite the events unfolding right above her head. Her ethereal encounter at Lucille's house seemed about to happen all over again, only she was fully aware of what was going on this time.

"Each half may roam freely where they wish to rule; however, they must meet as one once every century. If over by so much as one minute, each half shall perish. Agreeing that life in conflict with each other is better than no life at all, both must choose a realm as a basis to exist and agree to meet every hundred years to renew Gemini."

The witch continued, oblivious to the events happening to her guest in the living room. Margaret's human body could no longer fight off the disorienting effect of the whirlwind in her head, and her eyes fluttered and rolled to the back of her head. An unseen force lifted Margaret off the floor, her body limp as she hung there motionless. Madamé Hanté was still unaware that anything was happening around her.

"It is said the two shall arrive as one on a date—or time perhaps—containing twins like them. History shall record acknowledgement of their arrival, though it shall remain unknown by way of conscious mind. It is said there is a way to both summon and destroy the two halves, but to date no one has been able to successfully achieve this."

Up until Margaret succumbed to the vertigo as Madamé Hanté told the story, her voice had seemed altogether different. The look on the witch's face had made Margaret wonder if she was actually listening to the old woman herself, or if this was someone else speaking through the old hag. But now, as Margaret was caught up in a separate supernatural phenomenon, not only did the story fade out and the scenery change, but Madamé Hanté's voice grew distant and distorted. Even though Margaret physically remained in the living room with the swamp witch, her mind had been transferred into another plane of existence. As before, a liquid black shadow leaked from all about the darkness of the house, and pooled in a general humanoid shape in front of where Margaret's body was now suspended in mid-air.

As if in an out of body experience, Margaret's consciousness stood next to the wraith in both amazement and fear. A shadowy hand reached out and touched the woman's chin, running its clawed, bony finger down her throat and between her breasts. Margaret stood, jaw clenched, as she mentally screamed for the creature to stop. The shadow's form shifted, allowing more detail to surface from within the dark form. A male figure emerged from the phantom and stood by Margaret's side in silence. Though jet black hair crowned the man's head and his pallor emitted an unearthly aura, he could easily have passed as a human.

Who the hell are you? Margaret asked, though her mouth did not move. Even though she could see her physical body floating in the air before her, her attention was focused on the creature beside her. The man did not say anything at first; he only turned his head to look at the woman. As he turned, Margaret saw his eyes for the first time and was immediately entranced by the dazzling, deep emerald glow that came from them. *I asked, who the hell are you?!* Margaret asked again mentally, her mind screaming the words. The black-haired man's lips parted into an evil smile that sent shivers down her spine.

I am Hell, he answered as he turned toward her. *You think your pitiful mind can figure out this puzzle? You're better off forgetting about all of this and going back to your home, housewife! You're pathetic! You don't even know what you are. No matter; time is against you either way.* The man's demonic voice rumbled through the woman's astral projection of herself.

I don't believe you! Margaret exclaimed in denial.

Then perhaps you'll believe your witch here? Thyme goaded.

The demon reached out, placing his reaper-like hands upon the old hag's shoulders as he stared her right in the eyes. Margaret watched a look of horror spread across the old woman's face, and Thyme disappeared inside her. Silence remained a moment as Margaret and the old woman looked at each other.

"Dis evil ting...he cannot prevail! Chile, you must fight dis ting no matter de cost," Madamé Hanté pleaded, her voice wrapped in panic. Margaret looked at her, the old woman's eyes wide as saucers with fear.

"Madamé Hanté, what's going to happen to us if I don't...if I *can't*?" Margaret asked with worry-tainted words.

"Den all is lost."

"But why? I don't yet understand. What will come of this?" Margaret pressed for answers. Madamé Hanté cocked her head to one side and smiled broadly. With a hauntingly familiar voice the old woman answered.

"I will bring Hell to earth!" Thyme answered through Madamé Hanté's body. He laughed maliciously as his foul, inky form leaked out away from the old hag and disappeared.

At the end of the legend the old hag regained awareness, and she shook her head to shake off the grogginess. The witch looked around and rubbed her eyes before speaking again to Margaret; she appeared weakened but mentioned nothing of it as the imagery of another time and place faded out from their view. Just as Madamé Hanté turned, she froze a moment and stared as her guest was released from her hold in the air and the younger woman's feet touched the floor.

Margaret's eyes fluttered back, and she blinked her eyes to focus. Her head was not nearly as dizzy as before, and she shook off the strange cold feeling that remained as a tingle in her neck where it met her spine.

"I think dis be de last time dis story is told, no? Madamé Hanté has a feelin' dat you could be de one to solve dis cosmic mystery and bring balance back to de universe." The witch's voice had returned to normal, and it made Margaret shiver. The old woman laughed. "Oh, you be gettin' used to de magic 'round here, no? Certain forces are channeled through Madamé Hanté to make dis possible—you understand, no?" The old woman's grayed eyes peered out with clarity, reading Margaret's expressions.

"I understand enough on *your* part of things. I *don't* understand what is so goddamned special about me or my family line. Why us?" the younger woman said with a sigh. She looked at the grandfather clock that rose off the floor near the entrance to another room Margaret hadn't noticed before.

"Don't worry none 'bout de time. You will get to your aunt's funeral. You will understand, you'll see." The old hag reached into her pocket and withdrew a deck of playing cards. "Here. Might as well read your fortune while you be here, no?" Madamé Hanté spread the deck between dark fingers on hands that had been gnarled by arthritis and held the cards out for Margaret to choose. Margaret, while curious about such things, had never had any experience with a fortune reading. The witch sensed her apprehension and smiled but said nothing. After a moment's pause, Margaret placed her hand on a card near the center of the deck. An unusual tingle shot through her fingertips when her delicate fingers hovered above a particular card, and she hesitated before withdrawing it. The card was facing Margaret, and Madamé Hanté had not yet seen it. The old witch smiled as she shuffled the cards back into a stack and laughed to herself.

"Dat mean good fortune comin' to you from a family member death. De ten of clubs is a good card to draw. Interesting your aunt jus' die an' you draw dat one, no?"

Margaret's jaw clenched when she heard the old woman speak of her aunt's death—the way she said it just sounded so... final. It was the ten of clubs she had drawn, but the true test would be if the fortune reading came true or not. Margaret doubted it—

while her aunt Lucille had taken her in for a short time as a child, and had amassed a small fortune over her lifetime, there were so many other members of the family before her in line for a portion of the wealth in the will, she was sure. She had little faith she would receive any grand fortune.

"You understand I don' need to see de card to know. De card chooses you, and de deck speaks to me. And now, for Madamé Hanté's payment…," the old woman left off. Margaret had not thought about that aspect of it and worried the woman would ask for a large sum of money that she simply did not have.

"What about the chest? Aren't you even going to open it? Wait—payment? What is it that you charge? I hadn't thought to ask, since it was Mr. Flatts who suggested I should come see you. I-I'm sorry, I don't have much…," she began, nervous and embarrassed.

"Non, non, non! A lock of dat pretty, pretty hair. Dat's all Madamé Hanté need from you," the witch said, running her fingers through the silky chestnut locks. Even though the request was strange, it quelled Margaret's fear of owing a large monetary debt. "And as for de chest…chile, you forget I done seen dis box before. No need to look at what I already laid dese old eyes on."

Margaret was disappointed that the chest remained unopened, but placed it back into her large shoulder bag as the witch withdrew a tiny pair of silver herbalist's shears and carefully snipped a lock of hair from underneath the mass of tresses Margaret possessed. The old woman chuckled as she wrapped the hair carefully into a plain, white kerchief and placed it into her left pocket. And while Margaret did wonder if her lock would make it onto one of those little voodoo dolls, she did not dare ask, for fear her question would be answered.

"So, *exactly* when did my bloodline become so very special, anyway; and why did the legend take the form of this little box?" Margaret asked, tapping the chest through the cloth of the bag slung across her shoulder.

"Ah…dat be the right question, now! The mark upon your soul…it is not of this world. From what I know, it done be special since de very beginning, probably since before I even be born. I surprised you not opened de chest. Dere is much to be learned from within, no?" Madamé Hanté asked.

"I-I haven't had a chance to. When I do look inside, will I even know what I am looking at?" the anxious woman stammered nervously.

The voodoo priestess smiled broadly and nodded her head. "Dis whole ting be why you so attracted to de occult," the old woman said. "Or why it so attracted to you," the old witch added with a smirk. A silent shiver slithered down Margaret's spine, but she remained silent. "'Caus'n chile, you be born of de magic, no? You be raised with de *veil of blessings* o'er your head. When you open de chest, you find all you need to solve dis mystery, and bring balance to de world as you know it. De others before you, dey almos' right, but dey not fully understand de way it work. You must be willin' to 'cept de way you are…accept *what* you are and realize what you can do. You know, you look a lot like Agatha. *She* had de most potential out o' all de others before you," Madamé Hanté explained. Again, her answer seemed somewhat enigmatic. "Seek out de Devil's Promenade. You might find knowledge dere."

Margaret somehow knew this was the last of the information she was going to get out of the swamp witch. It did not matter how badly she wanted to ask more questions, her session was over, and she was on her own to find the answers. But there was just one more thing she thought the hag might answer.

"By the way, what does *Hanté* mean, anyway?" the housewife asked, curious. She was sure it had to translate into something.

The hoodoo woman showed Margaret the way out, and as she opened the creaky large door, a loud clap of thunder sounded, making Margaret jump. The old woman cackled melodramatically.

"It mean de haunted, chile," she answered. Margaret shuddered on the inside, and her mind was left to imagine what that could possibly mean.

Rain had begun to pour down heavily in a deluge just as it had the night before, and the sky was even darker now. Low lying areas in the expanse of the yard had attempted to recover from the flood on the previous night, but the ground's plea to remain puddle-free went unanswered.

"When'd it start raining?" Margaret asked, peering outside.

"My chile, it done be rainin' since you got here," the witch said as Margaret stepped out onto the covered porch. From the railing, Margaret could see the driver had pulled the car as close as possible in an attempt to keep her dry, but the wind was blowing the rain up underneath the carriage-style top to the car.

The stones and the landscaping that had led up to the cabin when Margaret first walked up to the house had all but disappeared. Instead, a worn path that had been carved through the Emerald Zoysia grass separated the rickety porch from the wild, unkempt lawn. The hoodoo priestess read Margaret's expression.

"Dat be de ting about magic…it make you see tings dat you want to see. An' other tings you don't," she said, answering Margaret's question though she hadn't asked.

"But I…. And it—but it…and it was sunny when I—that's *impossible*…," Margaret began to mutter to herself, frustrated. Margaret's footprints still remained in the muddy path, though filled with water from the rain. Muddy tracks led up from the ground toward the door, and Margaret glanced at her shoes to find mud caked upon the soles. As she looked back at the witch, the old woman had already begun to shut the door and had started laughing. She could still hear the hag's cackle as the door shut completely.

***

As Madamé Hanté closed the door, she felt the cold grip of whatever force had graced her home with an unwelcome visit. Being very much practiced in her questionable arts, it was unusual for her to feel that something was or had been present that was beyond even her comprehension.

She began to follow the sensation of the psychic pattern back into the main room where she and Margaret had shared the visions of Gemini. Remembering the quaking table, the voodoo hag returned to the place where Margaret had laid the tea cup down.

As the witch reached for the clay cup a flicker of electricity shocked her crooked fingers and made her jump. A thick wave of unease settled into the old woman's spine, and she looked nervously around the house. She reached past the electric wave and grabbed up the cup. Upon closer inspection, she saw that the purple-leaf residue of the tea had turned into blood, which Margaret had devoured.

The significance of blood in any ritual was always a very important but dangerous sign, and Madamé Hanté knew from all of her many years of experience that something more was afoot here than she had originally thought. As the old woman held the bloody clay cup a searing pain burned her palm, making her drop the cup to the floor where, even though it landed upon a plush carpet, it shattered and splattered blood all about the place.

The swamp witch looked over her burned palm to find Roman numerals of twelve, three, six, and nine respectively in a clockwise position seared into her old, withered flesh. She shuddered at the symbolism of time, and knew it could only mean one thing. Though she'd been visited by many dark spirits in her time, none could be darker than the half of Gemini whose name was Thyme.

As the old woman looked out over the bloody mess upon her floor, she knew she would have to light some cleansing candles and say some chants to banish the dark spirits that the spattered blood would invite. The withered witch picked up her layered skirts and headed up her creaky stairs to retrieve the candles she would need for the ritual. In this moment she envied Margaret, who now was on her way to her automobile, and completely unaware anything unusual was taking place just beyond the wooden door she'd exited moments ago.

***

Outside, Margaret secured the bag over her shoulder and tried to make it into the car before she got too drenched by the rain. The driver made sure she was in her seat before climbing back in behind the wheel.

"I left 'er running. I'd hate to crank that engine up in this downpour! Well, m'lady…that was quick. Find the answers you were seeking?" the driver asked with a tip of his hat.

"Quick? I was in there for —" Margaret sat back and thought. The witch had said time would not be an issue.

"Oh ma'am, it couldn't a been for more than ten minutes. Fifteen at the most. You *are* ready to leave, ma'am?" the driver politely asked, seeming to hope the answer was yes. Margaret could tell he just wanted to get out of there. She smiled and nodded her head at him. The driver let out a sigh of relief.

As the car pulled away, Margaret cast a glance back to the house. As she did, she caught a glimpse of Madamé Hanté standing in one of the upstairs windows, looking out. From this distance she was not sure just how well the witch could have seen her, but she was sure they locked eyes as the car made its way back down the hill and out of sight.

As the 1908 automobile chugged back down Flat Top Mountain, Margaret began to feel queasy. A lightheaded feeling led to feeling dizzy, which in turn led to her feeling very nauseated.

Never in her life had she felt so terribly ill, and she was surprised as she rapidly kept feeling worse and worse. Margaret felt the blood drain away from her face, and her mouth and eyes grew watery. The driver of the automobile seemed distracted and paid her no attention. The middle-aged woman's heart began to beat faster, and she swallowed hard to keep back the sensation to vomit. Drops of a cold sweat began to bead upon her forehead and trickle down the sides of her face. The clear, salty drops disappeared once they touched her clothing, and Margaret felt shivery. As the car continued down the rough road she fought to regain control over herself. She closed her eyes in the hopes it would keep everything from spinning, to no avail. She pursed her lips and began to take in slow, deep breaths. But with each breath she sucked in, the bile kept rising at the back of her throat.

Suddenly, a piercing pain stabbed at her belly, sending her doubling over in the seat. As waves of terrible abdominal cramps came one right after the other, she began to feel she might pass out. A million thoughts jammed themselves within her mind as she wondered what was happening to her, and though she thought about calling out to the driver for help, something in her gut told her it would be pointless.

As the pain grew to a limit that Margaret could no longer tolerate, she began to gag and cough. Her throat felt obstructed with something solid that was trying to make its way out of her gullet, and she began to quake with fear. Margaret began to retch violently, and at first a black, ashy fluid poured forth from somewhere deep within her. Horrified by this, she gagged even harder and more fluid poured out of her mouth. Her insides felt like she was going to turn inside out, and a deep, cold fear gripped her. Seconds later she had the sensation that something solid was inching its way up her throat; if she hadn't known any better, she would have sworn it felt like a ball of burlap and razors. As the solid mass laden with rough edges scratched her throat on the way up, Margaret felt she was choking. Slapping at her chest and grasping at her neck, she grew dizzy and neared hysteria.

After the lump was expelled, Margaret got her breath back and coughed; blood speckled the seat in front of her. She stared at whatever it was, coated in both blood and the black, ashy substance. She raised a sleeved arm and wiped off the residue from her mouth and chin. Her still watering eyes glanced at the driver, who was completely oblivious. While both relieved and puzzled by what was happening, Margaret was unable to speak. Her throat felt smoldering like it was on fire, and she supposed that it had been rubbed raw by what had just scraped through it.

Taking a deep breath, Margaret reached for the solid mass she had just vomited and was shocked when her trembling fingers touched a wad of paper. The paper was moist and covered with tiny dots of blood and the black, ashy fluid. Despite the impossible things that had happened to her lately, it was no wonder her instincts told her that whatever this was could be nothing good. She had not ingested anything of the sort, so how was this possible?

Her shaking hands flattened the paper and she prepared herself to see whatever might be on it. A sepia tone photograph began to unfurl itself as Margaret worked to smooth out the paper. More and more detail became visible to her; the impression of a woman in a high collared dress and hair pinned up presented itself to Margaret, though the look on the woman's face was laden with fear, loathing, and an unearthly disgust. The woman's eyes looked very distant and empty, even though they appeared wet with life at the time the photograph was taken.

Intrigued by the mysterious photograph, Margaret went on to unfold the rest of the crumpled picture. As she did the entire image came into sight, and Margaret's curiosity was replaced by the deepest horrific sorrow she had ever felt in her life. There upon the wrinkled photograph was the image of her own mother, from a time that she could not fully comprehend or remember. In the varying shades of brown upon the paper was burned the image of Margaret's mother in the act of slitting an infant boy's throat, while another child, a female, lay watching helpless at the woman's feet. Mortified by the nightmarish photograph, Margaret threw the rumpled picture to the side and screamed hysterically. Still the driver was oblivious to the chaos in the back seat of the 1908 automobile and continued driving down the road. Finally, Margaret's mind could take no more and the darkness of consciousness lost enveloped her.

Madamé Hanté had been quite correct in saying that Margaret would be back in plenty of time for the funeral. The driver returned her to Lucille's house in more than enough time for her to bathe and change into an outfit suitable for a funeral. He had a tough time waking her from her sleep once they arrived, but Margaret groggily thanked him and handed over a coin for his trouble. After the events in the motorcar Margaret felt wobbly and nauseated, but despite her ordeal, she wouldn't have the time to rest upon her return to the house.

CHAPTER 4

Once back in the house and in her old room, Margaret dug through her suitcase to take out the black dress and kerchief she'd brought along, Caroline came knocking softly at the door.

"Well hey, sweetie, you okay?" Margaret asked, looking at the girl's tear-streaked face.

With a sniffle, the young girl answered. "It's just so hard... going to funerals, you know? I-I've only been to a couple of them. What am I supposed to do?" she asked, very uneasy.

"You don't have to worry. Just be there to express your grief, your love, and your final farewell to her. That's all," Margaret answered, running a brush through her chestnut locks.

"My momma says that I should sit with them, but I want to sit with you. She yelled at me for crying too much. She said that I needed to save it for the actual funeral, and to stop being such a child," Caroline said with her eyes tearing up.

"Now, you don't listen to a word of that. Grief will come and go as it pleases, and no mortal can tell you when to cry. Just ignore her and you'll be fine. I know you still have to do as you're told for now, but we're going to a funeral. You have every right to cry if you need to."

"CAROLINE!" a shrill yell sounded out in the hallway.

69

"Oh no...," the younger girl groaned.

"CAROLINE! You get out here this instant! We need to put a comb through that rat's nest you call hair before we can leave. What would everyone think of me if I let you go to Lucille's funeral looking like *that*?"

"Coming, Mother," she called softly. She opened her mouth as if to say something else but closed it again and shook her head. She turned from Margaret and headed for the door. Margaret had no choice but to let her go and watched her walk out the door.

In the hallway, Margaret could hear Caroline and her mother's discussion.

"So, did you ask Margaret if she knows anything about Lucille's will?" the bitter woman asked, taking Caroline by the arm to lead her away.

"No, Mother. I-I didn't really have a chance to—"

"No matter! I'm sure Lucille was smart enough to leave those of us who really cared about her a nice piece of her fortune...." Caroline's mother's voice faded out as they continued down the hall away from Margaret's room.

"Poor girl...I feel so bad for her," Margaret muttered to herself as she continued to prepare for the funeral. As Margaret stood there, she felt something was missing from her morning. As she stood, continuing to run the brush through her chestnut hair, her mind grew fuzzy as she tried to retrace her steps after leaving the swamp witch's cabin.

Margaret turned her attention to the pallid reflection staring back at her from beyond the shiny, silver glass. She tried to remember the ride back to Lucille's house, and at first nothing came to mind. The longer she stared into her own amber flecked eyes, concentration began to ignite a headache in the center of her brow. Flickers of the inky wraith flashed through her mind, followed by images of the photograph.

Realizing more strange events had followed Margaret from

the hoodoo woman's house, her spine quivered with fear. A memory of coughing up blood and retrieving the photograph surfaced, and Margaret raised a hand to her mouth to wipe away the blood as she relived the moment in her mind. Margaret wished there was someone around in the family she could tell these events to, but knew she was pretty much on her own. Even Henry, her husband, would not be so interested in her tale, and would be likely to either blame it on exhaustion or dismiss it entirely.

As she stood there sinking deeper and deeper into the inner folds of the darkness inside her mind, Margaret wondered how something like this could possibly exist in a world where a great and powerful God was supposed to exist. How could a benevolent God allow such terrible things to happen? At that moment she felt so empty and alone, and when those sensations grew, so did the feeling that something truly terrifying was waiting inside the mirror for her.

In the next second after that thought, Margaret saw a decayed arm reaching toward her reflection from the mirror. Like a corpse reaching out of a grave, the gnarled hand threatened to grab her, and Margaret feared what this thing may be capable of. She felt herself grow ever more curious as to what was happening to her and was determined to get the answers even if it took the rest of her life. As Margaret fought for her mind to break free of this fear that gripped her, she slowly relaxed, and the images in the mirror and her mind ceased. Though she felt exhausted, she grabbed up the last few things she needed to be ready for the funeral and turned to head out.

About an hour later, a swarm of family members arrived at the parish where Lucille's body had been delivered earlier that morning. Large muddy puddles stood atop the saturated ground, refusing to take in any more water. It was evident that the gusting wind had had its fun overnight as twisted limbs on trees hung, now lifeless, among the canopy, while others dotted the ground.

The location of the memorial service had been decided by Lucille herself, long before her demise — it was to be held in a local, rural church. Some of the family disagreed with the idea of employing a minster from a smaller parish, as they thought great wealth demanded a large funeral at a larger place of worship. But the choice was Lucille's alone. Lucille had been a very bright woman. In her many years she'd come to know how certain things would play out if it was not directly stated how it should be in writing. The southern businesswoman had been smart enough to have an attorney draw up her plans and produce legal documents that could not be changed. So Lucille's funeral procession would be conducted at the small church with the small minister, and there was nothing anyone could do about it. Lucille was the only one who had the legal power to make changes and, since she was the guest of honor, that was something that would prove quite impossible.

Down a normally dusty brown dirt back road and off completely to itself stood the church. The road was overhung by a natural canopy of trees, while wild flowers painted with shades of amber and peach dotted the tall grass on either side of the road. The small rural church sat upon a meager plot of land just large enough for the building and the cemetery. The grass was in need of being cut, and large clusters of clover sprouted thickly in some areas while tall weeds of varying species poked up out of the taller blades of grass.

As for the church itself, it looked to have been built ages ago, and was badly in need of maintenance. Paint had begun to peel away from the termite ridden planks, hanging like drooping flesh from a zombie. Patches of green algae coated the siding, as well as places on the tile roof. The old clay tiles had been long baked by decades of beaming sunlight, and a multitude of fractures lined their once glazed and unscathed faces like cracks in sunbaked mud.

A large bronze bell teetered ominously above the bell tower at the peak of the church steeple, threatening to let loose its hold on the brittle ropes that once held the weight proudly. Though the bell had not been rung in several years, Margaret could picture the deep, echoing toll as the gong inside it clanged from one side to the other. How magnificent this little church must have been in its earlier days. Margaret felt a moment's sorrow for the way the building and its lot had been neglected. But perhaps it was this humbling effect that Lucille had been aiming for, and the reason she'd chosen such a rural setting for her final farewell.

To one side, near the rear of the church grounds, lay the small interment lot. The rows of stones were crooked, having been shifted with the moving earth over the years. Granite stones, weather-worn with age, marked the graves of some people, otherwise long forgotten. A pang of sorrow struck her soul as she glimpsed the ancient grave markers; awkward empathy left a cold, hollow sensation in the back of her neck, along with the feeling of déjà vu, as the cemetery looked extraordinarily similar to the one from her dream.

In the front entranceway to the church, Spathiphyllum floribundum — peace lilies — lined the walkway, beckoning grievers inward to find solace in remembrance. Margaret had studied horticulture on her own time and smiled to herself that she'd remembered the flower's scientific name; a small feat that made her feel educated somehow. From within the church, an organist played quiet spiritual hymns, though Margaret could tell the person at the keyboard was not an accomplished player.

Within minutes, the church was filled with the sound of quiet sobbing and whispering voices as the rest of family and friends gathered to wish Lucille a final farewell. Each took their place in the burgundy velvet-covered pews; the scent of dust and mildew rose up from the warped wooden floorboards that had seen water damage at some time or another. Margaret had the unfortunate pleasure to overhear some of the muffled conversations going on around her in the church. The bickering continued about which heirlooms would go to which family, arguments over who had loved Lucille the most, and talk about the desire to pose in photographs alongside the corpse — the idea itself was quite gruesome to her. It brought forth an unfortunate and not distant enough memory.

As a child, she'd been instructed to pose with some distant cousin and pretend nothing was happening except an ordinary day. But the cousin had been dead a day or two at least, and Margaret shuddered, remembering that terrible moment in her childhood. Though her aunt was very wealthy, it was the only way to justify the expense of the photograph, and the order to sit still next to a corpse had become quite difficult for Margaret to comply with, as she recalled.

As with any funeral procession, a preacher man read from the Good Book, while key phrases made a melodramatic person in the crowd of mourners break into unnecessarily loud crying. Those who wanted to share memories, or a farewell wish for Lucille more directly, took center stage behind the old woman's stiff, embalmed body.

Margaret was in the second row of pews, sitting to the left of Lucille's casket. She glimpsed around at the others present, silently judging who was truly sad to see the old woman gone, and those who were only there for their share of the Ordiki wealth. Her eyes were mainly upon those in the front row and found no other than cousin Susannah there with a melodramatic display of false grieving pouring forth. Margaret simply sighed to herself and tried to refocus on the preacher's words, though some nagging sensation in the center of her forehead made it nearly impossible to do so. Out of nowhere, an array of flashing lights danced before her aching eyes — swirling, spinning into infinity.

A howling, piercing scream ripped through the drone of the preacher's words, though Margaret could see that he was frozen in one spot. His eyes remained fixed upon the Bible as he continued to read from the worn pages, but his mouth no longer produced any audible sound. A picture formed in Margaret's mind of a hand that had reached through her chest, and her lungs squeezed shut, suffocating her for a moment. She fought to regain control of her breathing, but that was a trivial thing to accomplish compared to what she was about to experience. A thin band of freezing air snaked through the aisle between the rows of pews. Without looking, Margaret sensed the door to the church had been opened, allowing something inside that did not belong there, though no sound of the door opening had been heard.

As the breeze whirled into a stronger wind, the temperature dropped, and everyone froze in place, their behavior tied directly to the frigid air. Everyone present, except Margaret, was affected by the veil of freezing wind. Wide-eyed with curiosity and terror, the human woman fought panic with every fiber of her being. She desperately wanted to understand the events unraveling around her, and rather than just shut her eyes in fear, she opened them wider. The candles that had been flickering along the altar snuffed out in a violent gust, and the lanterns along the ceiling of the church faded out to nothing. Darkness ruled the atmosphere inside the minster, but Margaret was still somehow able to see quite clearly.

Her spirit ascending, she'd left her body, and Margaret found herself standing over Lucille's body, even though she could look back and see herself still sitting on the pew. A light began to glow behind Lucille's eyes, and poured outward like an inner fire yearning for freedom. Margaret knew something terrible was about to happen moments before a dark shadow began to form in one of the darker corners of the church. It made its way, bouncing from the folds of the dark clothing the mourners wore, until it reached the pine casket where Margaret stood.

Though the phantom ignored the live woman for the moment, she could not ignore it. She watched in horror and strange wonder as the wraith bent over Lucille, just as it had done back at the house; the specter was more interested in the black opal than in Lucille's body. Bony, clawed hands draped in leathery and decayed flesh reached toward Lucille, the hands passing through the corporeal shell into an unseen place inside the deceased woman. Margaret's breath caught in her chest as the creature withdrew its hands, holding onto a form that looked like the whitish-blue light she'd seen before.

The apparition in the clutches of this shadowy spirit seemed to writhe in an attempt to gain freedom from its death grasp; Margaret only concluded this must be some impossible-to-imagine death for the dead. As the phantom continued to rip this apparition from Lucille's body, it occurred to the fear-gripped woman what was happening. A shriek sounded from the spirit rising out of Lucille's body as the wraith nearly pulled it out of the corpse completely. Just as Margaret reached toward the dark creature to stop it, the thing succeeded in tearing Lucille's soul from her body. Only the universe knew what fate lie ahead for Lucille with her soul in the hands of this ebony specter, and Margaret screamed. This finally caught the attention of the phantom, who turned toward the human woman and laughed.

As Margaret looked around for help, she noticed a thick, dark water begin to seep upward from beneath the unsound floorboards. As the middle-aged housewife bent forward to gain a better look at it, she realized that blood was spewing up from some unknown depths below the church. The slow trickle grew into a steady flow, and in no time, Margaret found herself knee deep in blood. As she looked wildly about the congregation, everyone still sat frozen and oblivious to what was happening around them. As the people sat in the rows of pews, the blood first rose to their ankles, and then higher. Margaret tried to snap herself out of the nightmare unfolding before her, and struggled to return her attention to this foul thing that held her kin's soul in its hands. Powerless to save her aunt from eternal damnation, Margaret tried to ration out an idea to stop this demon.

"Thyme is against you," the creature hissed; the words uttered from the death encrusted mouth were purely ethereal and demonic.

"Time?" Margaret repeated breathlessly, misunderstanding the word. The foul breath of the wraith irritated her nostrils, and she turned her head to gag. In an attempt to regain her composure, she fought back the intense terror that seeped out of her every pore, and addressed the dark entity, her voice shockingly steady and bold. "Why do you do what you do? What possible gain could you have by invoking the evil in everything you touch?"

"Because it's what I do…it's what I live for. You should know *that*, human. You should know better. You're better than mere humans. They are but cattle. Pah! You disgust me. You have become so little and pitiful—what use have I for your attention? I only care to acknowledge your true self. But you…." The foul fiend stopped short and stared at Margaret. "Ahhhhh, you have forgotten…everything!" he said with a hiss. "Well now, this game should be more fun than the last time we played!" he continued before he erupted into insidious laughter.

Thoughts that had been brewing in the back of Margaret's head snaked their way toward the front of her skull, slowly at first, then rushing forward like a steam locomotive at full speed as flickers of memories flashed before her inquisitive eyes. With the information she was receiving too much for her human mind to accept and process so quickly, a splitting migraine pierced

Margaret's temples, and she knelt in the growing pool on the floor of the church, grasping the sides of her head in agony. She wondered where the lighter being she'd seen battle the dark creature in her vision the night before was, but it was nowhere to be seen. The phantom held Lucille's soul in its grasp, looking it over as he would inspect an article of clothing.

In the seconds following Lucille's separation from her body, a distinct glow began in the stained-glass skylight of the church. Though Margaret was silently wishing for this spirit's appearance, she could not help but feel a pang of fear streak through her body that spiraled outward from the pit of her gut. With no one to help her stop the madness that surrounded her, Margaret began to cry. When a delicate porcelain hand flew up to wipe away the tears, the woman found a black, ashy substance flowing from her eyes.

Not this again! Margaret thought to herself, fearful that there would be a repeat of the photograph incident. She tried to push all of her fear aside and listen to the voice of reason that she was sure survived somewhere within her. She could hear her heart beating in her ears, and could hear herself breathing. She listened for other sounds of humanity, but the only other thing she could hear was the sound of the monster that was forcing her Aunt Lucille's soul away from its departure into eternal rest.

In a panic, Margaret tried to think about what the swamp witch had said about magic being what you wanted to see, but dismissed this almost immediately. Why would she purposely want to see such horrors unfold before her eyes? But perhaps this was not magic after all, and therefore the rule would not apply in this case. As other darker thoughts began to form and pervade her mind, Margaret looked toward the skylight of the church and noticed the lighter being descending. The form had taken on a more humanoid shape than it had the first time she saw it. Margaret cocked her head to one side in curiosity, but was astounded that she felt afraid. The wraith remained steadfast with Lucille's spirit in its hold, but turned its attention away from the human woman and focused on the other apparition. The dark one drew back as the lighter one approached, but did not seek refuge in the many shadows harbored within the church.

From somewhere in the hollow of the church halls, echoed voices chanted some ritualistic words that Margaret could not make out. Voices spoken in both English and a foreign language met the housewife's ears, and though she was not able to speak it, she discerned from the sound that the other language may have been Latin.

Like the tall man at the voodoo hag's house had inquired, "'If you do not speak it, then how do you know it is French she speaks?'" While Margaret would agree to a point, she knew the sound of certain languages, and Latin was one she was more familiar with, though in these times was really only used in the church.

As the light apparition grew closer, Margaret expected to watch the wraith become weak and give up only to slither away into the darkness, releasing Lucille's soul to freedom. But to her amazement, the creature allowed the spirit to approach completely. The spectacle lasted for such a long time, though the clock in the church would testify that no time had passed in actuality. The sound of Margaret's heartbeat began to pound louder in her ears, and as Lucille's form writhed in the phantom's grip, the light dissolved from sight as it entered the decayed corporeal body that housed the dark creature.

A brilliant flash of light followed, growing frightfully large, filling the entirety of the congregation area in the church. The light danced wickedly off the bloody pool that continued to rise, reaching the chests of those still seated on the pews who were taller than others whose heads had already slipped beneath the dark liquid. A foul stench had begun to rise out of the mess, though Margaret hadn't noticed until now. The rancid odor of the scarlet fluid leaked inward to her nostrils, sending signals to her brain that the smell of death was in the air. Margaret choked on the offensive odor, helpless to do anything about it. She found it necessary to shield her eyes from the large, glowing orb that had once been the light spirit and the dark wraith. The light was becoming far too garish to look at, but just as it crossed to the point where Margaret could no longer look at it, the mass of light exploded into a million glowing embers, scattering into darkness.

Out of the midst of the explosion, Margaret watched as Lucille's spirit was released and rose gently upward and disappeared as it passed through the roof of the church. Her aunt appeared as a semi-transparent humanoid figure that really held no features of the deceased, but merely the suggestion of a female apparition surrounded in a light blue glow.

Margaret screamed as the projection of herself slammed into her body and ripped her out of whatever lurid nightmare realm she had somehow entered. All those present at the funeral snapped their heads around to look at her, and while some sitting on the same pew tried to comfort the woman, others simply shook their heads in embarrassment, refusing to make eye contact.

Margaret said nothing. She cleared her throat softly and shifted her gaze to the floor after taking a very quick glance around to find everything normal once more. After a few more moments of silence, the preacher began again, and the funeral service continued.

When the last prayer had been said and all those who'd wished to say a few words to send Lucille off had finished their speeches, the family was prompted to take their last looks before the coffin was sealed forever. As grief-stricken family members meandered by in their black garments, more tears flowed, and noses ran with sorrow. Margaret wanted to be one of the last to say goodbye, and purposely got in at the end of the line. By contrast, several cousins who expected a large share when it came time to read the will made sure they were right at the very front. Some people placed flowers, and the line moving by only got held up once by a young child who didn't understand why Lucille was sleeping so much. When it was Margaret's turn, she wanted to take her time and wish the old woman off in the most sincere way possible. As she bent down over Lucille's final bed, she whispered her final wishes for her aunt, planted a gentle but awkward kiss upon the cold skin of Lucille's forehead, and patted the old woman's hand.

The longer Margaret lingered over the casket, the larger the lump in her throat grew, until Margaret finally had to force herself to move forward. The preacher was behind Margaret and said a silent prayer to Lucille before he reached up and grabbed the lid to close the casket. Tears clouded Margaret's eyes as the preacher closed the lid and left Lucille in the dark confines of the pine box.

The six men chosen to serve as Lucille's pallbearers lifted the heavy box and carted it out toward the interment lot of the church. Each man's face held a grim, solemn expression, their eyes focused upon the ground to make sure the trip to the gravesite was as smooth as possible for Lucille. Those gathered had pretty well cried all their eyes would allow, and now just stood sniffling as they watched Lucille's coffin lowered into the six feet deep hole previously dug to accommodate the large box. The smell of the freshly broken ground met Margaret's nose; it reminded her of the smell inside the greenhouse back at Lucille's house. The connection made her shudder, and she looked away.

After the grave was filled in, those who had not yet meandered off remained to place wreaths of flowers upon the fresh dirt mound. In total, Margaret counted twenty-five wreaths and two memorial stakes containing pictures of Lucille in her younger years. Having nothing more she could do, Margaret kissed her fingers and lay them gently upon the headstone erected toward the top of the grave mound.

"Goodbye, Lucille," Margaret whispered. With her words the wind picked up and sent a chill through the graveyard. Margaret pondered if perhaps Lucille was answering her in the only way she could.

Three hours after the funeral Margaret finally found a moment to herself, but still no time to open the chest. Voices from other family members out in the hallway just beyond her closed door prompted her to think that she could have company at any moment. She was sure someone would have questions for her regarding her outburst during the funeral. She lay back on the bed, resting her eyes while her mind sorting through many strange things.

So distant now were the events of the morning, though they'd happened just hours earlier. What had happened at the church was the main topic of the friends and family present to gossip about, and while some saw a fit of grief, others saw nothing but a show for attention. From time to time she envied the other family members, and almost wished that her only concern was gossiping about a relative she thought might be going off the deep end.

As she lay there thinking, she wondered why, out of everyone in the universe, it was she that had been chosen to go through this. Was she really someone so special that she would have to worry about being haunted by angels and demons her whole life? Why did she have to be so different than everyone else? It had always plagued Margaret, and had made for a tough time growing up with supernatural thoughts running through her head. She had to spend a lot of time pretending to be a certain way just to keep a certain level of normality around her.

Margaret had done her best to apologize to everyone throughout the afternoon for her "fit," and blamed it on a wave of grief that had struck her. However much anyone believed her, she couldn't say. She only knew for certain that she was glad the funeral was over and done with. She was sure she wasn't the only member of the family who was completely exhausted.

So many questions whirled about in Margaret's head, and so many strange things were left unanswered. Like her grandmother Agatha. Margaret did not really know much about the woman, except to Margaret's knowledge, she was still among the living. Perhaps that could be a resource for getting some answers. And what about the playing card, and the prediction the witch had made that had since come true?

At the funeral service, Lucille's attorney had taken the podium for a moment to read the last will and testament of Lucille Ordiki. After a few words written by Lucille and signed by her before her death, envelopes addressed to certain family members present were passed around to each party named in the will.

The old woman had known about the types of people some in her family were, and did not want to cause a stir at the service meant to send her off into the peaceful arms of eternity. She did not truly wish to leave much to those who did not deserve or need the benefits of her good fortune, but in the eyes of society did not wish to have anyone think any less of her.

As family members opened the envelopes and read through the contents, various sighs, laughs, and moans of disbelief rose up about the place; some outright threw a fit, with a complete disregard for the solemn setting and feelings of others about them.

Ignoring everyone else, Margaret had discreetly opened her letter, but found it difficult to refrain from smiling, knowing that her aunt had to be looking down at her at just that moment. She'd never asked for any help, and had always been the one to struggle for every last thing she'd ever received throughout her life. For her aunt to have left her what she had made Margaret smile broadly, although it was only to herself.

Margaret gently folded the letter, with the check for a much appreciated one thousand dollars, and placed it gingerly into her breast pocket. She didn't bother to think that surely there were other family members who'd received a larger portion. Instead, she was very grateful for this little share.

Thinking back, Margaret smiled, knowing that the money would definitely help her family. But as soon as her thoughts began to drift toward the chest, she suddenly realized what time it was getting to be. She had to get back home soon. Her husband had been temporarily laid off due to severe weather that had flooded the quarry where he worked. He'd been out of work for nearly a month now, and their savings had been dwindling all the while. Unable to access the workplace for a while until the rain stopped and the pools of water receded, he'd stayed at home with their children, so Margaret could attend her aunt's funeral. But with the weather straightening up back in Missouri, she had to get back home, so her husband could get back to work. As it was, even with the newly acquired inheritance, their family could not afford for her to spend the amount of time she wanted to in Louisiana.

That night was going to be Margaret's last night in the house that she'd spent a great deal of her childhood growing up in. The house had been left to Lucille's own children, and god only knew what was to become of it. The plantation had been all but shut down in the last few years while Lucille remained alive, but with both Mr. and Mrs. Ordiki gone, Margaret could only guess what lay in store for the house and the property surrounding it.

With bittersweet thoughts floating about her weary mind, Margaret packed up all within her room she felt she could rightly claim besides the items that were her own. Her slender fingers untied the ribbons that had kept the bed curtains back for so many years, and packed them in with a few other things from inside her old room. She was going to miss the ability to come by when the occasion arose. She was going to miss the ability to sleep again in the room that housed so many memories for her. But like all things in the life of a mortal, it had to come to an end at some point, and the next morning it would do just that.

Margaret had retained the driver that would transport her to her home in Missouri, where a worried husband and anxious children awaited her return. Another thanks to her late aunt, for always ensuring she had a way home. And even after her death, Lucille's private motor car driver was still dedicated and loyal to her family, and had agreed to drive Margaret home despite the distance one last time. Though it was still a long journey, it beat taking a horse and carriage. After the events over the last couple of days, Margaret found herself doubting that things would be the same in her life. The only things she knew for sure were that something strange lie in wait inside that jewelry chest, and that she had a lot of work ahead of her to try to solve the mystery bequeathed to her by her dear Aunt Lucille.

CHAPTER 5

The car arrived very early the next morning. Not many members of the family had stayed behind in the house beyond the funeral, giving the place an empty and humbling atmosphere. Normally the place would have been full of so much life, but with Lucille and the mourners gone, all that remained was a mere shell of what things had been. So many empty shelves and missing family portraits, so many items stripped from the house where they belonged. Margaret was disgusted by the flagrant displays of mini feuds she'd witnessed throughout, as relatives disputed who got what beyond what Lucille's will detailed.

If her driver was able to drive straight through, the trip would take approximately two days, but it was just not possible. On the way there it had taken them three days because they'd had to stop and wait out rough weather a few times. Summertime in the Midwest was sure to show the ugly face of thunderstorms — that was just how it worked during the stormy season. Knowing the approximate time frame, Margaret knew she had to get moving soon.

She did not want to open the chest while sitting in the back seat of the motor car but knew she would finally have a moment to herself once they stopped off at a motel so they could rest.

She found herself strangely excited for this moment and could not believe the butterflies in her stomach that came with thinking about it; she felt like a child again in great anticipation for a long-awaited event.

She thought back to the visions she'd seen before her as the witch had gone into the story of Gemini, but she still did not understand just what it was that she was supposed to do. If previous family members in her lineage had been unsuccessful, how was it that she was supposed to get things right? The idea of seeking out Agatha had started the moment the swamp hag had mentioned the name, and it had been growing stronger ever since.

At long last Margaret found herself alone. The motel lobby's undecorated pale blue walls carried on throughout the whole of the building. Tarnished brass electric lights dotted the narrow halls, and every sound could be heard any time someone walked by on the creaky wooden floor outside her door.

Thin yellowed curtains did little to keep out the shadows from the overgrown shrubbery that invited themselves in and rested upon various pieces of furniture placed throughout the motel room. They had stopped somewhere between Arkansas and Oklahoma on their journey back to rural Missouri. Margaret had to admit she would inevitably miss the almost jungle-like appearance of the Louisiana swampland, compared to the miles and miles of boring farmland laden with prairie grass and corn fields.

Rural Missouri around her home in Jasper was all but exciting, at least for a dreamer like Margaret. Though she'd grown up near there and had spent many a day throughout the years as a child between her home there and with her aunt in Louisiana, she'd managed to leave home and still live mere miles away from her father's homestead. Through her thinking about what it was like living back home with her father, she began to remember something she'd long forgotten.

Tucked comfortably in the folds of the motel bed's blankets, Margaret sat in silence, holding the chest in her lap. She ran her fingers over the intricate metal work decorating the cherry wood box. A strange electricity seemed to course through her fingertips upon touching the old chest. As she sat there between the crisp linen sheets and an obviously well-worn homemade quilt, the static sensation seemed to heighten the intensity and clarity of the memory coming to Margaret's mind.

The mother of twins took a deep breath and withdrew the tiny key from around her neck. The bronze key slid easily into the lock, and a tiny click was barely audible, even in the still of the room. Margaret found herself shaking with anticipation as she pulled the lid open.

Images took Margaret back to about the age of eleven. While adventuring about the two-acre yard of her father's homestead, she'd happened upon a series of stones half buried in the dirt. Along the length of the acreage, wonderful, thick grass grew, perfect for bare feet. The child Margaret was left to her own time quite a bit, while her father worked in an attempt to keep up with the needs of a growing child.

Her father had always seemed so stern a man, so inexplicably sad. Well, not so inexplicable, as his wife had passed and left him with a small child to care for on his own. Margaret was never allowed to inquire about her, nor mention her name near her father. But she had always felt the need to learn more about her, and more about the secrets which her father seemed to harbor within his lonely heart.

As her feet traveled through the soft, lush emerald blades protruding from the summer-dry ground, a barren spot near the fence row caught her attention as it never had before. Curious, Margaret discarded the handful of wildflowers she'd gathered from her trek through the yard. These hints of stone beckoned to her like nothing she'd ever come across.

She knelt by one corner of the exposed rock and followed it across with her eyes. Whatever this was seemed both suspicious and deliberate, sending a quiver of excitement over the young girl. Margaret could smell the alfalfa that grew wild among the grass carpet, but the scent was tainted by reality taking over her memory.

Margaret could smell the musty scent of the crimson velvet that lined the chest. The hinges squeaked open, sounding as if the box had never been opened but she knew it had at some point through her conversation with Madamé Hanté.

Immediately inside were two scrolls, both wrapped tightly and held in place with a different colored piece of ribbon—one black, one white. The candle that Margaret had lit and sat on the bureau in the room suddenly puffed out; it appeared the flame had just been hit by a massive gust of wind, though nothing had disturbed the air as far as she could tell.

Eerily, at the same moment, the room seemed to shudder violently as a clap of thunder boomed out of nowhere. A large flash of lightning, which cast strange shadows across the room through the partially drawn curtains, quickly traversed the angry sky outside the window.

Margaret somehow sensed that this was not just a coincidence. Trembling, her thin fingers ran across one band of the colored ribbon. A jolt snaked through her; her fingertips had just met a considerable charge of static electricity. She jumped, startled at the sensation, though it had not harmed her.

Her memory continued. Odd, she pondered, that it would surface at the time she finally got to see what was inside the mysterious jewelry chest.

Her younger self, so massively intrigued with the line of stones, ran as fast as she could back to the barn where her father kept all of his tools. She remembered being quite out of breath and anxious that her father might come home and find her with his things — it was a very strict rule of the house not to touch certain things without permission. Her heart beat wildly and her respirations became ragged as she sat in the motel bed reliving this discarded childhood memory.

She had selected a spade and returned to the portion of the property she'd discovered. Casting a nervous glance toward the farmhouse, she decided that it was okay for her to start digging. And dig she would do, until beads of sweat rolled down from her determined brow and stung her chestnut eyes.

As she removed dirt from around the stones, she noticed the sound of metal scraping against something hard in the ground. Margaret stopped and tossed the shovel aside, beginning to dig with her bare hands. As her tender fingers scooped away the red clay and dirt, something sharp as a dagger sliced across her palm.

A shard of broken glass buried in the soil out of sight had split the flesh of Margaret's hand, and blood began to leak from the fresh wound. Dirt had already gotten into the cut, and Margaret pulled her hand back with a cry. With her intact hand she withdrew what remained of a whiskey bottle and tossed it aside.

Margaret wiped away the tears that had sprung forth from her aching eyes, smearing blood and dirt across her young face. As she sat in the grass surrounded by moved earth, she noticed a large, flat stone in the freshly dug dirt in front of her.

Ever curious, Margaret took her unwounded hand and brushed the dirt away; the stone appeared to have words engraved upon it. *Here lies beloved wife and mother Mary, with son Ad—* But dirt covered the remaining portion of the name. Margaret's "memory self" gasped, understanding she'd just uncovered a grave.

Recovering this forgotten event in her past, Margaret forced herself to remember what happened next. Stunned to see "son" on the grave marker, she rose to her feet, stumbling backward with tears of confusion staining her cheeks. The child Margaret's head began to spin, and she slumped to her knees on the ground.

A strong hand grasped her shoulder and she screamed. Her father had returned home and found the shed door open.

"The *hell* you think you're doin' child?!" his voice boomed. But Margaret only sobbed and stared at the grave. "I am speaking to you, Margaret! Stand up!" he yelled, grabbing the young girl by the arms and forcing her to her feet. Her legs felt weak and wobbled like jelly. "When I got home from work my spade was missing. Now I know why!" anger and anxiety both plagued the work-worn man as his furrowed brow stared down at his daughter.

"I don't! What *is* this? What *is* this?!" Margaret cried, looking up at her father.

"Honey…you just shouldn't know about such things yet. You're too young."

"Too young for the truth? Why is there a grave here with Momma's name on it? Why does the grave say something about a son? Do I have a brother?" the young Margaret asked sternly. Her tears had ceased, and she looked her father right in the eye.

"Did, Margaret. Sweetie, you had a twin brother. But he—"

"Died at birth?" Margaret asked with a sniffle.

"Not exactly. You see, something happened to your mother."

"What? What happened to Mother?" Margaret pressed.

"I can't say. I don't really know what the hell it was. I know it changed her—and not for the good. God only knows how awful it sounded when she said those words to me…," Margaret's father began, but trailed off.

"What did she say?"

"She said…." He sighed heavily and looked up at the sky. "'There can be only one.'"

"Only one what?" Margaret interrupted, her mind failing to

make sense of all of this.

"Twin. Only one twin. And then Adam—"

"My brother?"

"Yes. Adam was j-j-just gone," the man said, his words appearing to drain the very life out of him at that solemn moment. Margaret did not need her father to tell her that it was her own mother that had ended her young brother's life. There was nothing in the universe that would ever convince her otherwise, but Margaret refused to blame her mother without knowing all of the circumstances involved. As the sun set upon that terrible day, Margaret and her father spent the time in silence, filling in the grave that had been unearthed. There was a reason he'd wanted to keep it buried; but now that reason was moot.

She settled into the blankets, picked up one of the scrolls, and carefully handled the ancient parchment, untying the white ribbon around it. She took a few deep breaths to clear away the unfeeling emptiness that followed the memory she'd just relived within her mind. As she unrolled the yellowed paper, it took on a life of its own and grew rigid in her hands. Curious, she looked over the scroll, marveling at the intricate artwork on the paper. Margaret's eyes met the drawing of a being, equally proportioned but split into two halves. The right half was the figure of a woman. She was nude, perfectly formed, with flowing hair, enchanting eyes, and full lips. Her arm was extended up toward the heavens in a very serene sweep, her gentle nature gracefully flowing right off the parchment.

The perfect form of the beautiful woman morphed directly into the other half, which was not nearly as appealing to the human eye. The image faded into a hideous creature, obviously male in nature, but barely human. A long, pointed ear graced the still-fleshy portion of the male half's head, which otherwise was nothing but a rotted corpse. Portions of bone jutted out unnaturally across the ribcage of the male's half of the image, though Margaret failed to understand what it was she was even looking at. This half of the picture had no other purpose than to show the total opposite of the gentle beauty morphed on its other side. A gnarled hand with claws reached toward the ground, trying to grasp some unknown, unseen evil right out of the soil below it.

As Margaret poured over the symbols and the fine lines of the pentagram that encased the dual-being sketch, she felt herself losing her sense of reality for a moment. She felt she was being pulled into the drawing with the two creatures, and for a few seconds, she allowed the feeling to intensify with the hopes of gaining a better understanding of what she was looking at. She wondered carefully about the nephilim that the swamp hoodoo witch had mentioned, about the human cattle that Thyme had mentioned. Margaret began to wonder if the answer wasn't that the mysterious scrolls and the legend around them weren't the only things related. She began to ponder, what if *she* was what was related?

Then she saw it. At the bottom center of the scroll was the word "Gemini" printed in calligraphy. As she looked at the sketch, she began to make out other words hidden within the lines of the pentagram that she hadn't noticed before. It was fascinating and strange, but the longer her hands ran over the parchment, a feeling of déjà vu began to grow, and a new question had arisen from the drawing. Obviously, the scroll was quite old, but where had it come from?

Blinking, she looked away to clear her eyes. She hadn't noticed, but two hours had slipped by since she'd begun to look at the scroll's sketch. Needing to get a little rest, Margaret began to roll the scroll up, but paused just a quick moment to look at the wording. Much to her surprise, she found nothing else on the parchment, but the drawing of the half man-half woman centered in the pentagram. She decided that perhaps she was having hallucinations from being tired and going through what she had the last few days. She rolled up the first scroll and retied the white ribbon.

Though she was tired, she gave herself just a brief moment to look over the second scroll. Untying the black ribbon gave the same electrical sensation as the other, but Margaret almost expected it. This scroll also stood rigidly at attention in the grasp of her thin fingers. To Margaret's astonishment, the second parchment was blank, except calligraphy wording in an arced band across the top that read *The Face of Thyme*. The woman's tired eyes blinked back tears of fright that had come from her memory of that voice that had told her *"Thyme is against you"* earlier. As she held the scroll in her nimble fingers, a deep orange glow began to center itself upon the page, somehow emanating from within the paper itself and yet disconnected from it entirely.

Margaret had closed her eyes for a moment, slowly feeling herself succumb to the drowsiness expected to follow a long day. Margaret yawned deeply, completely ignoring the glowing light emanating from the parchment. Instead, she wondered if, in some twisted way, she was yet to discover that those words the voice had spoken to her had a direct connection to this scroll and how thyme was spelled. To her knowledge, ancient Egyptians used thyme largely for embalming and for flavoring in cheeses and wines. It was also thought to ward off nightmares if placed under one's pillow; even as incense placed into caskets at funerals.

She knew she was quite frazzled and would wait until her mind was more at ease before looking again. Like the first scroll, she rerolled the blank one and replaced the black ribbon around it. Her mind grew fuzzy — an after effect of the events of the long day she'd had — and Margaret thought it best to leave it alone for the night and take another look once she was well rested.

CHAPTER 6

Time was crawling toward the earliest morning hours when Margaret's weary mind entered dreamland. She found herself standing in the middle of a cemetery, looking over the grave of her deceased aunt. Everything was in black and white, and there was no sound despite leaves fluttering in the trees from the wind that blew through them. Though colorless, she blinked as bright sun rays were piercing her eyes, and as she strained to peer through the brightness, she noticed several people standing about the graveyard. Everyone was dressed in the ebony shades of unflattering funeral attire, but no one noticed Margaret's presence even though she stood in the center of them all. All the people remained silent—a deafening sound to her ears. In the back of her mind Margaret could hear the eerie cackle of some creature not of the earth, and every time the hideous abomination would appear to her, another lighter half would always be there to ward it off. As Margaret looked around at those standing about, the black of their clothes fluidly rippled, leaking outward like black ink before morphing into a shadowy being. Margaret knew full well what this was, and dared not look it in its shimmering, strange green eyes. A terrible feeling of utter cold and dread washed over her as the thing took shape and started making its

95

way toward her.

Margaret tried to call out for help, but those present in the cemetery were completely oblivious to her. As before, they would not move, look at her, or speak to her, though she was unsure if it was because they couldn't or that they were really not there at all. As Margaret stood between realms, locked somewhere on the line between life and death, she felt an untamed fear swelling within her. As she drew toward the cusp of what should have been sheer terror, she felt the horror begin to diminish as the shadow wraith approached.

"*What* are you?!" Margaret screamed out, though in the empty void around her the voice that should have echoed back manifested itself as a hoarse and breathless whisper.

"I am Thyme," the phantom answered, his voice clear, but sounding stressed and unearthly. As the black shadow drew ever closer, Margaret mustered the mental strength to thrust her arms upward and raise her eyes to the heavens, fighting the overwhelming urge to continue staring into the creature's glassy, soulless eyes.

At the moment the shadow was about to reach out and grab hold of Margaret, a brilliant flash of light filled the air around her, and an intense high-pitched squeal began in both of her ears. As the sound pierced Margaret's very soul, she realized this was the voice of an angel to human ears. She was not sure how she knew, but her gut feeling was correct. The sound was far too much for Margaret's ears, and they began to bleed. As the warm scarlet fluid trickled out, Margaret dropped to her knees, her hands slapped over each ear to block out the sound. Her mind whirled about with a vertigo unlike anything she'd ever felt as her human mind tried to make sense of what was happening.

As abruptly as the sounds had begun, all fell silent. There was no sound, no light, no air moving. There was, in that moment, nothing. Margaret paused a moment, cringing in the purest form of fear humanly possible, but slowly removed her hands from her ears and opened her eyes as her lungs expelled a breath she'd been holding a little while now. Confused when she felt no wetness on her hands, though her ears had been bleeding seconds ago, Margaret blinked in the darkness. She found no light to sting her eyes, but then it occurred to her—it was tears doing the stinging. A heavy sensation of grief washed through her, pouring forth from her mouth in the form of a sorrowful sigh. Like someone unseen was turning a dial slowly, dim light began to illuminate this cold place Margaret now found herself in. Margaret first inspected her palms, only to reveal that there was, in fact, no blood upon them.

Margaret looked out before her, finding a long tunnel-like structure that seemed to go on into infinity. The darkness of this hall was the richest shade of blue-black that the woman had ever seen, and it was only illuminated enough for her to find her way around. As she stood in the damp, dark tunnel, something hit the back of her head. Whatever it was seemed harmless enough. At first, she passed it off as a fleeting figment of her imagination, but a second later, something else brushed past her cheek. As her hand lifted to swipe where the thing had touched, a soft, satin leaf fell into her open palm.

Margaret jumped, startled, but smiled sheepishly to herself when she found it to be a rose petal. Confused, she looked around to find the floor coated with flower petals, and noticed they were floating down from the ceiling. Curious to find the source, Margaret looked upward toward the endless darkness that met her eyes, and as she assumed the ceiling had to be quite high to be so very dark, she felt thick, wet drops begin to drop onto her face. Perturbed, Margaret swatted at the fluid, not wanting the wetness to stay upon her bare flesh without her knowing what it was. As her fingers raked lightly across her face, a crimson smear followed, leaving tracks and spatters upon her fair complexion.

The light bright enough and her eyes adjusted as well as they were going to in the dingy tunnel, she withdrew her hand from her face, mortified when she saw the blood upon her fingertips. The drops of blood fell more frequently from the ceiling now, and the drops themselves grew larger. Streams of blood ran down Margaret's hair, and dripped from her clothing in a scarlet shower. Panic was swelling far beyond the tolerable bounds of the conscious mind when the ringing left from the piercing sound of the angel's voice began to vanish, and new sounds took the place of the partial deafness.

Sounding much like a leaky basement or sewer tunnel, drips of water resonated as they crawled off the dingy alabaster walls and into sporadic pools yet unseen upon the damp floor; Margaret wished it was only water that fell. The thought that pools of blood lay upon the floor for her to tread through was not appealing, and Margaret did her best to push that thought from her mind. Though no scent wafted about, Margaret suspected it would smell of mildew and stagnant blood, and with the light so dim, she squinted still to peer through the eerie darkness out in front of her. The high, arched ceiling of whatever this place was supposed to be was lined with recessed spaces tall enough for a large man to stand upon the shelf built right into the wall on both sides. The overhead arc of the structure should have housed stained glass windows, if windows of any kind had been present.

The sound of bird feathers fluttering echoed loudly in the near silence throughout the long, gloomy hall, startling Margaret and making her jump. The longer she stood there, the more detail became clearer to the woman's weary eyes. A few more seconds passed, and several figures came into focus. Upon each shelf inset into the walls sat human figures perched in different positions. Some stood about, some sat, either with their feet dangling off the edge, cross-legged, or with an arm hugging a bent knee. No matter the position, each gazed down the hall in the opposite direction of Margaret. These people were dressed in white linen that seemed to flow directly off their bodies, the fabric a part of their delicate skin. Thin-strapped sandals wrapped themselves about the ankles up to the calves of each person, holding a flat, leather-like plate against the sole of each foot. For the most part, each person looked about the same, though slight variances in hair color could be discerned even in the dim light. It was only when one man turned from his seated position and flew right off the edge of the shelf he'd been sitting on that Margaret better understood what she was looking at. Large white-feathered wings spread gracefully out from nubs that grew out of the skin between the shoulder blades; the sound of fluttering was not the sound of birds after all.

Throwing everything she'd ever known about angels into the darkness, Margaret's mind scrambled to make sense of where she was. She tried to think about everything she'd ever read—even about fallen angels, though she had to admit these did not appear to be that sort of angel. Despite the presence of an outsider, none of the angels noticed she was there, or even so much as cast a glance her way. Her imagination could not have conjured the images or atmosphere of this place, and she began to wonder if she was still in her dream or not. Curious, she thought perhaps they had simply not noticed she was there, so she called out in the loudest, most commanding voice the woman could muster. No effect. The longer she stayed within this cold, damp tunnel of angels, ideas began to expand within her brain that she knew, somehow, were not her own, but rather knowledge being absorbed from the hall of angels. No, this was not the hall of angels—it was the Hall of Judgment. The thought hit her mind like a tsunami, and at first it was overwhelming and too much for her to take in.

Little by little, she was able to see more details in the massive catacomb stretched out before her, making it less like a dream. She noticed her feet growing cold—she was without shoes, and the wet floor, which felt like concrete to her bare flesh, stung her toes with an intense frigidity. Margaret had always known everything about death to be cold, and the absolute, dark void that whirled about her even now made her start to think perhaps she had passed away. As Margaret took slow, steady steps, at the end of the passageway the light seemed to grow a bit brighter. To her utter amazement, out of the shadows came figures of those she'd known before — the faces of her deceased relatives waiting in the light for her. But was it for her? They were distracted and indifferent to her presence, almost insinuating that they could not see her. Then what was the purpose of her seeing all of this? More and more shadows climbed out of the darker shadows, and with each, another angel would loose itself from its perch on the shelf and fly toward the phantom to greet it.

With urgency wrenching inside her guts to reach the end of the hall, she ran faster and faster, but the angels ignored her that much more. Screaming out louder as anxiety raced through her body, only the sound of the fluttering wings resounded to her. She then realized that in the eyes of the angels there to judge those who passed, she was nothing. She did not exist. Not because of a lack of faith, or willingness to believe what she was seeing around her. But because of the simple fact that only one who'd passed from the living to the dead could be seen. So…she wasn't dead. Why, then, was she here?

And then one shadow reached at Margaret from behind; cold hands of some ghost slid against her warmth, sending chills down through her core. A whisper sounded in her ear as frigid air met the back of her neck.

"The hands of Thyme are against you." A sneer was buried in the voice.

As the arms began to grip tighter, Margaret could feel her body being dragged backward. The figure of a deceased family member from up ahead looked away from the angel who'd come to guide her down further into the Hall of Judgment, and straight into Margaret's eyes.

"Not yet." The voice sounded so clearly in Margaret's head, though no sign came that the person had actually spoken a word. Margaret focused long enough for her to see if it had been her Aunt Lucille, and with a gasp, darkness closed in on Margaret and everything fell silent around her.

The sound of knocking at her hotel room door drew her out of her sleep and back into the corporeal plane. It was time to get back on the road home. It was Margaret's priority to get to the bottom of this centuries-old mystery, and she didn't care how long it took her to figure it out.

***

It was a very early morning hour when Margaret's ride pulled up into the Glover residence driveway. Though still dark outside, light from a lantern in the tool shed meant that Henry was already up. No doubt he was inside gathering the necessary items in preparation to return to work. The muffled sound of the automobile's tires rolling through the gravel drive caught his attention, and he stepped through the already open door of the small shed. Henry hadn't been sure of exactly when to expect his wife but looked happy to see her arrive home safely.

The tall man lay down the pick axe he held upon the wooden work bench inside the tool shed. He stripped off the worn leather work gloves he frequently used to keep his hands from getting so calloused that they split open. He had learned that lesson the hard way many years ago. He balanced them atop the handle of the pick axe and grabbed the lantern he was using to find his way in the dark.

Inside the automobile, Margaret lay slumped to one side. Her deep smooth breaths let the driver know she was sleeping, but he didn't want to wake her. Henry stepped up to the door on Margaret's side and set the lantern on top of the motor car. As

101

Henry bent down to look into the window, he could see his wife resting peacefully. He took a finger and tapped at the window gently. Margaret stirred momentarily, but never opened her eyes. The driver stepped out from behind the wheel and went to retrieve Margaret's bags. Henry simply nodded at the man, who nodded back at him, but the two remained silent. As the driver grabbed hold of one of the bags, he suddenly jumped as if he'd been shocked and dropped the bag to grab at his arm. The jewelry chest within the bag crashed to the ground with a heavy, solid thump.

"You all right there, mister?" Henry called out softly, looking at the driver massaging his injured arm.

"Uh...yes sir. I...it's an...old injury. Nothing more," he stated, shifting his gaze to the ground.

"You sure? It looked like to me that you had some sort of —" Henry began, concerned.

"NOTHING more," the driver repeated, his voice stressed and stern. Henry noticed that the driver ignored the fallen bag and reached for another suitcase. Dismissing the driver's odd behavior, Henry rapped harder on the window, finally rousing Margaret. Bleary eyed from her deep sleep, and still on edge from the strange events that had haunted her in Louisiana, she jumped, nearly hitting her head on the top of the automobile.

"Jesus, Margaret! What's got you so tense?" Henry asked as he opened the door.

Margaret snapped wide awake and grabbed her husband with both arms, embracing him tightly, releasing a guttural sigh as she would if she'd just finished sobbing heavily. Henry pushed her back, so he could look at her. His steel grey eyes looked over his wife's fair features.

"Margaret, are you okay? I'm glad you're home...you must be exhausted from your trip. Come on, let's get you inside and get you comfortable," Henry offered, seeing the weariness upon her face.

"The chest. I need you to pick it up for me. I must keep it with me," she whispered in his ear, running her fingers through his thick, dark hair. As she leaned against him, he could feel her body quivering and the clamminess of her skin.

"Chest? What chest? What are you talking about? In that bag the driver dropped when he hurt his arm?" Henry asked, looking around.

"Yes. You will see...I will tell you everything," Margaret answered softly. Henry thought her voice sounded strange but said nothing. He sensed that something had changed about his wife but couldn't quite place what.

CHAPTER 7

About two hours after Margaret's return home, the couple sat across from each other — one sipping coffee, the other sipping tea. A clock ticked behind Margaret; the sound made her feel edgy. Margaret hoped that Henry would have some compassion and not expect her to pour details like a flood about her trip to Louisiana, the funeral, and this big news she had made mention of. But that was up to Henry, and so far, Margaret sat silently at the table, sipping her tea with an expression of weariness that could bring down the world's most positive optimist.

"OK, so are you going to talk? Or do you just need to go to bed to get some sleep? This isn't how I thought our first conversation after you'd been gone for a week would go. What's wrong, Maggie? Are you still shook up about your aunt?" Henry said, trying to break the awkward silence around them.

"I'm sorry. You have no idea what has happened since I—" Margaret began, her words carried on labored breath.

"No, but maybe I would if you'd say something," Henry interrupted.

"What I'm about to tell you is going to seem far-fetched. It's something you won't believe, but you *have* to, Henry," Margaret said. Her tone of voice had dropped, insinuating that what she had to say was something Margaret believed to be serious.

"What's wrong with you? You haven't been right since you learned of your Aunt Lucille's death. I know you just got home a couple of hours ago and that you must be tired, but the way you're acting suggests something else. You're just acting... strange. Are you feelin' okay?" Henry answered.

"No, it's nothing like that. I...look, there's something that happened while I was down south — something I know you're going to hate to hear. I just need to find the right words to tell you, that's all," Margaret said, setting her tea cup down.

"What? What happened that's so secretive?" Henry coaxed, but his voice held tones of sarcasm. Margaret swallowed hard. She wanted, just then, to call it hopeless and stop the story, but something inside her urged her to continue.

"That jewelry chest contains something I don't fully understand," Margaret said, giving a nod to the counter by the sink in their kitchen where she'd set the chest when they first got inside the farmhouse. Though it'd been sitting there the entire time they had, it was only when Margaret nodded to it that Henry's gaze shifted toward the small cherry wood box.

"Stop. This is something to do with the occult, or all that funny shit, ain't it? Margaret, you *know* I don't like that kind of stuff...I want no part of — " Henry said, but Margaret interrupted.

"Henry, you are as much a part of this, already, as I am. I don't know how you *can't* believe that maybe, just maybe, there's something bigger than you and I. Something man wasn't meant to fully understand."

"How can you?! This is nonsense. Foolish child's games!" Henry exclaimed, his fingers curling into fists of frustration. After holding each fist a few seconds, he took a deep breath and attempted to lose the temper that flared within him. He relaxed his fingers, working them open and closed, massaging the air around them.

"How can you *say* that? What about that hotel we stayed in on our honeymoon? How do you explain that specter we saw?" Margaret said, starting to dredge a memory that for Henry had been gladly suppressed for many years.

"I told you we will *not* speak of that. Look, we both had some wine—I can't say for sure what we both saw. But what has this got to do with anything, anyway?" Henry said, raising his voice.

"Shh! You'll wake the kids. You know what—just forget it. I don't want to fight with you, I just got home," Margaret suggested, shaking her head. She should have known that her husband was so closed-minded she would never make any ground with him about this strange situation.

"No, Margaret. You started this. Say what you've got to say," he urged, probably hoping if she poured her heart out, she would not bring up the subject again.

"Fine. Everything it is. What I'm about to tell you—I can't deal with this alone. I need you to support me, once I've told you everything," Margaret started again as she looked her husband in the eyes. She searched for understanding, but found a look that reminded her of a cross between weariness and cynicism.

"Margaret, God knows I love you, and you know I'd do most anything for you. But how can you sit there and expect me to support you on something that you, yourself, just said you didn't fully understand?" Henry said, raising a point.

"But you haven't even heard what I've got to tell you yet."

"Go ahead…," Henry said with a sigh.

"Look, I'll give you the short version. I was visited by a dark specter. I do not quite understand my connection to this being, but apparently Lucille's bloodline—*my* bloodline—is something special. Not of this world…."

Henry's hands flew up, blocking her words. "*Margaret!*" Henry said sternly, his single word sharp and commanding. But Margaret did not stop her story. As before, she seemed to enter a trance-like state, and details began to pour from her quickly and in detail. Henry had no choice but to try and follow her words.

"At Lucille's house, Arnie—my aunt's butler—brought me the jewelry chest. He was very nervous—so...anxious—he couldn't wait to be rid of the thing. Like he was...afraid of it," Margaret began. Henry's face had already tensed with a look of skepticism that Margaret was all too familiar with. "I was told that my bloodline is very special, and that what lay inside was—" Margaret continued, but Henry interrupted her.

"Look, I'm willing to hear this story of yours, but please skip to something that was actually strange," Henry requested, not impressed with her tale so far.

"I believe I may be from another time or place. I believe my ancestors were chosen to fight some evil force," Margaret said, skipping right to the core of the story.

"*What*?!" Henry exclaimed, taken off guard.

"Just wait...I've had these visions. Something is trying to get my attention to stop me from discovering the truth that lies inside that jewelry chest. An evil presence has plagued me ever since Mr. Flatts handed the box to me at Lucille's house."

"Come on, Margaret, something *evil*? We are talking about reality, not some biblical story meant to frighten children," Henry said with sarcastic disbelief.

Margaret scowled at him. "Henry, this was...is real! Damn it! Listen to me, please! There are two of them—two beings that come together every century to form a single, greater being. One is an angel, the other is a demon. I am here to stop them, and the answers to the riddle lie inside the velvet confines of that cherry wood box. I have seen such hideous sights, Henry, things that a human was not meant to survive seeing. Gore...blood...death. Lucille was trying to tell me something when I watched the evil spirit pull her soul from her body at the funeral. I went to visit a medium, who was suggested to me at Lucille's house, in the hopes she could enlighten me, and she told me the story of *Gemini* and pointed me in the right direction. I think I may be someone reincarnated as—" Margaret explained, her words making little sense to her husband.

"Margaret Ann Glover. I…you…you shouldn't be…." Henry seemed to be fighting to find the right words. "Look…sometimes we have dreams that lead us to believe we have experienced something, when in reality, we have not. But—"

"Henry! *These* are not *dreams!* I know how it must—" Margaret began, but Henry interrupted once again.

"Stop! Just stop! You'd best be careful…talkin' out of your head like that. *That* is how you wind up in those sanitariums!" Henry warned.

"Damn it, Henry! I can't explain this. God only knows I've always wondered why I believe in half of the things I do…." Margaret trailed off when she noticed that Henry's stern look was not fading. She just shook her head.

Trying to think of any possible way to convince her husband, she remembered the photograph of her mother killing her infant brother. She'd left the photograph crumpled up in her overcoat pocket. She jumped up from the table, jogged over to the coat rack just inside the kitchen door, retrieved the picture, and returned to the table where Henry still sat.

"You don't believe me?! Here, take a look!" Margaret tossed the photograph at Henry. "I don't know *how* it's possible, but I vomited…." she continued as Henry reached for the crumpled paper.

"What's this? You never told me you were sick…," he asked, as his work-calloused fingers worked to unfold the paper.

"Look—just *look*, if I'm so crazy!" Margaret instructed.

"I never said you were crazy…."

"Henry…this is very difficult for me." Margaret's voice dropped to a tone that was both pleading and urgent.

Henry smoothed the severely crinkled picture and looked at it. He remained silent a moment, then looked at Margaret. His eyes held both disgust and bewilderment.

"Jesus, Margaret, what's your obsession with death, anyway? You know, photographs like this ain't normal. You're lucky I don't put you in the sanitarium myself, woman."

"Henry, I can't explain how or *why* my mother would have a picture like this taken —," Margaret began, but Henry interjected abruptly; his face wore an expression of puzzlement upon it.

"Your *mother*? Margaret, Lucille was...," he said, looking back at the photograph and shivering.

"What? What has Aunt Lucille got to do with...?" Margaret hurriedly retrieved the picture from Henry and looked at it closely. There before her eyes was simply one of the three pictures she'd taken of Lucille with her camera. Margaret stared at the photograph in utter disbelief. She hadn't taken the film to be processed yet.

"I-I don't understand," Margaret said. The longer she stared at the photograph, the more she knew she was losing ground in convincing Henry of what was happening. Margaret's slender fingers began to shake, and she dropped the picture as she rose silently from the table.

"Come on, Maggie. Let's get you to bed. I think you've had a very tough time losing your aunt. I know you were very close with her. I'll help you work through this, but you've got to get this voodoo stuff out of your head. Even if something strange *did* happen, you're home now. Nothing will harm you here. Grieve however long you need to, honey, but no more of this weird stuff," Henry said, doing his best to comfort his wife.

Chapter 8

About a week after Margaret's arrival home, an afternoon arrived that seemed fair enough. A pleasant warm wind blew softly through the fragrant summer blooms in the trees. Not a single fluffy cloud dotted the crystal sky, and not a thing felt wrong in the world. For a moment Margaret felt almost normal for the first time since the whole ordeal at her aunt's homestead back in Louisiana. Her husband was back to work at the quarry, and her dear twin children ran about the east yard on the Glover farm. Though their farm was actually quite small in relation to the hundreds of acres of fields and pasture belonging to the Heiberman's—the wealthy neighbors just ten miles up the road—they still benefited from the modest assortment of items harvested every summer from their gardens.

Corn stalks lined the northern-most edge of the Glover property, while poles of beans and rows of cabbages, lettuce, and carrots lined the ground beneath them. Everything that could have been planted was, and this year's garden was more productive than ever before. There was even a small barn which housed a couple of horses, and beyond that, a tiny herd of cattle that were destined for the market before much longer. Winter fell hard in rural Missouri, and their poor family would profit greatly from the bounty of food and income their small farm provided.

Margaret hung freshly washed clothes that had taken all morning to rake across the washboards and wring out. Her aging hands, though not terribly old, ached slightly from gripping the creaky crank that pulled the clothing through the wringer. Tonight she would have to break out the peppermint oil and rub them down, she feared. As Margaret smiled lovingly at her children, she watched them play, oblivious to any problems in the world.

Her skin erupted unexpectedly with goose bumps when a ribbon of cold air mixed out of nowhere with the pleasant summer breeze. The unusual chill in the air made Margaret switch her attention to the sky to see thick, white clouds began to drift into view where no clouds had been minutes before.

"Hmmph. Figures...," Margaret said to herself, and returned to her laundry.

The puffy white clouds began to pile up, climbing higher upon themselves and spreading outward, like a river overrunning its banks. Soon large towers of cumulonimbus clouds dotted the entire sky above, and the shiver in the wind returned, sliding its invisible hands over Margaret's bare forearms. As Margaret looked up again, she was taken aback. Her perfect summer sky had traded itself in for the look of an impending severe storm. Stark white clouds grew darker with the tint of gray moisture inside. On the edge of Kansas at this time of year, it was not unusual for thunderstorms to come popping up out of nowhere. But the way the cold chill snaked among the warm air caught Margaret's attention more than the ever-growing thunderheads up above her. As the wind picked up and began to shake some of those summer blooms down over the head of her children, she noticed that their laughter had ceased.

"Momma, that air don't feel right," Henry Jr. said, looking up at the sky.

"Ma, are we gonna have a cyclone?" Ann asked, her eyes wide with worry. She hated storms. Sometimes it was the thunder that scared her, but mostly it was the lightning.

"Well, my littles, the sky isn't looking green yet, and it's not yellow like it's about to hail, either. I sure don't like how that warm and cold air are mixing up there, though," Margaret answered, eying the sky suspiciously.

"It'll probably rain any second!" Henry Jr. exclaimed excitedly.

"I hope not!" Ann cried, giving her brother a dirty look.

"I hope not, too—my laundry's not dry," Margaret said, agreeing with her young daughter.

"What if it does?" Henry Jr. asked, curious.

"Well, my dear, that just means you'll have to help me bring in the clothes and hang 'em over the stove," Margaret answered with a grin.

"Oh…not *more* chores!" Henry Jr. groaned as he kicked at the ground.

"I'll help you, Momma!" Ann chimed in excitedly. She loved to help with the chores her mother did—it seemed to make her feel more grown up and responsible.

"Thank you, Ann. Listen you two, why don't you wrap it up and head on indoors? I'm sure with the way that storm's rolling in it won't be much longer 'til it rains."

"But…," Henry Jr. began in protest.

"But…," Ann said, mirroring her twin brother.

"We'll come grab those wet clothes at the very first sign of rain. But I want them to get as dry as they can before we take them in," Margaret explained.

An hour later, when Margaret was in the kitchen tending to a pie, the wind abruptly died down. In her experience this was not a good thing with storm clouds in the sky, and she stepped to the window to investigate. The rain clouds had finished gathering and boiled like black smoke in the sky. A nervous chill ran down her spine, but she knew it was not because of the storm. Her gut told her that the darkness outside was not merely the threat of a tornado, but something unearthly. Something…evil.

Henry Jr. and Ann remained at play, oblivious for the moment. A motionless storm hung over the Glover farm, and Margaret needed to keep an eye on it. As thick, fat drops of rain began to fall, Margaret remembered she needed to get the clothes in. But at that moment she found that she really didn't care. Entranced by the boiling black clouds, Margaret's stare fixed upon a tower of storm clouds. Before her very eyes a dark shadow seemed to churn and twist its way out of the swirling clouds. A human-like figure — arms outstretched — loomed ominously in the face of the sky to the west. Margaret felt a sudden need to get outside in order to see this dark cloud-wrapped figure closer. Like the drive of a hungry animal to eat, the urgency grew, and Margaret flew from the house with wings on her feet. She flung open the door to the farm house and bolted outside. As she rounded the corner of the house and caught full view of the black shadow man in the clouds, she halted dead in her tracks. The form peered directly at her, but was disinterested. The smoky figure shifted and turned away, floating along as the rest of the rain clouds swirled about.

"No, come back here this instant! Who are you? What do you want with me?!" Margaret called into the sky. Half expecting an answer, she found herself disappointed when there was none. As the dark figure picked up speed, Margaret began to run across the yard after it. She was intent only upon the cloud man, unaware of the heavy downpour of rain around her.

***

From inside the house, Margaret's children could see her outside in the rain, but supposed she was out to gather the laundry. It occurred to each twin at nearly the same moment that the laundry was on the opposite side of the house than their

113

mother.

"What's Momma doin' out there?" Ann asked, frightened by the way the storm looked outside her window.

"I don't know, Ann, but we're going to go find out!" Henry Jr. answered.

"No, don't go out there! I don't want to go out there!" Ann cried, grabbing up her ragged doll for comfort. A large bolt of lightning crackled across the sky out in front of them, making everything turn as bright as daylight for a brief moment. A tremendous clap of thunder was not far behind. Henry Jr. jumped, and Ann screamed. She wanted to watch out the window, but was too afraid and backed away.

"Fine. *You* stay here!" Henry Jr. instructed. After all, since their father wasn't home from work yet, he *was* the man of the house.

Henry Jr. ran out of Ann's room and went to go flag down their mother. While Ann did not want to be left alone in the house, she was content to stay inside the house and out of the storm.

***

As Margaret ran her boots slapped the water out of the puddles forming on the ground. The rain was falling too hard for it to soak in; water flew upward in multiple droplets with each splash. Making no headway on the quickly disappearing monster in the clouds, Margaret tried to think of some way to regain its attention.

"I know who you are!" Margaret yelled into the sky, bluffing. As she took a step to begin running again, the wind picked up, whipping about wildly from all directions. Leaves, grass, and debris on the ground flew up, blinding Margaret as it flew into her eyes.

***

Margaret continued to run, but her footing slipped in a muddy spot in the yard, and she fell flat onto her back. The force was enough to knock the wind out of her, and as she lay there attempting to regain her breath, she noticed a tiny, distant voice. As she tried to focus on it, she felt pressure across her chest, the feeling of a large hand pressing her onto the ground very real. She was unable to sit up, and unable to speak loudly.

"What is happening?" Margaret croaked weakly. Then she noticed the sharp pain at the back of her head. The sensation of warm liquid ran down the back of her neck, despite the cold driving rain falling in droves down upon her.

Margaret lay upon the muddy ground, bleeding and blinking as she tried to peer through the rain. The dark cloud shadow had turned back around and was quickly descending down upon her. A blast of freezing air washed across her face, sending shivers across her soaking wet body. All around her sounds were muted like muffled background noise, except the voice of the shady being wrapped in black clouds.

"The Hands of Thyme are against you…," the voice said, sending quivers of terror splintering through Margaret. The black cloud shadow hovered inches above her, then seemed to dissipate into nothingness before the echo of its words ceased to ring in her ears.

Margaret's vision grew cloudy, and everything happening around her was quickly growing fuzzy. Wet footsteps sounded behind her head, and a small hand reached out and touched her forehead.

***

It was some time later when Margaret woke up. She was in her bed, but had no idea how she'd gotten there. She didn't remember walking back to the house. Her last memory was of her son, Junior, standing over her asking if she was okay. She remembered his little voice sounding so scared as he asked her what had happened. She remembered calling out his name weakly before everything went black.

Pain hammered hotly through the back of Margaret's skull. Her lips puckered as she winced when she rolled over onto her back. Though her eyes were open, darkness plagued her still, and a gentle hand full of panic flew up to touch her face. Her shaking fingertips relaxed when she felt the wash rag across her eyes, and she swept it to the side. Evening had fallen early as the angry thunderclouds settled in across the mid-western sky. Buckets of rain poured from the heavens like tears all of the angels were crying. The wind still whipped about, rattling the windows of the farmhouse now and again.

"Honey? Maggie?" her husband's voice inquired quietly.

"Henry...what happened?" she asked, looking into his furrowed brow. His gentle gray eyes swirled with a cloudy concern that made them look like the sky outside.

"I was going to ask you the same question," Henry answered, sitting at the edge of the bed. "What's the last thing you remember?"

"I remember the laundry still hanging out on the line, and the rain. But...," Margaret began.

"Anything else? Junior said you ran out of the house and was wandering around in the yard — away from the clothesline."

"I...," Margaret said, thinking hard about it. Her mind was mostly shadows and fuzziness. "I thought I saw something in the clouds," she finally answered.

"The cyclone," Henry said, shaking his head. "Honey, why did you run outside? You've been through tornado weather before."

Suddenly Margaret's memory flooded back to the shadow man coming out of the clouds toward her, and that awful voice echoed once again in her head. But she knew better than to tell her husband *that* story, even if it was the truth. She knew all too well how he would react to such a thing.

"Well...I just couldn't see well enough, what with that hard rain pelting the window. I thought I saw some circulation in those clouds and wanted to get a better look, that's all," Margaret explained, and her story seemed to satisfy her husband's inquisitiveness for the moment.

"Yes, but look what that got ya, Maggie—a big ol' hole in your head," Henry retorted, touching her face gently.

"What happened?" Margaret asked again.

"Well, Doc said the rock you slipped on and fell onto wasn't too sharp. It was a hard enough hit to slice you open, though. You'll have to take it easy for a few days. Give it some time to heal up."

"Doc was here?" Margaret asked, still groggy. She tried to blink away the heaviness in her eyelids.

"Don't you remember? I told you this morning before I left that Doc was going to follow me home to look at one of our horses," Henry replied, probably thinking her forgetfulness may have well been in part to Margaret hitting her head.

"Oh yes, Dusty. How's she doing?" Margaret asked, genuinely concerned for the old mare.

"Doc said her wound where that barbed-wire caught her will heal just fine. Good thing, too—I really didn't want to have to put her down," Henry said with a sigh.

"Yes…that is good news." Margaret answered with a yawn. "So…I thought I heard you say something about a cyclone?" she added, recalling Henry's statement.

"I could see it cutting across the Heiberman's pasture. Looked like it might've been headin' this way, but it turned back north and kept goin'," Henry answered. "And now there's more rain to contend with. Ain't that my luck?" he groaned. Margaret knew she would be unable to say anything to comfort her husband, because she knew he was right, and decided instead to change the subject.

"So, Doc's already gone?" Margaret inquired softly.

"Yeah, had to head back to town for other appointments."

"Well, perhaps I should drop him a card to say thank you for tending to my head," she suggested, wincing when she went to move.

"That would be nice—maybe even take him one of your apple pies, honey," he added with a wink.

"Where are the kids?" Margaret asked, suddenly realizing she hadn't seen them since before she left the house.

"Oh, they're fine; already in bed, I'm afraid."

"Dang. I wanted to see them," Margaret replied, disappointed.

"It's probably better if you just rest. You've got all the time in the world to talk to them."

"*Time*?" Margaret asked, finding the word strange and unattached to what Henry was saying. How could the word, the name, stand alone and mean so much?

"But now, just get cozy and try to get some rest," he continued, pretending Margaret hadn't said a word.

Margaret had begun to feel woozy and closed her leaden eyelids. Henry kissed her gently upon the lips, careful not to press her onto her pillow. A whirlwind of sensations crawled through her body, first making her feel like she was falling, and then nauseated from a swirling, spinning flickering of light all around her.

A vibration seemed to rise up through the mattress, bleeding into her skin, making every muscle and joint ache deeply. She felt herself draw up, as if her body were seizing, though she lay as still as a corpse. Henry must have thought she'd fallen asleep from the rhythmic breaths his wife took. He stood, pausing a moment to watch the rise and fall of her bosom before quietly leaving the room. A darkness fell over Margaret as Henry closed the door, and a series of fragmented nightmares plagued her mind before mental exhaustion overrode her senses and swept her subconscious into a lonely and lengthy nothingness.

CHAPTER 9

It was around the beginning of July, when the hot, humid days of summer were on the verge of peaking, that Margaret caught word of a parish in a neighboring town that might listen to her plea for help. With excitement for the prospective assistance, she began to compose a letter, choosing her words ever so carefully as not to sway their thoughts.

As Margaret looked at the notes she'd scrawled out about the church, she remembered there was a telephone number she'd copied down. Rushing to the kitchen to place her call, Margaret's anxiety rose up from the pit of her stomach. After many weeks of rejection, she was nearly at her wit's end trying to piece this puzzle together. Her gut told her it was through the church that she would gain all the rest of her answers; but first, she needed to find someone who would listen to her. The operator patched through the call and the soft voice who greeted her on the other end boosted Margaret's hope for help. Searching for the right thing to say, she fought the urge to come up with some story just to get her in the door, and chose her words from her heart.

"I need your help with an urgent matter that I'd rather not discuss with you over the telephone," Margaret began, her voice cracked as her throat suddenly ran dry.

119

"You know our doors are always open, my child, do you not?" the soft voice inquired.

"Well…yes, but I've attempted to speak with another parish, and once I revealed my reason…," Margaret began again. She hoped the woman on the other end could not hear her voice quivering.

"My child, whatever your trouble is, you may rely on the good Lord to help you through it."

"No, you don't understand. I seek guidance on a matter of…." Margaret tried to choose her next words carefully because of her previous experience earlier in the past few weeks.

"A matter of what, my dear?"

"…the soul," Margaret said, completing her thought. Surely that would not deter this church from speaking with her. After a long pause, the soft voice invited Margaret to come in person. Margaret got the feeling whoever was speaking to her had been deciding whether or not to grant audience with the appropriate church members. Tomorrow, mid-afternoon. Henry would be at work in the quarry, so she would have to leave her children with his sister for the afternoon.

***

Margaret walked slowly toward the door of the church. The large wooden doors were propped open to allow some breeze to flow inward on such a hot day as it was. An older woman beckoned her in without a word at first, and Margaret stepped through the threshold of the door.

"You must be the woman who called?" the same soft voice from the telephone call asked.

"Yes. My name is Margaret. Margaret Glover," Margaret answered, swallowing the lump in her throat.

"Well now, what was your question, my dear? Something about a matter of the soul?" Soft, kind eyes matched the quiet tone of the old woman; she reminded Margaret of a church mouse.

120

"You see," Margaret said, withdrawing one of the scrolls from her shoulder bag. "I was given these when my Aunt Lucille died." Unrolling the scroll with the half demon, half angel sketch on it, she handed it to the outstretched hand of the old woman.

"Oh?" the old woman asked, taking the scroll from Margaret. As she unrolled it a breeze blew in from any number of drafty spots and flickered the flames on the candles. The flames shortened, nearly snuffing themselves out as they tried to hide.

The old woman of the church seemed so small against the large hollow room. Several rows of pews began a few feet past the greeting area just inside the large wooden front door. Without more than a couple of tiny windows lining the wall on either side of the church hall, no light could shine in, which made the place quite dark. Like any other church she had ever been to, Margaret noticed an empty feeling with the lack of a large congregation gathered to sing their praises and participate in worshipping the Lord.

One picture of cherubs graced the far wall across from a rather large painting of *The Last Supper*. Aside from the small fragments of sunlight from the miniscule windows, some old rumpled white curtains, and a couple of small green plants, the dark walnut pews and dark hard wood floor really brought out the loneliness inside the minster.

When the candle flames nearly died down to nothing more that amber embers, shadows seemed to ooze outward from the darker corners inside the church. It was amazing that a house of God could seem so empty, and be infiltrated by something evil. How could this building harbor such cold feelings when the teachings spoken here were quite the opposite?

***

Even amid an already uneasy atmosphere, Margaret was unimpressed by the flickering candlelight, but the old woman noticed. Right away she knew something was with them that

121

did not belong. As the kind-eyed woman spread out the scroll, the half angel-half demon sketch opened up in front of her. The faces of both beauty and peace and pain and death presented itself to the old woman, and her heartbeat caught a moment in her chest. The gentle eyes widened into saucers of horror before her nervous fingers let loose their grip on the parchment. Mid-air the scroll rolled back up and landed on the floor, rolling toward Margaret before stopping at her feet.

***

Margaret stared at the scroll, as it seemed to know to return to her. It stopped exactly at her feet as through by instinct.

"What sorcery is this that you would *dare* bring into a house of God?" the grey-eyed woman asked.

"I…. I…," Margaret stammered, shaking her head. She had no choice but to comply. If God was going to help her figure things out, he would have already done so. "Thanks anyway," she muttered quietly as she scooped up the scroll off the floor.

As Margaret reached for the door to the church, she felt sinister eyes upon her lurking somewhere in the shadows. She turned slowly to peer back behind her, only to meet the sight of the old woman stamping her foot upon the floor and pointing rigidly at the door with her index finger. It was obvious that the old woman had not felt the dark eyes upon her, and was only intent on Margaret leaving. Having nothing more she could do or say, Margaret had no choice but to exit the church empty handed, and that much more frustrated. She stood a moment just outside the church, staring silently at the ancient-looking scroll in her hand.

"Damn you," she cursed the parchment roll. Since she had no other prospects of places or people to turn to for advice, Margaret found herself contemplating destroying the scrolls and the chest altogether. That could surely provide a way to end her obsession, and perhaps end the terrible visions and dreams running through her mind. But it was only pure speculation that it would even work.

In her own secret time, between the needs of her children and her husband, laced among the chores of the house and her duties on their farm, Margaret turned a burning match to the parchment scrolls. Neither the paper nor the colored ribbons would accept the flame, and each match simply burned out, an eerie trail of smoke escaping the orange glow of the match head before going dark. The next attempt was the fire place. The wood crackled and popped as the fire consumed the dried timber, and with a good, healthy fire roaring away inside the hearth — gray smoke puffing up and out of the chimney — Margaret knew this had to be the end of the scrolls. But as her slender hand released the rolled parchments into the flames, they too died down into nothingness, as though someone had doused the fire with water. The half-burnt logs smoldered a moment, and wisps of white-gray smoke snaked up into the chimney and away from the house.

Margaret stared at the accursed scrolls as they lay amid the scorched tinder unharmed. A small bit of black soot was smudged upon the white ribbon as it lay against one of the charred logs. She retrieved the parchment rolls and shook her head in disbelief. How could paper survive fire, unless it came from Hell itself?

Desperately trying to obliterate the scrolls and the chest, Margaret made one final attempt to destroy the cherry wood box itself. Raised high in her anxious hands shined the silvery blade of an ax from the toolshed. Summoning the strength from within, she swung the ax with all of her might and brought it down upon the center of the small jewelry chest. As the shiny metal blade struck the top of the small wooden box, it simply bounced back with a force that nearly threw Margaret off her feet. The ax head slammed to the ground outside the toolshed, and Margaret's arm ached from the vibration that shook through the wooden handle to her flesh. How her husband chopped wood for their fireplace was beyond her comprehension; she couldn't stand the sensation the impact of the ax had sent through her hands.

Margaret dropped the ax down upon the ground to her side and stood looking over the chest in utter bewilderment. How could smashing a newly sharpened ax upon mere wood not splinter the thing into a million shards? And then a thought crept through her angry mind that perhaps the chest itself really *was* from another place; an unearthly place that had allowed it to survive for these many, many years. Haunted and unnerved by this thought, Margaret realized that if she indeed could not destroy the chest, she would simply have to endure its lure, and hoped that she could withstand being drawn deeper into the occult to come out solving this puzzle and putting a stop to this mystery.

Her confidence crushed, and her hopes deflated, she adjusted her mindset to the alternative. Margaret felt she had no other option than to continue with the obsession the small cherry wood chest and the mysterious scrolls within it brought. As the days continued she prayed that some answer would come her way. She pleaded with the heavens to provide a source — someone willing to see her long enough to answer some questions. Feeling she had no place to turn, Margaret was on the brink of giving up hope.

As days rolled by into weeks, the madness that washed over Margaret's mind grew ever more intense. Like a spike through her skull, the aching desire to unlock the secrets of the mysterious cherry wood chest pounded in her head. Even on the most brilliant sunny summer days, Margaret seemed only to see darkness. Deep within her heart she doubted she would succeed, but a nagging voice inside her mind urged her on, telling her that she *had* to succeed — not only for her herself and her own need to know, but for her daughter, Ann. Margaret knew that if she failed, she would in turn fear for Ann's future for passing along the apparent curse that had attached itself to their family's bloodline. With each letter she'd written asking for assistance to research information about the scrolls came silence. No answers, no visits with clergymen or scholars, just silence. And with each day that passed without answers, it was just one more day Margaret had to dwell on things and sink deeper into the hold the darkness had on her.

On a summer afternoon when the blazing sun took its perch at the highest point in the sky, and the UV rays made their invisible journey to the earth to scorch the ground, Margaret and her children sat at the table and enjoyed the lunch their mother had prepared earlier in the day.

"Momma, how do angels know who needs help?" Ann asked suddenly before taking her last bite.

"What? What do you mean?" Margaret asked, startled, puzzled by her daughter's out of place question.

"Well, people in trouble get rescued by angels. So how do angels know who needs help?" Ann elaborated.

"Well dear, angels are a lot smarter than regular people. You see, they have a connection to a higher power," Margaret began, choosing her words carefully.

"God?" Ann asked, her innocence obvious.

"Y-yes…I supposed there are some who would believe that sort of —," Margaret answered, growing uncomfortable with the conversation.

"Do you believe that's how it is, Momma?" Ann asked, watching her mother's expressions change.

"I…," Margaret began, searching on the inside to answer the question. She could feel her heart beginning to beat faster and her head began to grow dizzy.

"I think angels could help you," Ann said, looking down at her now empty plate.

"Why do you say that?" Margaret asked, uncharacteristically defensive.

"Oh...I don't know," Ann answered, the tone of her voice seemed to carry on the innocence.

"What do you mean by that? Tell me!" Margaret exclaimed, immediately furious for no apparent reason.

"Momma...?" Ann muttered, her lip quivering. It was apparent that Margaret's young daughter did not understand her mother's outburst and seemed afraid.

"I can't believe you'd say a thing like that!" Margaret exclaimed, slapping her hands down hard upon the table. She rose, tipping her chair over as she stood up. "I think you two should go outside and play and leave me be for a little while. I don't...I don't feel well. Let's just get along with our day, shall we?" Margaret suddenly stopped with the fury and lightened the tone of her voice.

"Okay, Momma. We can go play a while in Henry's room. It's too hot outside," Ann suggested quietly.

"Fine," Margaret answered, waving her off. The family stayed apart for the remaining time of that afternoon; unspoken uneasiness filled the entire house, but Margaret pretended not to notice. She would make it up to her children in her own time, in her own way.

After that uneasy outburst, the children were unusually obedient and seemed to try to steer clear of doing anything to upset their mother, as if deep inside they knew something was wrong, but dared not make mention of anything unnecessarily. They played a lot, and Margaret continued with her search for answers, leaving family matters on the back burner.

CHAPTER 10

Many weeks passed, and the peak of summer threatened to turn into early autumn. Time had passed silently into the future since Margaret had returned home from Lucille's funeral with the mysterious chest, and with the strange events happening within her weary mind, the middle-aged housewife lost count of the number of churches she'd contacted for help to decipher the scrolls' writing. She often wondered how she could ever show it to anyone if the writing was not apparent all the time. She'd taken so much of her time aside from tending to the farm house and her children's needs that Henry had begun to feel their relationship had taken a back seat to her obsession with this matter of the occult.

Margaret was willing to meet with anyone who would give her the time of day on the phone, but despite what Margaret told them, once she brought out the scrolls, suddenly it was time for her to leave—and sometimes quite hurriedly. Doors slammed shut in her face, even at churches, where doors were supposed to be open to everyone. She had attempted to express her dismay and frustration to Henry, who'd all but ignored her requests for his help. She could not give up hope on her journey to recover the truth about her family line. She had plans to make things up to her husband, though sometimes she feared it may be too late by the time she would be able to dedicate herself solely to her family once again.

Be that as it may, Margaret's mind was dead set on locating assistance from someone who might know a thing or two about demons and angels. By telephone one theology scholar was willing to meet with her, but upon arrival at the church, the man she'd spoken to simply handed her a book, then shut the door without a single word. Margaret peered down at the leather-bound volume before walking to a bench by the cemetery in the church yard.

As Margaret sat and read from the book, she gazed up from time to time to look over at the cherub statuettes that lined the outside of a small family mausoleum. Her innards quivered as their cold, granite eyes stared lifelessly into nowhere, but she fought hard to focus on what she read. The book title was nothing she could pronounce, though what she gathered from the forward inside, it seemed to be a book along the lines of theology versus the occult. As she flipped through the onion skin pages, she realized that several references had been made to thyme, though all were in the typical use, as in incense. Throughout the tome were black and white depictions of historical scenes, like Daniel in the lion's den and so forth. But this book held notations to each story that attempted an alternate theory or more scientific approach to each biblical story.

Margaret had skimmed through at least a dozen, hoping to find even the mention of the Hall of Judgment or any other helpful references, before randomly turning through several chapters at once and landing on an intriguing item. There was mention of a creature born of half angelic and half demonic energies thousands of centuries ago. It told of long lines of historical disasters in chronological order that pointed to a century's lapse between them. Though no mention of this Thyme character was noted in the passage, there was a notation of the *Geminus Lingua* — or, according to translation provided next to this notation, Double Tongue; apparently, the ancient art of speaking something in two languages at the same time. Margaret did wonder what types of circumstances would ever call for such a thing, but thought back to her vision at Lucille's funeral. Perhaps some ritualistic chant? Margaret concluded this would take more reading and further research. She would just have to continue her quest to unlock the secret of the scrolls in the chest, but she hoped it would not be long. In the months since her aunt's funeral, the chest's mystery had become her obsession as Margaret's questions remained unanswered. Despite all of her efforts and the time she had invested, she was no closer to finding the missing piece of the puzzle than when she was first handed the small jewelry box.

By August, as the weather grew intolerably hot, Margaret returned to the thought of Agatha. Across the state of Missouri, in St. Louis, her grandmother resided in a sanitarium. It was previously unclear to Margaret why she had been admitted as a patient, and remembered having asked that as a child, only to be shushed once the words slipped off her tongue. Margaret had always been curious about Agatha, and no one would ever talk about her or acknowledge her existence. The subject was not only met with an immediate attempt to silence it, but with a feeling of unsettling fear as well.

Henry, Margaret's husband, had not liked the entirety of his wife's research as it was, but knew that once she was set upon accomplishing something, it would take something like the magnificent power of divine intervention to stop her. Once more the woman set out, some of the money from her inheritance coming along to pay for the trip. Across the state by passenger train, to St. Louis, Margaret had plenty of time to reflect on more pleasant memories for a little while. The last time she'd been to the city was back in 1904, when they hosted the World's Fair. The entire family had gone — herself, Henry, and their twin son and daughter, who were only three at the time.

When they'd gotten there, they could not believe how many peopled had travelled from all across the plains to attend; but then again, it was quite the event of the year, having been the centennial anniversary of the Louisiana Purchase. Though they'd had a wonderful time, and returned home days later full of memories and loaded up with souvenirs, that trip was the last trip they'd taken anywhere. It was unfortunate that it had taken something dreadful like Lucille's death to draw Margaret away from their home. And had it not been for the reason she was on this train now, the inheritance money could easily have paid for another vacation for the entire family.

Margaret counted down the minutes as she left the train depot and hailed a taxi to take her to see her grandmother. She mindlessly read street signs as they passed by, though she'd no idea what she'd just read. She was so entranced by the scenario playing out in her head of how their conversation would go, the taxi driver had to turn around and raise his voice to catch her attention.

"Miss? Miss?! We're here…this is where you wanted to go, right?" he asked, trying to get her to answer him.

"Um…yes. Yes, thank you," she answered after a pause, then simply sat there, staring at the white, multi-story building.

"Ma'am?" the driver said, placing an unspoken request for her to get out within his voice.

"Oh, of course…yes…," Margaret said, grabbing her travel bag and shoulder bag and stepping out of the taxi.

"Your fare — " the driver began, but Margaret interrupted.

"This will cover it?" she asked, thrusting the bills toward the driver. A large smile spread across his greasy lips.

"Yes, ma'am."

He greedily accepted the large overpayment and pulled

away from the curb, leaving the woman, hands and mind full of baggage, staring dumbfounded at the stairs leading to the door. Margaret was glad she'd not packed too many items, as her bags would be quite heavy to carry by herself. As the woman looked over the building, gray clouds began to creep across the perfect azure sky above her, and the wind picked up ever so slightly. For some reason, Margaret could feel another bad storm approaching, and thought it best to hurry and get indoors.

As she climbed the many narrow stairs to the entrance to the sanitarium, images began to crawl across her mind, seeming to be flashbacks of memories from the past. At first, Margaret was confused by the images she saw — a girl with chestnut braids, marching solemnly by the side of a woman dressed in drab colors. Voices were distorted in the memory, and the vague connection to a letter received previously began to return to Margaret's mind.

She had been to the sanitarium before, only as a child far too young to understand the reason behind the visit. The memory was broken, and too many pieces were missing to fully recall why they'd come. As Margaret climbed the last few steps, she replayed the events out further. At the top of the staircase, Aunt Lucille had bent down to look Margaret straight in the eyes.

"Whatever your grandmother says, you just forget, you hear? This woman has no business being alive, and I will not have you corrupted by her veil of lies." The words were spoken in such a cold, wicked tone, and it scared Margaret, for she'd never known Lucille to act this way before. She could only muster the bravery to nod her head in understanding. The two turned and disappeared inside the building. The Margaret remaining in present time lived the moment again, and her fingers flailed outward, her hand trying to touch the ghosts from the past dancing before her eyes.

"Why all the mystery?" Margaret asked herself aloud, as she bit her lower lip, puzzled. The only other thing she remembered was when they returned home from their trip. It was the day she first laid eyes on the black opal necklace that Lucille would later wear to her own funeral.

Stepping through the doorway between the past and the present, Margaret breathed in the scent of the lobby inside the building. Floor wax, ammonia, and she thought perhaps the stale scent of urine met her olfactory senses, and she coughed. Though she knew she'd been there once before, nothing about the interior seemed familiar, thought it had been many years and such things were prone to change.

Everything was as one might expect in a hospital—stark white as far as the eye could see. Narrow, intimidating hallways, to those not familiar with the building's layout, could easily lead one to be lost, and they offered an almost claustrophobic sense sometimes, even to those who worked there. Margaret managed to find a receptionist hiding behind the thick lenses of a pair of glasses, her hair pulled as tight as the scowl that pursed the older woman's lips. A dry sarcasm met Margaret's eager ears when she'd asked for Agatha's room number, and those scrutinizing eyes behind the glasses squinted to follow this new visitor as she walked away in search for the room.

The place was plain enough—the idea was to keep distractions from upsetting those of feeble minds who found solace in nothingness. Only necessary sounds were allowed—breathing, footsteps, the sounds of occasional quiet conversation. A few of the residents of the sanitarium were allowed to roam about freely, each wrapped in a white robe of fleece despite the hot temperatures outside. Slipper covered feet shuffled about while arms hugged their own chests, and others rocked themselves back and forth as one might to do soothe an infant. Margaret could instantly feel the woes and troubled minds polluting the already stale air inside the hospital. She moved as quietly but as quickly as she could to locate Agatha. There were questions that needed answered.

Margaret found the stairs that led to Agatha's floor. At the top stood two orderlies keeping watch on those shuffling around below. Because Margaret was obviously not a patient, they paid her no mind, and remained locked in their private conversation as they poked fun at those less fortunate. As Margaret gazed up from the base of the staircase, she looked at each door to the patient rooms that lined the second floor to the sanitarium. Only patients that were unable to move or were less mentally disturbed were allowed on the higher floors, as a safety measure. As Margaret climbed the steps, she could see the door to her grandmother's room. Her breath caught in her chest as anticipation welled within her. Would Agatha finally shed some light on things?

There it was — room 33. The door was propped slightly open, and as Margaret stepped out from the top stair onto the landing, the sound of wheels creaking caught her attention immediately. The room was still four doors down from where she stood, and she walked quickly toward the door so she could investigate. With the door knob inches away from Margaret's hand, the door flew open and two orderlies emerged pushing a gurney out of the room. The wheels creaked, as did the entire rickety body of the metal stretcher. Upon the wheeled cot was an ominous body-shaped mound blanketed with a blood-stained shroud. Margaret's jaw dropped and she gasped loudly, quickly trying to correct her outburst by slapping a hand over her mouth. Shocked, she could only manage to shift her gaze between the cot and the two orderlies.

"Ain't you never seen no meat wagon before?" the orderly asked with a sour grin.

As the orderlies began to push the gurney past Margaret, one hand of the body underneath slid out and brushed against hers. On contact, an electrical surge swept through Margaret's entire body. Tiny forks of lightning lashed out unseen through the ends of every nerve, sending a startling and paralyzing streak of fear down her spine. Images began to flicker at an ungodly pace, bringing Margaret to her knees. Agatha's face flashed among them, only vaguely familiar from rare visits as a child. The old woman appeared just as Margaret remembered—stringy, yellowed hair, thickly wrinkled face, her eyes covered with milky white lenses. And those haunting blind eyes seemed to peer directly at Margaret. The image neared the younger woman, and fear kept Margaret kneeling in terror. Her heart beat faster and faster until she was convinced that it would burst…or simply give out.

Agatha seemed to be saying something, and her face bore the look of panic and a strange urgency, radiating like an attempt to escape from someone—or something—terrible. And then the image of Agatha disappeared, slipping into Margaret's mind. Margaret somehow knew what she was about to see were the last events that Agatha had witnessed. Much like the chaos that was revealed at the swamp witch's house in Louisiana, the images from a nightmare played out before her. A young woman held a scroll in her hands, reading off an enchantment that seemed to have written itself out before her very eyes. A priest was also present, translating the words being spoken by the younger Agatha from Latin into English; the sound of two languages spoken at once was quite disturbing. A giant creature began to pull itself together from two beings so that each was the immaculate depiction of perfection and living damnation in the center of a candle darkened room. The creature hissed words that spilled out more like gibberish than actual spoken words, as they stemmed from languages so unearthly that human ears could not properly translate the sounds.

Time was warped, for a lack of better understanding on Margaret's part, and the hellish scene playing out before her very eyes came to an abrupt end when the chant that Agatha was attempting to finish was overcome by her sudden and inexplicable inability to speak, hear, or see. Margaret shuddered. It was like some of her worst dreams come to life. The sensation of having Agatha inside her mind was intensely disturbing, to the point that Margaret had to physically shake her head and close her eyes tight to try and remove the nightmarish images from her mind.

"Agatha? Are you under there? It...it's me...Margaret," the woman said with a shaky voice. She tried to push Agatha from inside her mind and lifted the sheet up off the body. Her honey brown eyes peered, astounded at what lay before her, and tears of fright blurred her senses. An older woman lay silent and still, just as Lucille had. Strands of yellow-white hair seemed thin and scraggly as the locks draped themselves over a thickly wrinkled face. The withered old woman who lay before Margaret seemed so lonely and haunted. Margaret was horrified that the woman had died with her eyes wide open; large white veils scarred the once clear lenses of the woman's eyes, while her thin lips seemed somehow sealed; the flesh from both had melted onto each other. Margaret had no idea how much time had passed. It could have been seconds, it could have been hours. She only knew that once again her quest for information would be halted because of death. But as she knelt there, engulfed in the awkward uneasiness that filled the atmosphere of the sanitarium, an overwhelming sensation of energy leaving her body left her weak, and everything went black.

Not quite an hour later, Margaret found herself sitting in the office of Mrs. Mary Weatherby. A woman, unconscious and moaning something about the dead speaking to her while visiting a sanitarium, was enough grounds to wind up in the campus counselor's office. Bitter, black coffee was offered partly for stimulating purposes, but mostly out of the lack of sugar and milk to spare. Margaret sipped very slowly, looking over the rim of her cup at the older, obviously stressed woman across the polished oak desk at which they sat. Well-manicured nails tapped impatiently upon the hard, wooden surface in front of them. Judgmental eyes peered over round glasses that seemed to focus the condescending waves streaming from them somehow.

"Mrs. Glover, are you all right?" Her voice harbored a more gentle tone than her look suggested it could. "I'm terribly sorry, but I had to look through your personal effects in order to find out who you are."

"Yes...I'm fine," Margaret answered with a sigh. "I've just been through a lot lately, and thought I could come here for some answers."

"To what, my dear? What kind of questions could you possibly think could be answered in a sanitarium?" Mrs. Weatherby asked dryly.

"Well, ma'am—" Margaret began, clearing her throat gently.

"Mary Weatherby. *Mrs.* Mary Weatherby," the stern woman clarified.

"My grandmother Agatha, she's a patient here. I came with my Aunt Lucille to visit her once when I was a child. I have come here to ask some questions regarding a family matter," Margaret answered, taking a sip of the strong coffee. The sanitarium's counselor looked troubled by Margaret's answer, and cupped her chin with her left hand. A look of intense thought pressed the lines on Mary Weatherby's face closer together, and Margaret would have bet the counselor had a headache coming on.

"What's wrong? Do—do you know my grandmother?" Margaret asked, puzzled by the counselor's behavior.

"Yes. Her name was Agatha Mary Gruenwold. Never really caused us any problems," Mary Weatherby answered stiffly, looking away.

"You *do* know her! Did she ever speak of family? Tell any stories of—" Margaret began, excited.

"Mrs. Glover...Margaret...she was never able to talk to us.

I'm afraid what you're looking for never existed."

"What do you mean? She can't remember, or she wasn't allowed to talk?" Margaret asked, not understanding.

"No, dear. Perhaps you were too young when you visited before. You see, Agatha had been in some sort of fire or had some kind of accident. We were never very clear on exactly what happened to her. When she came to us she was in no condition to speak. That's why relatives brought her to us. Her condition was so severe, it was far too much of a burden for them to care for her…properly," Mrs. Weatherby began to explain.

Margaret's heart fell. "Didn't she get any better?" Margaret asked, nearly pleading with the woman sitting across the desk from her.

"Gracious dear…no. Her face…. Her—she had been burned. Her mouth was nearly sealed shut, her eyes had been blinded, and something had deafened her. She could not hear, see, or speak. No one knew what happened to bring her into such a state. And when she arrived, she had only a small jewelry chest with some old keepsakes inside, and the tattered, bloody clothes on her back."

"I…I see. Do you know what sort of keepsakes were in the box?" Margaret said, tears springing to her eyes.

"Nothing really—a couple of rolled up pieces of paper and a list, I believe. I think it was some names of family members. But if memory serves, that was all there was. Your aunt, Mrs. Ordiki, took it with her when she left that day," Mrs. Weatherby answered, indifferent to the whole thing.

Margaret rose from her seat and turned toward the wall to gather herself. She could almost hear the hag back in the Louisiana swamp laughing at her defeat, but Margaret refused to give up her search for the truth. Though she would have to return home to her side of Missouri empty handed, she had one last place to visit that the haunted witch had suggested may unveil some answers.

"Oh, Mrs. Glover...," Mary Weatherby said, remembering something from long ago. "She did have this on her, with instructions from Lucille that it was to be sent to you at a later time. I guess since you are standing before me now, I can give it to you. I honestly don't know why I've kept it all these years. I suppose it just slipped my mind. My apologies." The stuffy woman reached into a drawer in the desk and pilfered through some papers before retrieving a dingy envelope. The name Margaret was scrawled hastily upon the outside in what looked like a brownish-red ink.

Mary Weatherby handed the envelope to her, curious to see what was inside. Margaret's slender fingers trembled with anticipation as she broke the seal across the back of the envelope. A simple slip of paper was inside with the same hasty writing in the same brownish-red ink.

Be wary of the light.

Margaret frowned. Yet another subtle hint that whatever was happening had been a long time in the making. She crumpled the paper in her hand and turned to return to her seat.

"It's a shame I couldn't get here any sooner than today. I might have been able to—I don't know...talk to her, even if she couldn't answer me. Perhaps if I'd made my journey last week...," Margaret said, thinking aloud.

"Last week? Why, my dear, whatever good do you believe that would that have done?" Mrs. Weatherby asked, curious.

"Well, maybe if I'd gotten here last week, I could have at least visited Agatha before this morning's events," Margaret said, sitting down. She reached for the coffee to take a sip of the pungent black fluid.

"Pardon me if I seem confused, but what on earth are you talking about? "

"The—as your orderlies called it—*meat wagon* taking

Grandma Agatha away. I guess I just must have—" Margaret began to explain, but Mary Weatherby interrupted.

"Mrs. Glover, I hate to tell you this, but Agatha died two years ago. Our orderlies said they found you passed out on the floor in front of room 33—Agatha's old room. I am sure what you think happened to you this morning was nothing more than the dream inside a weary mind," the counselor suggested in a stern tone that left no room for additional comments.

Margaret stared over the rim of the cup even as it left her fingertips and crashed to the floor. Mrs. Mary Weatherby rose from her seat, startled. She quickly scanned the area of her office for something to mop up the mess until she could have one of the maids come by to clean up properly.

"Oh my god! I-I'm sorry. I didn't know Agatha was already dead. I know what I saw...I know—" Margaret interrupted herself. She had to remember where she was. She was sitting in the counselor's office in a sanitarium. This is the last place she should allow herself to speak of anything supernatural, or she'd wind up as a patient there herself. "I'll help you clean it up," Margaret said, choosing to redirect the conversation. "I think it best I should go back home and take some time to rest. I just lost my Aunt Lucille. I guess I haven't recovered from that yet."

"Understandable. I agree, I think it would be the best thing for you. You are apparently weary, exhausted, and in a state of grief," Mrs. Mary Weatherby said, waving her off. "Don't worry about the mess. I have staff to clean around here. So, before you go, is there anything else I can assist you with?" Mary asked, obviously hoping the answer was no.

Margaret rose to her feet and headed for the door. "You said Agatha died two...years ago?" Margaret asked, in denial that she'd heard Mrs. Weatherby correctly.

"Yes. Two years," Mrs. Weatherby answered, her voice and expression stoic. "I'm sorry," she added, including a small hint of sympathy in her voice, although it seemed sarcastic.

"No then. I guess there isn't anything you can help me with. Thanks for the coffee," Margaret said dryly, and opened the door. She slipped out quickly and headed for the exit with a step quicker than her normal walk. She had a feeling that Mary Weatherby was questioning her sanity right about then. Despite all of her efforts and all of the disappointment, Margaret's curiosity alone fueled the energy for her quest in a very inexplicable and profound way.

With a heavy sigh, Margaret walked away from the sanitarium empty handed, except the hastily scrawled letter from her dead grandmother, and a growing suspicion that something truly terrifying and indescribable had happened to Agatha.

CHAPTER 11

The month had since become late October, and Margaret would pay the town of Hornet, Missouri a visit. It was not far from her home—just a few miles out—but the time of year was better to try and see the mysterious light that served as the basis for a local legend. Because autumn had removed most of the leaves from the trees that lined the country road, Margaret had waited all summer to seek out the Devil's Promenade. She was unsure of what could possibly be learned from a fabled "ghost light," but at this point, she was willing to investigate any aspect she could if it would help her solve the mystery of the scrolls. But as the summer had begun to draw to a close and the strange things happening to Margaret had failed to cease, she had conveniently thought of a few things to ask her father about. Having told her husband Henry she would be visiting her father in Joplin, her plan was to ask her father some questions, but he just happened to live very close to the mystery light. Before Margaret went any further on her quest to learn the secrets of the chest and the scrolls, she wanted some things answered, and there was only one person still living in her family who could shed some light on a few things. But Margaret questioned whether he would respond to her or not.

141

With a flock of butterflies flitting about inside her belly, Margaret wished that her childhood and family life had been normal. What she would give to pull up in front of her father's house and be greeted by a loving father, mother, and twin brother. Instead, Margaret was greeted by a man broken by fate and bent by time. His face wore lines that told a harsh tale—lines she'd never seen before. She could not help but notice how much his hair had been painted white in the many years since she had last laid eyes on him. The stink of booze wafted about the scraggly old man, and Margaret could barely believe this man to be her father.

"What do you want, Mag?" he asked, rising from his perch in an over-sized rocking chair parked on the front porch. Though it had been many years since he'd seen his daughter, he knew who she was in an instant. It seemed that time had not yet changed Margaret, as it had for him.

"I've got questions about Mother," she answered, skipping the traditional kiss and hug.

"No. That will never be brought up again…not as long as I breathe. Ain't nothin' to say," he said, glaring at her. His red-rimmed eyes seemed glazed by the haze of the alcohol in his system.

As Margaret looked around she could see empty whiskey bottles lying on the ground everywhere. "I see you have started drinking again," she commented with a shudder.

"Again? Pah! Never really stopped. What the hell do you expect me to do? Huh? I'm sure your life's been easy—*you* didn't know…!"

"What—*them*, Father? *Mary* and *Adam*…that's their names! Not ever talking about them and pretending nothing ever happened won't make what happened go away!" Margaret retorted, her amber-flecked eyes flashing.

"And it don't help talking 'bout it neither! I don't know what you want from me…," the broken old man began, looking away.

"Answers," Margaret stated clearly.

"Don't have any," he snorted, looking up at her briefly before shifting his eyes away again.

"Yes, you *do*! What happened? Why can't you just tell me everything?" Margaret asked, her voice desperate.

***

The withered man before her turned his grayed eyes back to his daughter. Ever since the rest of his family was ripped away from him, he'd felt so alienated. With the rest of his family dead, he had never known how to act around her. So much in her face reminded him of Mary, and only brought back more details of the nightmare in his mind that he relived in every waking moment.

"Because you can't possibly imagine…," he began softly. His chest heaved as he recalled the events. "What it would be like to watch your wife — your children's mother — go crazy, like she was possessed by the devil himself," he said, his voice becoming angrier. "What it would be like to hear your infant son *screaming*, and walk in to see the woman you love in the middle of slitting his throat!" His voice was saturated with seething hatred and soul-shattering sorrow.

***

"*Jesus!*" Margaret gasped under her breath, reliving the horror of the image in the vomited photograph in her mind.

"Ain't no Jesus. Ain't no *God*. It's all bullshit!"

"Father, what happened to Momma? Why was — IS — everything so screwed up? What the hell happened?" Margaret asked, worried he wouldn't tell her, and worried that he would.

"It all started with that goddamned jewelry box. I can't say exactly what the hell was wrong with her, but I know it had something to do with that cursed thing," he answered, reaching for a whiskey bottle that was sitting on the porch by the rocking chair. As he raised it up to take a drink, he noticed it was empty.

143

Only small brown droplets coated the inside of the glass bottle, but it wasn't enough for him at that moment merely to have a tiny taste. Dismayed, he threw the bottle across the yard, and it smashed when it landed among some stones that lay upon the ground by an old wagon wheel.

Margaret looked around at the yard, only to notice the entire place had seen better days. The yard had absolutely no upkeep, and all sorts of trash littered the ground. White paint hung in strips off the old wooden planks of the house, and the fence that lined the edges of the property was in great need of repair. She sighed, her heart heavy, knowing that the man who was once her father had disappeared. Left behind was a mere hollow shell of a man who had all but given up on everything. Margaret could feel his angst — a thick blanket draped around the entire property. She couldn't really blame him for shutting down, but she also kept in mind that he'd shut down on her, too. Ignoring a burning sense of aggravation linking her past to this place and the broken man before her, Margaret choked back the anger she felt and pressed on for answers.

"Where did the chest come from?" Margaret asked, taking the subject further than she'd ever taken it with her father before.

"You know, when a man has a daughter he hasn't seen for nearly ten years, you would think it would be easier to talk about something pleasant," he said, ignoring Margaret's question. He scratched his head and looked down at the ground.

"Father, this is important. I *have* the jewelry chest. I wouldn't be asking if I didn't need to know. Some things have been happening to me…," Margaret began to admit.

Her father's eyes narrowed, and his brow furrowed deeply. He turned away from her. "It arrived as a package. Some young guy in a buggy come by the house, said he'd been instructed to deliver it to Mary. She was expecting with you two, nearly ready to burst. She felt it necessary to take a look inside, thinking it might have been something for the babies," he explained, his voice seeming to sober up. "There was an immediate change in her—never was the same after that. And then…." He stopped, shaking his head. His gaze shifted up to the clouds.

"What…? Please…!" Margaret said. Urgency dripped from her plea.

"Girl, you're gonna get yourself into some trouble. You'd best get rid of that thing right now!"

"I've tried. It won't let me," she answered softly. Her father shook his head, as if he knew it was already too late. "What happened to Momma?"

"Don't know. After she killed Adam, she disappeared. Went to some church. Said there was something she had to do that I wouldn't understand. Next thing I know I got a wife with her eyes and mouth burned shut, and deaf as a doornail. Damned church looked like all hell fire rained down over it, too," he continued, his body beginning to shake. Margaret was unsure if it was the whiskey wearing off or the reality of what happened washing over him. "She died later. Don't know if it was from her injuries or if she starved to death."

"Like Agatha…," Margaret said in disbelief.

"Don't you mention *that* name. Whole goddamned family's line been ruined by whatever the hell that damned chest is," Margaret's father warned.

"That's why I needed to know. So the same thing won't happen to me!" Margaret said, a new worry surfacing. "I'm sorry…that all this happened like it has," she added, thinking she might try to make amends with her father after all he'd been through.

"No need to apologize. Whoever started this bullshit—THEY need to apologize. But I got to ask you, as one last thing you can do for me as my daughter. Don't come here again. And don't bring up this shit again. I ain't gonna have neither!"

With his words, Margaret walked away with so many emotions swirling around in her guts. Feeling sick, angry, sad, and some strong emotions she couldn't even name, Margaret turned her back on her father, and in that lonely moment, Margaret knew what it felt like to truly be an orphan.

Prior to reaching her father's house, she had stopped at a nearby farm and offered the farmer's son there a nice payment if he would take her to the road where this fabled light was supposed to appear. She had heard vague stories about the mysterious "spook" light, but in her youth had never made the venture to go see it. Their deal was set, and at ten thirty the evening before Halloween, Margaret took a ride up to road E50 — The Devil's Promenade. While the story of the mysterious light on this road attracted visitors on a regular basis, the cold October air welcomed no other guests, save for Margaret. The housewife found herself alone in the cold darkness, facing a long dirt road before her. The moon had been full on the 22nd, so no soft glow from above was there to comfort her. The farmer's son agreed to wait for one hour, but then would have to return home with or without her. Margaret, uneasy about this, did agree to make her visit short.

The boy was about fourteen years of age, and while he lived in the pocket by the state line, he had never been to see the light, nor did he want to. Just before turning onto road E50 he stopped, and there it was he would remain for at least the next few minutes. The idea of a supernatural light with no confirmed source had scared him at a young age, and after the stories he'd heard, he had never even been curious about it.

Margaret looked about cautiously — no sane woman would be out this time of night or year by herself on a lonesome country road. But she had to see what Madamé Hanté had spoken about. The road had a slight incline partway down, so the view was not a straight shot. Bare tree branches clicked against each other

146

every time the breeze picked up. Cold wind threatened to bite at Margaret's earlobes, and she did her best to snuggle down in her scarf to block the bitter gusts. She wondered if she would see anything; and furthermore, would she know what she was looking at if she did?

About ten minutes into her visit, Margaret thought she caught a glimpse of a dancing white orb just over the rise of the incline down the gravel road. Her breath caught in her throat and she paused, listening and watching the glow intently. As in stories she'd read before making the trip to see the legend for herself, the orb grew brighter and larger in size. At first it hung motionless even with the tree line over the rise, but Margaret noticed that it had begun to make its way toward her.

Terrified something would attack her out of the solid darkness around her, she took a step back. Her eyes darted back toward the corner of the road where the farmer's boy was waiting, wondering if he saw it too. She snapped her head back, only to see the orb had grown into a fog of misty, white clouds, and as she looked closer, figures in a ghostly vision grew more distinct. Images of a giant entity being pulled together out of two smaller and clearly separate ones were the backdrop for the foreground image of a woman. Margaret could not clearly see the face, but from occasional side profiles, she would have sworn it was one of the great grandmothers in the picture book Lucille had kept. As the image shifted and the brightness grew more intense, the woman seemed to phase from one face to another, and Margaret could see the likeness of more than one ancestor. Suddenly the wispy image of the woman grew more three dimensional and solid in appearance, and the figure turned its head, looking straight at Margaret. She was astonished to see her own face in the vision, but her features quickly dissipated into a monstrous, demonic form. Margaret was horrified, yet intrigued, and in a trance, took one step closer.

The new demon face turned away to face the giant form being created behind it. A dark shadow began to be pulled away from the body, just as Lucille's soul had been ripped from her body in Margaret's vision at the funeral. And yet a faded light revealed the spread of what looked like wings behind both images. Confused and shaken, the feeling grew too intense for Margaret to handle.

"No!" Margaret cried, as the memory nearly made her sink to her knees. She was not sure of exactly what was happening, but she was beginning to have a better idea. She was the nephilim, just as Madamé Hanté had suggested back in Louisiana.

"Ma'am? You all right up there? You ready t' go?" the young farmer boy called out into the darkness.

His young adolescent voice broke Margaret out of the spell she was under, and she sighed heavily. "Y-yes! I'll be right there!" she answered, trying to hide her fear, but her voice still shook ever so slightly. Everything Margaret had discovered and experienced, this far, seemed to be making more sense to her in that moment. If she truly were a half-angel, then there had to be something within her that was super-human. And this was what she had to find out.

A thought arose in her head, and in that moment, she realized the secret of the ghost light. It wasn't a matter of simply seeing the light, it was what you needed it to be. Whatever the experience was for an individual, that was the key. It was different for every person, so no one would ever understand or be able to corroborate what happened to her there. Acting like nothing special had occurred, she would have to go home the next day, celebrate Halloween with her children, and tell her dear husband Henry she was just fine, though he would know she was not.

As her mind wandered about contemplating the events over the last few months, Margaret began the drive back to their farm. Back down the dusty trail cut into the countryside on her way back to rural Jasper, and back to her family, with whom she was feeling quite detached lately. As the same strange feeling began to creep over her once more, Margaret found herself beginning to realize the connection between that inner voice, the odd sensations that wrapped themselves around her insides, and the blackness that would follow. Anxiety started to rise like a tidal wave within her, and she fought to focus her attention to the road ahead of her. She knew she would have to pull over before she blacked out, but it was too late. By the time the realization hit her, and Margaret pieced things together, the nightmarish vision of the dark shadow creature manifested itself in the road. The abrupt appearance of the hideous thing made Margaret swerve sharply, sending the thin-tired vehicle sideways.

The crank style auto lost balance and rolled up onto just two wheels for a few yards before toppling over on its side. As it slid, Margaret was tossed about as she tried with all of her strength to hold onto the steering wheel and stay inside the motor car. But her grip was not strong enough to hold on and gravity pulled her down, slamming her against the window. Panic gripped Margaret as she scrambled inside the auto car to climb up the seat and out of the passenger side window.

As she struggled to grasp onto something to pull herself up, she found her skirts caught on something beneath her. As she reached around her high lace up boots, her tender flesh raked against broken glass. A large shard of shattered glass cut deeply into her left hand, slicing it open and allowing blood to flow outward freely. With an injured hand, Margaret was no longer able to grasp onto anything in order to climb up and out of the wreckage. Blackened areas in her vision made it very difficult for Margaret to focus. It was hard to fight against the nagging dizzy beckoning of surrender to the darkness she knew was going to envelop her any moment. A voice echoed in her head from inside the darkness that Margaret could barely understand.

Remember what you are, the voice cried out to her, but its message was detached from her current situation and Margaret did not understand. As the brink of unconsciousness edged itself closer and washed over her, Margaret found that she was no longer concerned with getting herself out of the overturned vehicle. With the fold down top completely crumpled and blocking her from simply crawling out from the front of the motor car, Margaret let gravity take her to the bottom of the automobile. When she closed her eyes, a forceful sleep took its hold and she slumped over as her hand continued to bleed.

Margaret awoke sometime later. Had she been out very long? She felt she'd been thrown from a great distance and slammed against the ground. The mangled wreckage of the auto car was several feet away from where Margaret lay on the ground. She rolled up onto her side; blood smeared across her brow and into her chestnut hair from the still bleeding wound on her hand. As her torn flesh burned and throbbed, Margaret felt a queasy nausea begin to well up and churn around her insides. Battered and bruised, she tried to pull herself up into a sitting position, but her body was far too wracked with pain to abide, and Margaret simply collapsed back onto one side.

The sound of insidious laughter erupted all around her. As her darkened vision flickered between blurry and clear, black shadows in front of her morphed into the demonic creature she'd seen far too many times for her taste. Severely weakened and frightened, Margaret found the inner strength to call out to the evil being as she tried once more to prop herself up.

"Leave me alone!" Margaret demanded angrily.

"Oh, I mustn't do that...," the creature hissed. A decayed hand reached out and pressed its clawed fingers against her forehead, absorbing the very thoughts flowing through her mind. "Pitiful human creature. Why can't you understand what you really are? How little you've become. I love your fear—the hot, animalistic smell of terror calls to me."

"Why do you continue to plague my mind? What the *hell* do you want with me?" Margaret exclaimed, frustrated.

The creature smiled and pressed its fingers harder against her clammy skin. "The hands of Thyme are against you," he sneered as his claws dug into her forehead.

As the phantom's physical form began to dissipate, Margaret could feel him pass through her, leaving a cold ache throughout her entire body. The lingering shadow disappeared underneath Margaret as strangers approached when the wreckage of the motor car was spotted by travelers on horseback.

CHAPTER 12

As Margaret came to, white walls surrounded her on all sides. The dim light of dawn or dusk hinted beyond pale pressed curtains hung on a small square window across the room to her left. Panic rippled through Margaret's skin as goosebumps sent chills down her aching spine.

No! Margaret thought, first about her nightmare that took place in a hospital ward, and then secondly about a sanitarium. "Henry would never…," Margaret muttered under her breath.

The middle-aged woman sat up quickly to take a more thorough look. Margaret really was in a hospital room. The smell of clean linens and freshly scrubbed wooden floors met her nose. But there were no eerie shadows, no gore or corpses on gurneys. Nothing about the room seemed malevolent at all; a sanitarium was not the answer either, as she was neither restrained nor medicated.

Sock-covered feet swung out over the edge of the bed, though Margaret was not sure she should get up. As she looked around a bit more she discovered her hands and arms were wrapped with bandages. Thinking back, she remembered the accident and looked around the room for a mirror. Had that damned creature left marks upon her face where its clawed inhuman hands had touched her?

Toward the foot of the bed on the far wall stood a pedestal with a wash basin, fresh bath cloths, and a small polished oval looking glass. Margaret carefully placed her feet upon the cold tile floor and stood up slowly. She paused a moment to correct the feeling of unbalance that flowed over her, but the wooziness passed quickly, and she took steps toward the mirror.

Reaching the wash basin, Margaret held her breath as she looked at her reflection. Expecting to see stitches holding scarring wounds together all over her face, she was pleasantly surprised to learn her fair complexion was only a little scratched and bruised. A small bluish-purple spot had come out on one cheek, and red marks on her skin dotted her forehead in three places.

With a quivering hand Margaret reached up to touch them as nightmarish images of the dark phantom touching her face danced behind her amber-flecked eyes. She could still feel prickles of pain as she recounted the claws pressing into her flesh. But as she gazed harder, a different vision pervaded the mirror's reflection and showed her a curious sight. Margaret peered harder into the mirror.

Like gray-black smoke drifting upward, a pair of vaporous feathery wings appeared and spread out behind her; it appeared that Margaret were some sort of spectral angel. She shook her head and closed her eyes—the vision was just that much more confusing. A heavy breath caught in her chest as she lingered a moment, trying to figure out exactly what she was seeing. Nothing made any sense to her these days, and she wished it would all just leave her alone.

As Margaret stood in front of the mirror, she opened her eyes and again searched behind her own eyes for answers. This time there were no wings, and no flickers of terrible creatures trying to grab for her. Gazing deeply into the face that stared back at her, mimicking her every move, she jumped when the face of a young boy appeared suddenly in the mirror in the open doorway to her room. Knowing she had definitely not dreamt what had happened, she tried to gather her thoughts and figure out what her next move should be. She still had no idea what had happened, but knew there were even more questions to ask now. It occurred to her that she really was in a hospital, and with the sudden appearance of the boy in the mirror, her heart felt that it had come to a screeching halt within her chest.

She spun around quickly on her heels and found herself nervous about what would actually meet her eyes. The boy she had seen in the mirror grinned at her and waved as a giggle escaped his young lips.

"I'm sorry if I scared you," the boy said as he apologized. A small hand went up to push back a stray strand of his shaggy, sandy hair.

"I just wasn't expecting to see you there, that's all," Margaret said with a smile. Her insides calmed down and the nervous feeling began to go away. "What's such a handsome boy like yourself doing here?" Margaret asked, curious. The young boy reminded her of her own son Henry Jr. and the two looked to be of about the same age.

"Momma says I'm real sick. Doctor don't know why, but all I know is that I don't feel too good."

"What's your name?" Margaret asked, her tone gentle and soft, in the manner she would speak to her own son.

"I'm Peter," he answered with a cough.

"Pleased to meet you, Peter. I'm Margaret," she said as she walked over to shake his little hand. "And that beautiful young lady next to you there...," Margaret said, motioning toward the blonde haired, fair skinned woman standing at the boy's side. "Is this your mommy?" The blonde-haired woman remained silent and looked down at the child.

"You can *see* her?" the young boy asked, puzzled. He took a step closer to Margaret and looked up at her.

Margaret knelt down by his side, so she could talk to him easier. "What?" Margaret asked, bewildered.

"You ain't 'posta be able to see her. That's my angel; she's here to make sure I don't die," Peter explained. The blonde-haired woman continued to remain silent, but raised her head and seemed to look straight at Margaret. "She sees you could use her help, too," Peter commented.

"Oh my...," Margaret said, sucking in a breath. The angel looked at Margaret, and though silent, sent a feeling of warmth and peace throughout the room that seemed to chase away the darkness that had been pervading Margaret's mind of late.

"She's real pretty, huh?" Peter asked, smiling up at the angel. As Margaret looked over the woman's face, she seemed more and more familiar. "You shouldn't be able to see her, though," he whispered. His words carried a quiver that was very unsettling to Margaret.

"What do you mean? Why do you say that?" Margaret asked, questioning the boy further.

"'Cause you ain't 'posta see angels 'less you're dying!" Peter cried, tears bursting from his hazel green eyes.

Margaret sat back on her heels. In that moment she felt truly sorry for the boy, and was empathetic as she thought of how she would feel if it was her own son standing before her, having to face his own mortality at such a young age.

Down the hallway voices could be heard calling for the boy. Peter seemed startled and began to cough — a symptom of whatever sickness plagued the child, Margaret supposed. As the voices grew closer the boy turned his attention toward them, and the figure of the angel stepped closer to him. It appeared she was going to pass right through the child, but she vanished into thin air.

"She says she cannot be seen by others — they must not know

she is here," Peter said, obviously sad to see her go.

"But why is it that I could see her?" Margaret asked herself, knowing the child could not possibly provide an answer. As Margaret stood there with the boy, there was a voice in her ear; the angel was sending her a private message across a great distance, despite her appearance near the boy.

One of us, sounded in Margaret's ears out of nowhere, and she blinked at the warm sensation suddenly filling the hall. And then the angel was gone.

"Maybe 'cause of the same reason you can see that black shadow—he *scares* me," the boy said with a quiver to his voice, just as those calling for him took him by the hand and led him off.

"Huh? H-how strange…," Margaret stammered to herself as she focused her attention back to Peter.

"Come along now, Peter—you need to be in your bed resting," one of the voices coaxed as their footsteps disappeared down the hall. Margaret hadn't had much of a chance to see who'd said what, but watched as a woman and a man led Peter down the hallway away from her. Margaret felt bad for the child, and hoped he had a loving family he could count on to give him support. She wondered if the black shadow he referred to could possibly be the same deathly wraith she had been envisioning over the last few months.

"Nah, it couldn't be," Margaret said, dismissing the idea. But perhaps Peter was having a close encounter with the father of death as the boy's illness drew him ever closer to the arms of the Grim Reaper. The angel would be there to protect him and keep him safe, she hoped.

As she stood up, her thoughts turned from the young boy to her own family—they must be so very worried about her. But why hadn't they come to see about her? A rush of nervous thoughts flooded her eyes and tears welled up behind them.

"Oh Henry, what have I gotten myself into?" she said to

herself with a heavy sigh.

"You tell me," Henry's voice said from somewhere behind her. Margaret turned slowly to see her husband Henry standing in the hall, and though she could tell he was not thrilled to be there, she was happy to see him all the same.

*****

"Oh, you should've seen—" Margaret stopped and peered down the hall, but there was no one in sight. "Peter—the cutest little boy...," she continued, but trailed off.

"Who?" he asked, looking around. "Maggie, I really do worry about you sometimes."

"He's a patient—I was just talking to him. I-I guess he already made it back to his room," Margaret explained.

Henry took her by the arm and guided her back to her bed. "Maggie, I think you're exhausted...just plain tired. It's been a hard year for you. Now I know I ain't been the most supportive, but when the sheriff...when he said.... Well...," Henry began, his eyes tearing. "I thought maybe I'd lost you."

"Where are the kids?" Margaret asked, glancing around, hoping to see them smiling at her.

"With my sister. I didn't want to leave them—I thought it'd be nice for you to see them. But a hospital is not a place for children," Henry answered, shaking his head. "Looks like you've got a couple of nasty marks on your forehead there." His finger reached out to touch them, and as his flesh brushed hers, it occurred to him he hadn't made love to his wife for such a long time.

An incredibly potent sensation swept through him, and an urgency filled his body the likes of which he'd never felt before. Could it be that his wife's vulnerable state had stirred a suppressed lust he was on the verge of rediscovering? Was it wrong of him to want to take his wife right there in the hospital room? At that moment he didn't care. His hands touched Margaret's face ever so gently. His fingers cupped her chin and his thumbs brushed softly across her lips. Margaret's breath caught in her chest and she began to look flushed. Henry leaned toward her and kissed her gently and slowly, caressing her neck with one hand. Goosebumps spiraled out across her skin, and she ran her fingers up into his hair. His lips brushed her ear and then down the side of her neck. Margaret's fingers curled tightly around stands of her husband's hair.

***

"Henry...yes...," she whispered as she felt herself getting completely swept up in the moment. As he went to lay her back, quick footsteps echoed down the hallway and stopped just outside her door.

"Mrs. Glover, the doctor is releasing you to home now. You may gather your things. Just check out at the clerk's desk down the hall. They'll answer any questions you might have," the young volunteer announced cheerfully. Her cheeks were still blushed because she'd walked in on the kissing couple.

"Thank you. I'll be ready shortly," Margaret answered, looking at the younger woman. The girl didn't linger in the doorway, but simply nodded and walked away. "Goodness, I'm very glad that wasn't one of the sisters who came by. I'm sure they would not approve of this," Margaret said, looking at Henry with a smile.

"It don't matter to me. We're married, we ain't got nothin' to hide. Now...where were we?" Henry answered, kissing her neck. Margaret's eyes fluttered as he lay her back down upon the hospital cot. Margaret's body rose with anticipation of a long-deserved moment of ecstasy. With each kiss, each caress of her husband's strong hands, she could feel the weight of the last few months melt away, and for a few passionate, though rushed, moments, her world felt balanced and whole, as if she'd not a care in the world. And though they both knew the moment would be fleeting far too quickly, they each sought to savor each sensation, seeming like it would be their last intimate moment together.

It took a total of three hours to check out of the stone, volunteer-run hospital, load up in the wagon, and head to Henry's sister's house to pick up their children. Since it was nearing noon, the family decided to stop off at Sally's Place, a small family owned café on the edge of town, for lunch. It was not often the Glover family had a meal prepared besides at home, and the children were thankful for the treat of ice cream sodas. Margaret felt this could be a second chance at mending the holes in the fabric of her family's life, and smiled to herself behind her cup of coffee.

Over the next couple of weeks after the journey back home and settling back into more of a routine around their farmhouse, things seemed to return to normal quite quickly for the Glover family. The shadows of dread that had followed Margaret home from Louisiana had simply vanished into dust. She felt a calming peace within herself, and looked to her children and husband with a renewed sense of energy and gratefulness for still being alive to be there with them after all of the foolishness over the past summer. Everyone about the house seemed happier; eggshells had been swept up from the floor and a weight had been lifted off their shoulders. The darkness that had clouded Margaret's mind shriveled into a distant light, like a bad dream fading in the mind of a child in the night. Smiles abounded, and despite the edge of a winter's chill coming soon, the drafty farmhouse felt warm and inviting, unlike the whole of the summer they'd only recently left behind. A new hope grew deep within Margaret's heart, and like a firestorm a new passion for her life and family brewed as well.

Over supper one evening Henry decided to tell Margaret of some news that he'd brought home from his work in the quarry. "Maggie, you remember Harry Brendleman? Works out there in the quarry with me, you know?" Henry began, taking a bite of biscuit.

"Vaguely, dear. Why?" Margaret asked, unable to clearly remember exactly who Henry was talking about.

"Big guy…tall…red hair," Henry explained between bites.

"Oh yes…Nancy's husband. What about him?" Margaret inquired, the man's face popping into her head. She'd only met him twice before.

"Well, he and some of the fellas been talking 'bout all that jack down south—" Henry began.

"Jack?" Margaret interrupted.

"Zinc…them fellers been zinc mining down south in Joplin. Anyway, word is coming up out of those mines that there's some jobs and good money to be had."

"I suppose it is well more lucrative than the quarry?" Margaret asked, genuinely interested.

"Of course. If it wasn't, I wouldn't even be giving this another thought," Henry answered before taking the last bite of biscuit.

"Golly, Henry, Joplin seems such a long way to ride the horses or drive, don't you think?" Margaret asked, worried. "Would you really want to run the horses that far every day? That's a far piece from here—especially for an everyday ride. And in the winter…," Margaret began, the idea beginning to seem less attractive to her already.

"Well, Maggie, you bring up some mighty fine points. I thought about those things. Any man would be crazy thinking them horses could take that trip back and forth like that. You know, I was thinking more of gettin' ourselves a house down that way and migrating south just a tad. Just make a fresh start of it. They've got some nice schools down that way, I hear. The kids could get a good, solid education and have a chance for a brighter future than this ol' farm could provide," Henry said, looking over at Margaret.

"Joplin is an awfully large city compared to our farm life now. Do you truly believe this would be a good move for us?"

Margaret asked, skeptical.

"Maggie, we wouldn't have to live in town. The mining don't take place in the city, you know. It'd be a new start — a chance for new opportunities. What do you think?"

"What would we do with the farmhouse? I thought we had a pretty good life going here," Margaret commented softly. She felt strange talking about moving away.

"We do. It's just some talk about doing even better for our family. There's a lot we would need to look into and discuss, but it does seem very promising. And with zinc mining you wouldn't be shut down and out of work during the rainy season like with the quarry," Henry added with a wave of his fork.

"Do you want to look into things now? I personally would rather wait until at least spring. It'd be easier, I believe," Margaret answered; the decision had already been made.

"Well, there don't seem to be too much rush to get down there — the way Harry talks, that jack will be pouring out of those mines forever and a day," Henry agreed. "Besides, I'd like to get past the holidays first, and I'll most likely spend a good week down there to try my hand at it before we just up and move," Henry added, chewing his last bite.

"I suppose that would be wise," Margaret agreed. And while Margaret did believe this could lead their family into easier times, she wondered about where the road would lead her if she were to solve the questions the jewelry chest still posed.

"Say, what's the date today? Is it time for the news cast?" Henry asked, suddenly changing the subject as a stray thought entered his mind.

"Today is the tenth," Margaret answered, swallowing a mouthful of water. "The news cast should be tomorrow."

"I'll have to remind myself to go by the drug store in town and pay this week's voucher," Henry said aloud to himself. "Thanks for supper, darlin'; I'm going out to bring in the cows. I'd better check on those roastin' hens to see which one'll be the fattest for Thanksgiving, too." He bent down and kissed Margaret on the forehead. "Looks like those red spots are finally fading away," he said with a smile as he brushed over them lightly with his thumb.

She simply smiled back up at him. Margaret wanted very badly to believe this meant the encounters she'd had with the black creature were going to fade away as well. As good as things felt at this moment in their home, Margaret was sad to know that sooner or later she would have no choice but to once again face the horrors the small cherry wood box contained. And that meant she would have to endure the darkness that would attempt to take over her very soul as it had tried to do once before.

Tired from the day, Margaret began her chores and checked in on the kids. As she looked over their peaceful faces, she envied them and their innocence and ignorance of the world. To be young and unaware again would be a bliss incomparable to little else, Margaret thought to herself. A certain hypnotic charm washed across Margaret as she watched the children's rhythmic breathing in their own separate rooms as she looked in on them both. She wished them pleasant dreams, though she knew her words would never reach their sleeping ears. It really had been a long time since she'd felt this close to her family, and at least for tonight, she wanted for nothing more in the world than to keep this feeling going as long as she possibly could.

Margaret turned down the lanterns mounted on the wall in the hallway outside the children's bedrooms, and prepared the house and herself for the night. Margaret knew Henry would be a while yet bringing in the livestock and preparing their farm for the night, so she took that opportunity to clear the supper dishes and get the floor in the kitchen swept up. Later that evening, with tired children sleeping and the Glover farm shut down and secured for the night, Margaret and Henry sat by the fire place and talked of their plans to move their family toward the promise of wealth through zinc mining. The absence of the children's voices would allow their parents to speak with each other uncensored. But just as the dark of night had devoured the light in the blue sky of the day, shadowy dreams wove themselves into a nightmare that entered the sleeping and innocent mind of Ann, halting the restful sleep she had only recently fallen into.

***

The young girl found herself standing outside a lonely looking house, barefoot in knee-deep snow, with gentle white flakes falling into her dark hair. Shivering, Ann looked longingly into a large picture window with fine, parted draperies. Inside, where it was obviously warm and inviting, a girl about her size danced about a grand carpet full of rich reds and golds. A multitude of strange people unknown to Ann twirled and swirled in a whoosh of black fabrics that flowed about as they danced. As Ann watched their rhythmic display she seemed completely mesmerized with their bending and swaying. A sound like a distant music box tune tinkled in the background, and the sound began to fill her ears.

Suddenly Ann noticed it was she who wore a black silken party dress, the likes of which Ann had never owned. A black lace veil drooped lazily down over her curious eyes, and she looked through the material as she stood in the center of the group of dancers. With panic not yet at her doorstep, Ann took a good look around. As she found herself surrounded by very fine things, the music box tune stopped playing and laughter erupted from somewhere amid the others dressed in black garb.

The laughter sounded like it could have come from a child at play, gaining Ann's curiosity that much more. She stepped into the mass of people, though they didn't seem to notice or care. As the laughter continued, Ann darted in and out between people, dodging moving bodies the best she could, though no one seemed to acknowledge her when she did bump into one of

163

them. Through her efforts and her dismay, Ann found nothing.

Just as suddenly as the laughter had begun, it stopped, and Ann found herself lost in a sea of people. From her short height all Ann could see was dark clothing. Even the brilliant reds and golds in the carpet upon the floor had disappeared. The dancers had quit dancing, and each darkly dressed stranger stood still. With black gloved hands they began to reach out for Ann; slowly at first, only reaching. Ann began to grow afraid; something in this room did not feel right. The hands began to grow more and more desperate to reach out and touch the young girl, and Ann's fear finally welled up and poured forth. Tears clouded Ann's gentle, innocent eyes and she began to peer through the crowd for a way out. She saw no clear path, so she closed her eyes tightly and dove into the swarm of people.

Ann began to run as fast as she could, but she felt her legs weighed a ton. With each frightened stride Ann struggled to move forward. The inside of the house changed and shifted all about her, and the panic inside her grew ever more intense. All of the lights began to fade into nothing around her, and Ann found herself running down a long, dark tunnel with hands grabbing for her. The once black gloved hands began to change as well, becoming more deformed and corpse like in appearance. As those trying most desperately to grab ahold of Ann passed by her, they began to disappear into the darkness that surrounded Ann inside the terrifying tunnel. It had grown so dark that Ann could only see those terrible creature hands grasping for her as she fled by them; the darkness was quickly overtaking the little light that remained. Suddenly, voices from every direction began to whisper words Ann could not quite make out at first. The voices whispered over each other, but it would soon become clear what the voices were saying.

"The hand of Thyme...," the voices whispered hurriedly again and again over each other.

"Stop it!" Ann went to scream as she found it more and more difficult to move. At this rate any number of clawed, deformed hands could reach out from the pit of the shadows and take hold of her. But only panic-ridden silence escaped her wide-open mouth. She seemed to be running in slow motion now, and the whispering voices grew louder and louder.

"The hands of Thyme…," they kept saying, once so very softly, now so loud, like thunder rattling her ear drums.

"STOP!" Ann screamed with all of her might, and the sense of urgency that flooded her one single word broke the young girl free of the nightmare's hold.

***

Ann's scream sounded all the way down the hallway into the living room, alerting Margaret and Henry that something was wrong. Both rose quickly to go check on their daughter, but Margaret put a slender hand up.

"I'll go…it's probably just a bad dream. You sit and relax, I'll be right back." Henry nodded and sat back down.

When Margaret opened Ann's door she half expected to see a horrifying specter hovering over her daughter for the way Ann had screamed. Instead, she found Ann resting peacefully. The girl only stirred slightly, and Margaret concluded Ann must have had a nightmare, but had since moved on to another dream. Margaret stood there looking in at her daughter and smiled. How lucky she was to have such wonderful children. As she stood there in contemplation, she thought she felt a fleeting presence lurking somewhere in the shadows of her daughter's room.

"You leave her alone," Margaret demanded in a hoarse whisper into the darkness. The out of place feeling lasted only a brief moment longer before it vanished from the room. "You'd better run," Margaret warned aloud.

Satisfied that her daughter was safe, she turned and stepped back into the hallway and closed Ann's door. No matter what

165

the future held in store for her, Margaret would welcome death for herself if it meant her children would never have to endure anything like she was going through.

"Sleep tight, honey," Margaret whispered. She kissed her palm and placed it lightly upon the child's bedroom door before walking away to rejoin the company of her husband waiting by the fireplace.

"What was that all about?" Henry asked as Margaret walked back in.

"Like I thought, a nightmare…that's all." Margaret answered. "Ann seemed to be sleeping fine when I walked in—I just let her be."

"Nightmare, that's all? Sheesh, with that scream, you'd think she was being murdered," Henry commented jokingly.

"Yes…that's *all*," Margaret confirmed, though she suspected otherwise. She didn't even want to start any conversations about the sensation she'd picked up in their daughter's room.

The household settled into their beds and into their individual sleeps.

CHAPTER 13

At midnight on the morning of November 11, 1911, a shift occurred deep within the universe. Like a thunderous clap from the heavens, two comets shot through the stars, blazing at speeds far beyond the speed of light itself. Glowing with the intensity of a billion stars, each comet raced forward in a direct bullseye aim for Earth. Should anyone have been out scanning the sky at such an hour on that cold November night, one might have been fortunate enough to have viewed the luminous show above.

Across the dead stillness of the Midwestern plains of Missouri, no one felt the ground jolt with the impact of the comets. Only miles apart, each comet left in its wake a large, smoking crater in the ground. Upon impact, the earth shuddered uncontrollably until the shockwaves ceased to emanate from the site. Perhaps the cattle in the countless pastures were the only living creatures to feel the effect, but soon the good people of the earth would know something was happening.

The first comet landed in a quiet grassland approximately forty miles west of the Kansas border into Missouri. Brilliant orange embers glowed fiercely at first, but began to fade as the crisp, late autumn air cooled them. In the dark night, a hand reached out from the edge of the crater. Slender, alabaster fingers shakily feathered outward and grasped the charred soil. A perfectly proportioned female body pulled herself out of the seared hole in the ground, wiping dirt from herself as she stood up. Waist-long blonde hair whipped about her face in the breeze, making sapphire eyes blink. The woman looked around, filling her lungs with the cold night air; firm, round breasts heaved with each breath.

Making a motion with her fingers, a wispy fog formed all around her. Swirling and smoky, the thin clouds seemed to wrap themselves around her naked body, solidifying into soft, white linen robes. Her palms facing toward the ground, the woman forced energy through her body, lifting her up off the ground. Hovering merely inches above the terrain, then being began to float off through the tall prairie grass, leaving the sensation of a gentle, warm wind that cut like a knife through the bitter cold. In minutes the woman disappeared into the night, setting out to explore her environment. There was much she wanted to learn and accomplish, and only twenty-four hours to get it done.

***

Not even a hundred miles away from the first, a second comet collided with the earth, it's embers an eerie red against the darkness. Unlike the first crater, a bony hand with decayed flesh clawed at the dirt in its attempt to escape the blackened pit. Emerging in a forceful, upward thrust requiring unnatural strength, the creature—more than a man—landed, one hand upon the ground, sending a puff of ash flitting away into the breeze. The man-thing drew in a deep breath as it stood covered in decay, ash, and dirt at the edge of his smoking crater. Catching a scent carried by the wind from a hundred miles away, the corpse-like creature emitted a low, supernatural growl as his cataract-covered eyes narrowed. With a grunt, the demon took off—in the opposite direction of the scent, however, for he too had a mission to accomplish, and only twenty-four hours to do it.

***

As the early morning hours passed and the people slept, changes had already begun to take effect, though most would not be aware of them for a little while. In the distance, a church bell tolled three. A tall, thin man in a black suit walked quickly, book tucked neatly under his arm, down a narrow, white hallway. Dim light flickered as an out of season thunderstorm raged outside. The tall man whisked past several women dressed in white, the whoosh of his overcoat breaking the restful quiet. Whispers flew up as a lingering result of the skinny man's presence. His quiet, quick footsteps pattered on the tile floor as the hallway drew to a dead end.

At the far end of the hall, a large window allowed strange shadows to crawl inside and sprawl across the floor. As the mysterious man cast a glance outside, a bright bolt of lightning illuminated the courtyard outside brightly, momentarily making it daylight. To the left of the window was a door, and a woman, shawl about her shoulders, standing half out of it, waving the tall man in. Candlelight from inside flickered outward with a soft, glowing effect.

As the tall man entered through the doorway, all those present, including a doctor, hurriedly stepped aside, not wanting to get in his way. This was a room in a small hospital just southeast of the Kansas border into Missouri. The room was quite plain—stark white walls, no carpet or pictures. Only a wooden crucifix hung upon the otherwise bare walls. Against the opposite wall was pushed a single hospital bed, where a small boy lay. It was obvious family members were gathered to support him; however, the looks upon their faces were curious about the situation. Rather than tear-streaked faces of worry and angst, lips were smiling, and expressions of amazement graced the eyes of all those present. The tall man solemnly removed his wide-brimmed hat and looked around the room, then up at the ceiling. He sat on the edge of the boy's bed and looked at him through gentle eyes before speaking.

"You say the recovery was immediate?" the tall man asked, directing his gaze toward the doctor for the moment as he spoke with the man.

"Yes, Father McKenzie. He...we gave him no chance. I must say I am skeptical—perhaps we misdiagnosed...." The doctor's voice trailed off. It was painfully clear he was uneasy about the situation.

"NONSENSE! How *dare* you question my son? You're saying he's not really been sick this whole time?!" a man exclaimed as he rose to his feet. His anger toward the physician was misplaced, but it had been a long road and he was desperate and at his wits end. In his heart, he knew that the physician was just as puzzled and confused as the rest of them were.

"Franklin...hush! Let the man speak," a woman commanded in a bold, harsh tone.

The man looked at her, but said nothing more. He remained standing, crossing his large, obviously strong arms, and nodded at the doctor without another word to say.

"The boy's condition, to our collective medical knowledge, was irreversible at best...terminal, if you will. But this incident, when the nurse came in to do her nightly check— What she said she witnessed...." The doctor shook his head and cleared his throat. "Well, I don't quite know what else to think," the doctor left off, unable to put the event into proper words.

"Excuse me, Doctor Goldman. Exactly what was witnessed, and what are you suggesting?" the tall, skinny man asked, looking at the man in the long, white lab coat as he raised a curious eyebrow.

"Father McKenzie...," a small voice interrupted as the priest felt a light tug at his sleeve.

"What is your name, my child?" The father returned his

attention to the boy. The young hazel eyes of the boy met the aged, gentle brown eyes of the older man. The boy peered around him a moment to get permission to tell the story. The boy's mother smiled and motioned for him to go ahead. The room remained silent to allow the boy to speak.

"My name is Peter. Well, Father...sir. See, I was real sick. No one was really 'spectin' me to feel better, but the nurse tried to make me think so anyway. But every night I would say my prayers like Momma tol' me, an' ask Jesus to find a way to help me," the boy began to explain, propping himself up on his elbows.

"Well, Peter, that's very good of you, saying your prayers every day. Then what happened, my child?" the lanky priest asked, urging the boy to continue.

"Well, Father, sir, tonight I was feelin' real tired, and it was gettin' real hard to breathe. The nurses were actin' funny...like they knew somethin' was wrong. And that's when she showed up. I've seen her before, but this time she was different," Peter continued. It was obvious he was excited to be feeling better, and even more excited to tell about what had happened. If it was possible, the room grew even more silent when "she" was mentioned. It wasn't natural, what the boy was talking about, and the grown-ups had a hard time with the thought that maybe, just maybe, the boy had seen an angel.

"*She*?" the father asked, raising an eyebrow.

"Oh sure...the lady from the sky that helped me get better. She said —" the boy answered, but was interrupted.

"Wait...she *spoke* to you?" the preacher man asked.

"Well, it was more like I heard a voice in my head, not from her mouth. She didn't talk like we do. I just kinda knew what she was sayin'. She told me that the Lord sent her to me from Heaven to take away the illness and make me better, so I could go outside and play with the other kids again. And then I just...felt better," he said, seeming amazed as he relived the events in his head.

171

The priest sat at the edge of Peter's bed in silence. He'd studied many teachings of miracles and researched the theories on angels, but in a small corner of his heart he had trouble admitting that perhaps, just perhaps, a miracle had actually taken place in the very facility where he made his rounds when he was called upon.

"An' she was real purty too. Long blonde hair…and eyes that looked like the sky. Just *so* blue. I got the feelin' that she had to go away once she helped me, so I probably won't ever get to see her again." The boy's gaze shifted into nothingness, almost appearing that he was trying to see her through the ceiling.

Still pondering the possibility, the priest knew there was much to be written and investigated regarding this incident. It was considered a privilege and honor to be directly involved with a proven miracle. And a meeting in person with the pope was almost always a reward — a dream come true for a dedicated man of the cloth.

The family members present fluttered around the priest and began asking questions, leaving the conversation to turn from one direction to another as the night ticked away. Once daylight broke, the priest intended to contact his colleague — Father Talbert — to gain another perspective.

***

Hidden away in the shadows, no one in the little boy's room noticed that Sky sat smiling, satisfied with her work. It had been a century since her presence had been among the people of the earth, but a flicker of disturbance burned in the back of her skull. She didn't yet know what the sensation would translate into, but she could feel something different with this visit. Slowly she allowed herself to pass through the constraints of the building and set out toward her next objective. Fortunately, she'd found this case to start with and hoped to find others in her short time, but even more pressing was to watch out for events related to her brother Thyme, and to try to make contact again with her sister,

Margaret. Over the course of the day, the angelic half had been fast at work. She had brought food to the hungry, wealth to the poor, and love to the lonely. Though the world was a wide, wide place, it seemed the good on Earth was ignored by eyes blinded by the greed and loathing of others. She was painfully aware that as she existed on this plane, so did her brother. Her angelic heart would not allow her to be weighed down by sorrow, for by doing so she would begin down the same path as Thyme, and that she *could not* allow. She swam among soft clouds, enjoying the warmth as she contemplated how much the world could benefit from a source of pure goodness. She dreamed of how to persuade the demon's half to surrender his evil, though she knew it would be an eternity—if ever—before he would come over to the light. The beat of her heart sounded like the sweetest melody ever sung, and nature's creatures responded quite well to her presence, yet through the warm, uplifting breeze blowing, undertones of darkness wafted up now and again, reminding Sky why she was there. After enjoying a quiet moment of peace in the natural harmony of the earth, she moved on toward her goal.

***

But not everyone on Earth was fortunate enough to see good times come of the unearthly beings' visit to the planet. Miles and miles away, a darker soul was hard at work, avoiding the trail of his angelic counterpart and wreaking havoc. Darker times were brewing, and to those involved, there seemed to be no end to it all, and no way out. A crushing weight of oppression, hatred, and anguish pervaded the air no matter where the demon went. A veil of darkness and chaos rose up about the land as the evil—free to roam wherever it wished—crossed city and countryside alike. Those who were ill suffered seizures and coughed up blood; animals, if not mutilated, went rabid. Children went missing, lost to unimaginable, unspeakable acts for all time.

Near dawn, the dark creature wound his way through

endless acres of pasture, and found great pleasure in taking the life he came across. He happened upon one particular farm, rich with livestock and looking quite well for the time of year. The demon slinked through the dark and into the rear door of a large barn toward the eastern edge of the farmhouse grounds. A heifer was chewing her cud quietly in the night as her months-old calf lay sleeping by her side. The monster's slimy lips spread open in a gaping smile of horror as he leered toward the warm-blooded animals. If the barn had been closer to the farmhouse, its residents may have heard the terrible cry that rose up from within, but that was not the situation, and not a soul stirred. The wretched creature smoothed the cow's fur back as he looked over his prey.

Choosing a soft patch on the animal's neck, he threw back his head in a cackle of hatred and smashed his fist right through the bovine's flesh, tearing open a large hole, and allowed the life contents to spill all about. The demon positioned himself so he would be immersed in the gush of hot blood that poured forth; steam rose in contrast to the cold night air. The beast bellowed in pain and writhed in fear as it felt its life slipping away under the creature's touch. But there was nothing the cow could do but drop slowly to its knees and lay on the ground by the undisturbed calf to die. The demon, draped over the dying carcass, began to tear at the flesh hanging loose at the sides of the heifer's neck, where his fist had torn chunks of meat loose and left them hanging outward. His pointed, monster teeth tore at the gore, his face smearing totally in the warm crimson sauce pumping through the wound. Once finished with this one, there were plenty more to massacre—solely for the fun of it. And he thought to himself, why stop with the animals?

When the sun finally rose, the earth noticed the changes taking place and responded the only way it knew how. Across the central plains, the mercury began to climb—unusual for November, and seemingly out of nowhere. Once dawn finally hit, the air had warmed considerably compared to the frosty coolness it had been just after midnight. Kansas City saw sixty-eight degrees by sunrise, and the thermometer rose steadily from there. As households began to wake, families began to discover the horrors left behind in the demon's wake. It was not long before calls to the local authorities began to flood in, and the police began to feel overwhelmed by the revulsions that rocked the Midwestern plains.

***

It was the same for Margaret — her day began with a nightmare. A figure bathed in golden-blue light appeared floating on a misty cloud. Margaret could barely make out the figure's features, as it was so very far away. An unnatural stillness pervaded the air; the sight was quite ethereal. A wind blew out of the stillness that wisped the figure's long hair and shroud about. As Margaret looked over the figure with intense curiosity, it began to move toward her. Like a flashback from her vision at her aunt's funeral, Margaret prepared herself for the half with the death-face. The angelic creature arrived in no time to a distance of just three feet in front of her. The aura began to brighten, but Margaret squinted against the glare to glimpse the face beyond it.

Piercing blue eyes sat like sapphires in the sockets of the pale-skinned being. The long platinum tresses caressed a face that mirrored intense purity, though those eyes were haunted with sadness. A thin hand raised up toward Margaret and pointed, as if choosing her out of a crowd, even though Margaret stood alone.

"Me?" Margaret asked, pointing to herself. The angelic apparition nodded. A feeling of peace washed over Margaret as a warm breeze blew about her. Images surrounded in a pink aura of love danced before the woman's eyes — a mother rocking her baby, children laughing, a young girl playing with a kitten in a large field of flowers. Margaret began to wonder if this angel, perhaps, was to represent all that was good and pure.

A voice sounded off, speaking from the heavens, and a single word was uttered. "Sky."

The voice and the word echoed in Margaret's head as she drank in the warmth of the peace. The figure advanced and vanished—it had simply walked through Margaret. Just as this happened, a withered corpse hand grabbed at Margaret's throat. Cockroaches crawled from the creature's skin and onto hers. Margaret tried to scream but was unable. The scent of death stung her eyes and she gasped for air. Dark shadows crept over her mind as she tried to resist the demon's grasp. Visions of destruction and war overrode the lingering aura of the light. A virtual land of waste and sin and death opened up in front of her; piercing screams and moans shrieked in her ears. Margaret tried to remember the good half and push away the dark, but fear gripped her very soul and she could not.

The human woman found herself dressed in wedding clothes; the scarlet stain of blood tinged the once shimmering white satin fabric. As she grasped at the clothing, the dark fluid ran between her fingers; her gullet had been ripped open, and the blood flow was coming from her own body. The creature turned Margaret to face it; tears blurred the already terrifying sight around her, adding to the sense of panic she now felt. As Margaret faced the thing, the visions of hell intensified. The woman tried to figure out what her wedding dress had anything to with what was going on around her, but found no other clues.

The creature's solid black eyes sat inside a mostly human face, but quickly changed into a more human look, and harbored a deep emerald color. Jet black hair edged eerie chalk-white skin, and as the mouth opened to speak, maggots poured forth and fell in large numbers on the ground. Gagging, Margaret turned her eyes away in an attempt to shut out the evil. The creature laughed with a deep demonic tone. His hand grabbed the back of

Margaret's head and forced her toward him. Without warning, that strange feeling Margaret had experienced on a couple of separate occasions now returned. The demon's eyes began to bleed, and the sound of sobbing women seemed to come from all directions. He extended a long, forked tongue and forced Margaret into a kiss.

At first she felt a hot flush building through her core, and she kissed back, her body lust-hungry. In the seconds that seemed like an eternity, the mother of twins felt compelled to surrender everything she knew and flow into this creature's very being. But a small voice inside her urged her not to give in...not just yet. As the kiss continued, maggots squirmed off the forked tongue and into Margaret's mouth, writhing about in the search for rancid meat. The demon pulled back and laughed hysterically, and as Margaret regained control of herself, she began to choke and gag as she spit out the fly larvae when she realized what was happening to her. The creature's eyes went back to the solid black color and glared at her; a demonic voice boomed, "Thyme is against you, sister."

With that, the nightmare around her stopped. All went as silent and black as a tomb. Margaret woke with a jolt, grabbing at her throat as the feeling of choking from the dream lingered in the physical realm. Margaret frantically patted the empty space beside her as her heart pounded in her chest. A great weight sat heavily in her chest as she fought the drowsiness that came with being ripped out of a deep sleep. She battled with Thyme's words at the end of the dream — she wasn't ready to accept the possibility that she was related to that monster. Groggily she looked over at the clock to see that it was nearly ten in the morning. Through a cracked window she could hear the voices of her husband and children playing out in the yard. It didn't immediately occur to her that the window was open. She propped herself up on her elbows, half sitting up, and listened. The children were laughing, and it was obvious they were hard at play. Margaret realized that the window was open and shivered before she noticed the breeze blowing in was pleasantly warm. Blinking at the bright light flooding in, she shielded her eyes with one hand as she reached for her housecoat, which hung on the back of the chair at her bureau.

CHAPTER 14

Shaking off the effects of the dream, Margaret shuffled sleepily to the back door and stepped outside.

"Henry...what is going on out here?" she asked tiredly with a big yawn. Her husband, busy with the kite he'd built the past summer, passed the roll of string to their son.

"Good morning, dear! Sleep well?" His tone suggested he didn't expect an answer.

"Henry...you're playing out in the yard?" Margaret asked as she looked around. The site was simply shocking, and she knew something just didn't feel right about it.

"Yeah, I know! It's great, huh?!" he answered with a boyish enthusiasm. It had been a while, but Henry seemed as giddy as a school boy for some reason. Perhaps it was simply the relief from the freezing temperatures in the month already, albeit out of season. But Margaret suspected something she could not explain. Margaret looked around, her mind fuzzy in a dream land, and wondered at first if she was still in bed asleep.

"But...but it's *November*. It should be cold!" she said, scratching her head as she tried to find reason in her mind for the situation.

"I don't know, sweetheart...it is how it is. Say, why don't

179

you go get dressed and come enjoy this fine, warm day?" her husband suggested, trying to bring her out of her grogginess. Margaret looked over the flawless blue sky and sighed heavily; the air seemed stale. Something about this just didn't feel natural, and the feeling welled deep within the pit of her stomach. It burned like a coal with remaining hot embers that sought to char her insides. Nodding her head, she shifted her gaze to Henry and smiled. Henry gave her a quick kiss and Margaret's thoughts momentarily flashed back to the kiss in the dream. Shuddering, Margaret drew back.

Henry looked her over a moment. "Maggie, are you feelin' okay? You seem—I don't know...distant, distracted. What's wrong?" he asked, looking her in the eyes.

"Oh, I'm fine, Henry. Just trying to wake up yet. I'll bet once I get dressed I'll feel much better. I'll be out in just a moment," she answered, pretending to yawn and be sleepy. Margaret kissed Henry on the cheek and disappeared back inside the house.

***

Henry watched her go inside and shook his head. He had noticed that ever since she'd come back from her aunt's funeral, months ago, she wasn't the same. He had tried to talk to her several times about what was wrong with her, but each time he broached the subject, he noticed a very strange look in Margaret's eye that was both wild and wicked—a manner that was completely out of character for her. He never pushed for any further details and left her to her research, though he disagreed with the nature of it entirely.

She spent a good deal of time making drawings of the images on the scrolls and writing letters to priests and scholars for help to decipher them. He noticed that she seemed more preoccupied with her project than with her own family, sometimes even daring to think she might be obsessed. It had been months with no word in return from the many letters she'd written, and Margaret had started keeping a journal about the scrolls, her visions, and the dreams. Henry secretly worried about her, having found and thumbed through one of her journals, but figured that she would eventually let it go. He returned his attention to Henry Junior and Ann Marie, and praised them for doing such a great job with the kite.

In less than ten minutes Margaret joined them, and they spent a good portion of the morning running around outside. It felt nice to be a little more like her old self, like the times they'd spent as a family before the death of her aunt and the receipt of that damned chest.

As the morning passed by and gave way to noon, the temperature had reached seventy-six degrees, and they had decided to take advantage of the freakishly warm weather and have a picnic. Halfway through an oddly pleasant and completely out of season lunch outdoors, an automobile chugged up the Glover residence's long drive and stopped out in front of the farmhouse. Margaret and Henry looked at each other, then toward the vehicle, puzzled. From the thin-wheeled machine a rather round man sporting a thick moustache climbed out, bearing a metallic star on his chest.

"Afternoon folks!" the man called toward the side yard where their spread lay. Henry and Margaret rose to their feet, walking to meet the man as he moved closer to them.

"Afternoon, Sheriff. Nice weather we're havin'," Henry said, greeting the uniformed man; the brass star on his chest glimmered in the sunlight.

"Yes, too nice, if you ask me," the sheriff commented as he stopped just in front of the residents. "Ma'am," he added, removing his hat in the presence of a lady. Margaret nodded back. "You folks hear anything last night? There seems to have been some disturbance down the road at Farmer Wilson's property overnight," the sheriff continued, fanning himself with his hat.

"Well sir, that's almost five miles out, and I don't know if we *would've* heard anything. Wish I could help you out, sir," Henry answered with a shrug.

"Oh, that's all right, Mr. Glover. Just have to stop by and ask everyone. Standard procedure...you understand," the sheriff said with a wave of his hand.

"Sheriff, if you don't mind my asking, what happened?" Henry asked, sharing in some of Margaret's curious side at that moment. The difference was that Henry was curious about potentially important things, while Margaret was curious about... well, *everything*.

"Oh, it's a shameful mess, I'll tell you. Someone came last night and mutilated half the livestock. Tore 'em up *real* good."

Margaret's hands flew up and covered the gasp escaping from her mouth. "How *dreadful!*" she mouthed, her words muffled by her hands.

"Any idea who would've done such a thing...and *why*?" Henry asked, curious.

"Didn't find so much as a footprint. You know, you'd think with all the crazy storms we've been having, there'd have been *something* in the soft mud around the barn at least," the sheriff answered, shaking his head.

"Well, it was just the livestock, right?" Henry said, "You can replace that...expensive, but replaceable."

The sheriff's already troubled face fell. He took Mr. Glover aside, as his next words were far too disturbing for a lady of the house. "Now Mr. Glover, what I'm about to tell you goes no further than between you and I. But I figure since your residence is the closest, you deserve to know so you can protect your family if necessary," the sheriff said, worried about their safety.

"Sheriff, you sayin' my family could be in *danger*?" Henry said, careful to keep his voice down.

"Well, I'd only say just be sure you keep your windows

closed at night and your doors locked when you go to bed. See, whoever trespassed on the Wilson property last night didn't stop with the livestock." He shuddered as he thought about the sight he'd encountered in the Wilson's farmhouse. "Mr. and Mrs. Wilson are both no longer with us…." His voice trailed off.

"And their children?" Henry asked slowly, though judging from the sheriff's demeanor he already knew the answer. The sheriff just looked at Henry for a moment in silence before lowering his eyes and shaking his head.

"*Jesus!*" Henry exclaimed.

His voice carried just a little too loud, and Margaret's gaze turned to him from the distance.

Henry instantly regretted what he'd said, and looked sheepishly back at his wife before returning his attention to the sheriff.

"Well, Mr. Glover, I'd best be getting along. There's a lot of things to be done. Just do what you must to keep your family safe." The sheriff turned to walk back to his automobile, but paused briefly after a few steps. He cast a glance over his shoulder at Henry. "If you've got one, I'd keep your shotgun loaded, Mr. Glover."

Henry stared blankly at the sheriff as he turned back away and finished the walk to his vehicle. Margaret joined her husband, and they watched the sheriff drive away together.

"What did he say?" Margaret asked, curious but afraid.

"I'll tell you later," he answered solemnly.

"Look, I know it was something bad. I can't tell you how I know this, but there is something really terrible happening," Margaret said, her tone almost pleading with him to tell her what had happened, though she did not press the issue.

"You may just be right about that…," Henry agreed. He left it at that for the time being. He didn't want to upset his wife, and he certainly did not want to dwell on the picture that the sheriff's words had painted in his mind.

***

Like the cold hand of death reaching toward the planet, arctic blasts began to form and the skies became overcast. The winds shifted to the northwest and the temperature began to plummet. Earlier Oklahoma City had reached a record-breaking high of eighty-three degrees. But as the afternoon crept past two o'clock, it became clear to the residents in the Midwest that their welcomed heat wave was coming to an end…and fast.

By three that afternoon, what had been the temperatures of mid-summer began to turn colder and colder, until it reached a degree mark cold enough to snow. At first it didn't strike anyone as odd, since it was November after all. But soon, as it began to drop at an intense rate, people became aware that something was very wrong. Southeastern Kansas across to southwestern Missouri and a large portion of the greater mid-western plains — halfway over toward the eastern half of the United States — dropped from a very pleasant eighty-three degrees to a chilling thirty-three in the matter of that hour.

***

Margaret and her family had long since gone back indoors, and Henry kept an eye on the sky through the kitchen window as the gray dome above them grew angrier and angrier. Though much earlier in the day than he usually would, Henry walked over to a small desk where he would use the leased headset to listen to the "telephone tribune," a subscription-based version of the world news. For just five cents per day, continuously updated news was broadcast over the dedicated telephone line. The subscriber could listen seven days a week between eight in the morning and ten-thirty at night.

Margaret sent the children to play in their rooms, so she could sit with Henry and listen to the news, something she didn't normally do. But in this case, she was interested to know if mention of what was going on would be made. A strong, masculine voice repeated the same loop of news twice over as Margaret and her husband listened in disbelief.

"After a rather large earthquake felt by the areas such as San Jose, Los Gatos, and Morgan Hill back on July first this year by the Calaveras Fault, California, residents are reportedly experiencing waves of aftershocks. So far they are estimating an incredible several hundred-thousand dollars' worth of damage. Some say they expect the aftershocks to last well into the next month.

"Across to the far east our neighbors in Manchuria, China are reporting a new total of sixty-thousand fatal cases of the pneumonic plague.

"Visoko, Bosnia — a raging fire is burning through the entire upper city and heading toward the main streets alongside Beledija. City officials estimate some four hundred-fifty houses and businesses have already burned, but at this hour local fire brigades have not made much progress in stopping the flames.

"Central Plains in the United States — an arctic blast is cutting through from the northwest, coming down from the Canadian border and dropping down across the Midwestern states. The Mississippi Valley is reporting an outbreak of severe thunderstorms and tornados due to the sudden and extreme temperature drops. At this hour meteorologists are unable to explain where this intense weather pattern has come from.

"Additionally, the Ohio Valley is experiencing a series of spontaneous blizzards, while across the way in Oklahoma a dust storm is clouding their skies. And here is a report that southeastern Kansas and southwestern Missouri are currently enduring a massive temperature drop. Their day began with temperatures near seventy, rising quickly to nearly eighty-five degrees. Currently sources report a temperature sitting just above the freezing mark...."

With each portion of the newscast being read, Henry and

Margaret's eyes grew wider and wider. Unable to keep listening, Margaret rose quickly from her perch on the edge of the desk and went back to stand in front of the kitchen window. As Henry hung up the receiver, he cocked his head to one side, listening intently to something.

"What is that?" he asked, unable to determine what he was hearing.

"What is what?" Margaret began. She stopped to listen, but heard nothing.

"Shh! There it is again…hear it?" Henry said in a hoarse whisper.

"No, I—." Margaret began, but stopped.

A crackling sound seemed to suddenly fill the house in all directions. As Margaret peered outside, she noticed everything seemed to have a layer of frost on it. As she watched, the window seemed to fog over with a thin layer of ice before her very eyes. The sound became louder, like the sound of ice cracking. Margaret turned and looked at Henry for a moment before realizing what was happening. Her eyes snapped wide open, and the look of pure panic spread over her face.

She suddenly made a bolt toward the children's rooms. She stopped frantically by Ann's room, but found the room empty. Margaret quickly continued down the short hallway to their son's room. She stopped abruptly at the door to find both children by the toy bin on the floor in front of a large picture window. Margaret startled Ann, and the little girl stood up and began to walk toward her mother. Henry came running up and stopped at the doorway just behind Margaret. Henry Junior stood in front of the window and twisted around to look at the commotion.

"Maggie…what the—?" her husband began, confused.

"Henry! Get away from the window!!" Margaret screamed at the ten-year-old.

Before he could process his mother's command, his attention

was drawn to the grating, popping sound coming from the window. A long split appeared at the top of the window, splintering outward. As the temperature outside dipped below freezing, the dramatic shift proved to be too much for the delicate glass, and windows around the house began to implode into jagged shards. Margaret wished at that very moment she had the power to freeze time, but Fate was unleashing its fury without delay or bias.

Henry Junior spun toward the window to look just as the window exploded inward, and a large shard flew toward him among a thousand smaller ones. The young boy's arms flew up in a feeble attempt to shield himself, but his tender flesh proved to be no match for the razor edges of the clear, spun sand. In utter horror the family watched, helpless, as the broken glass sliced the boy square across the throat. He grabbed at the wound as other smaller pieces buried themselves in various places of the child's body and the room. Henry Junior collapsed to the floor as a scarlet flood began to spread out onto the floor around him.

Despite her own small wounds from the flying debris, Margaret rushed forward in an attempt to aid her son. "Henry, dial the operator and have her get the doctor!!" she screeched over her shoulder to her husband, but he was already headed on his way to the kitchen to use the telephone. Ann was crying and asking about what happened to her twin brother, but Henry had dragged her away to shield her from the gruesome sight.

As Margaret kneeled over her son the boy gasped for air, but only blood filled his lungs. His mother, not quite sure what to do, grabbed at a curtain hanging from the fresh shattered window to try and use it as a bandage to stop the blood from gushing out. With a handful of the cloth, Margaret tugged the long curtain free of its hold on the long metal rod, sending the curtain rod crashing down to the floor. The long metal pole clinked on the shards of the broken glass as it landed, scattering a few of them across the floor. There was blood — so much blood. The doctor was coming from town seven miles away. Margaret's blood rushed through her ears, thundering, pounding like a steam locomotive.

In the next heartbeat — perhaps it was the next minute or two, Margaret was not sure — her son grew quite gray in the face. She slapped at the boy's face, trying to keep him awake.

And then….

Henry walked through the doorway to let Margaret know the town physician was on the way; Henry Junior's eyes set and glazed over, staring out into nothingness; Margaret sat by her son's side, now covered with his blood. Ann, despite her father's order to go to her room, ran in between her father's legs and saw the horror and screamed; and Henry Junior died.

"It's too late…," Margaret said. Her body felt heavy and numb. But there was something else…something else.

There was a knock at the door a few minutes later. The doctor had arrived.

CHAPTER 15

It was about an hour later, after the doctor had helped Henry move the boy's body and the floor had been swept clear of glass and scrubbed free of the blood, when the telephone rang. Margaret, still with bloody clothes on, walked to the kitchen and picked it up shakily, thinking the sheriff might have some questions. Instead, a hauntingly familiar voice crept through the receiver.

"H—hello?" Margaret answered weakly, her throat tight from sobbing heavily.

"*Vous devez agir rapidement. Je vois que quelqu'un vous contactera bientôt que vous avey dû parler avec pendant longtemps maintenant.*"

"Madamé Hanté?" Margaret asked, still weak and full of grief, but curious.

"*J'ai vu la mort de votre fils. Mais vous devez comprendre que la force que vous comptez avec n'est pas normale. La loi insiste sur le fait que le prochain sera femelle et il ne peut pas y avoir tous deux. C'est trop parallele lointain á leurs propres qui sont pour que ceci soit,*" Madamé Hanté's said to Margaret.

Margaret kept speaking past the voice, but it did no good. She went completely ignored and Madamé Hanté's voice continued to droll on in French. Suddenly, it occurred to Margaret why the

189

witch had wanted a lock of her hair; it was allowing the swamp hag to contact Margaret in a way other than conventional means. Such a personal item was a powerful link between the sorceress and her quarry.

***

Henry walked around the corner into the kitchen where Margaret stood. He stopped short when he saw his wife standing like a zombie in front of the telephone. Her hand was reached out toward it, grasping for the receiver, but her hand touched open air as it posed motionless mid-air just in front of it.

Henry was frightened and shocked as he watched Margaret standing there, locked in a stillness like being frozen in time. More disturbing was the fact that she was mindlessly pouring out words to herself that were in a language his wife didn't even speak. It was then that her husband realized something had happened to his wife when she was gone, though he could never possibly understand what. He tried to step forward to make an attempt to break her out of the trance she seemed to be caught in, but found he was unable to move or speak. Helpless, Henry was forced to watch as the spectacle continued before him.

***

"*Quand il est temps pour la jointure, sois circonspect de la lumière,*" Madamé Hanté finished, and the call disconnected. Even though Margaret didn't speak French and didn't understand the words she'd heard, she still somehow understood in her mind what was said to her, just like from the effect of the tea back in New Orleans. Margaret placed the receiver on the hook and turned.

Startled, Margaret jumped. She hadn't expected anyone to be standing there. "You scared me!" she exclaimed. She hadn't heard Henry enter the kitchen.

He raised an eyebrow. "*You*? Maggie, *what* was *that*?" he asked, his face pale.

"Madamé Hanté. She told me —," Margaret began, but Henry

190

interrupted abruptly, quite confused.

"*Who*? Maggie, you were just standing in front of the telephone talking to yourself in a foreign language!" her husband exclaimed.

"What? No, no I...," she began, but stopped. A cold chill crawled down her spine. "What is happening here...?" she trailed off. Suddenly lightheaded, she sank to the floor.

Henry knelt beside her—it had been a strange and tragic day. He put an arm around her shoulder in the best attempt he could muster to console his wife, but he knew it would not be of much consolation, just as it would not be for him if roles were reversed.

"Did you understand any of it?" Henry inquired.

Margaret remained silent a moment, thinking back to remember the conversation. While strange, Margaret was able to recall the words in French, and put them into a brief explanation so Henry could understand.

"She said I needed to act quickly. That someone I've needed to speak with will contact me soon. She said—" Margaret stopped. Tearing up, she tried to continue through sobs. "She saw Henry's death, but said that the law insists there can't be twins. Only one...female...." Margaret tried to continue, but was unable to.

"What the *hell* are you talking about?! Has this got anything to do with those weird scrolls you brought home from the funeral? I *told* you I didn't like that stuff. And what does this have to do with our children—our *son*?!" Henry exclaimed in anguish; his voice was tainted with bile and shook with anger. The tragedy was far too fresh for it to be remotely easy to speak of.

"Please, lower your voice! I don't know. I...," Margaret said in a hoarse whisper. Her throat was still very dry and sore from sobbing so hard; she fought to choke back another wave of tears.

"Well, you'd better figure it out, now! Whatever is happening might be tied to this. You'd better find a way to solve this mystery. I won't stand by and watch our entire family be destroyed by this!" Henry yelled, his anger growing stronger the more he thought about it.

Henry rose to his feet, his heart too full of sorrow and anger to be of any use to his wife at the moment. He went down the hallway to check on their daughter, Ann. She hadn't left her brother's side since her father and the doctor had placed him in his bed until they could figure out what needed to be done. Margaret sat slumped on the floor in tears as Madamé Hanté's final words to her echoed in her head.

"When it is time for the 'joining,' be wary of the light." Margaret pondered what she'd meant by this, but the day had been too harsh and far too overwhelming. Margaret's world began to close in around her, and everything went black.

"Be wary of the light...."

***

As the weather on Earth continued on its destructive and extreme path, the angel and the demon's own separate paths seemed to be discreetly leading them to the same place. Events continued around the world, equally shared between good and evil. The being's mere presence on the planet was powerful enough to spread outwardly, though the two were centered in central North America. Hours had passed since the shift in the universe, and both entities knew that only a handful of hours remained. It would not be long before they would meet up once more for the century and become Gemini, if only for a moment.

***

By now the time was approaching six. The sun had long since set on the suffering in the Midwest. The Glover's son had been dead long enough for rigor mortis to set in, and no matter what they tried, Henry and Margaret could not pry Ann away from the grotesque sight of her brother's body. The poor girl seemed connected to him, even in death. Her father had noticed she held the same fascination with atypical things as her mother; "an unfortunate fate," Henry had always thought. He had secretly hoped that Ann's intrigue would die down and eventually fade away, but with the events of the day and Ann's reaction, he began to doubt that would ever happen. It was then that he began to pray for the miracle it would take for Ann to grow out of her fascination for stranger things. It was the only trait she'd inherited from her mother that Henry resented.

***

Tired of the mystery, Margaret had brought out the chest. She emptied the contents completely out onto the kitchen table and wildly began to rummage back through them for clues as to what was happening. She looked at the clock; an hour and a half had already slipped by, and the time was nearing eight in the evening. Finding only what she'd found before, Margaret paused, panting, as she thought a moment on what she needed to do. She'd written dozens of letters, made phone calls and several trips to various churches in the hopes that *someone* would — or could — be able to help her figure out the scrolls. The only thing that had been somewhat useful was her trip to the ghost light back in October, but from other sources so far, rejection and silence had been her only answers.

Suddenly, Margaret had a thought — there was only one more place to look in the chest. She spun on her heels and dashed to the counter, where there sat a block of knives. She loosened one sharp-bladed knife from its slot and returned to the table. Margaret began making slices in the burgundy lining of the chest, releasing the fabric from its ancient hold against the cherry wood; bits of crimson dust rose up and Margaret waved it away. The newly bereaved mother tore every shred of the lining away, but revealed no additional scrolls or clues. Margaret, with nearing hysterical frustration, slammed the knife down on the table and pressed her knuckles against the wood as she thought some more. She could feel the veins in her head throbbing, threatening to explode any second.

It was at that moment that the telephone rang, startling her. Because of her experience earlier, she stared at the phone, but didn't move. The sound drug Henry away from his daughter's side, which left the girl by herself. Margaret's husband made his way to the kitchen, past his wife, and answered the ringing telephone. He only answered with a weak hello, listened briefly in silence, then turned toward Margaret.

"It's a St. *Something's* Cathedral—Father Talbert?" he announced, motioning for her to come to the phone, his voice weakened with weariness. Margaret made her way from the table and took the receiver slowly from his gentle hand. They locked teary eyes a moment before she spoke.

"H-hello?" Margaret asked slowly. She paused and hoped the telephone conversation was really taking place this time.

"Mrs. Glover of Jasper, Missouri?" a man's voice inquired, sounding scripted, like he was reading the name off something.

"Yes. Who is this, please?" Margaret asked wearily, ignoring that Henry had mentioned the name to her.

"Father Talbert. I thought I told your husband that. Anyway, I work out of a church here in Joplin. You wrote some time back regarding some scrolls, correct?" a gentle voiced asked, pausing to give her time to answer.

"Y-yes. I've sought help with something important…you aren't calling me to poke fun, are you? Because now is not the time to…." Margaret stopped, leery. After all of the negativity from her previous attempts to gain help, she did not take anybody's reaction for a genuine response, even if they seemed receptive.

"My child, such derision is not something the Lord would take lightly coming from a priest like myself. I must admit I initially had some doubt about the seriousness of your request, but it seems the events of late point all too clearly at a more divine basis," the priest explained. showing some pity for Margaret's

194

distrustful disposition.

"When can I speak with you in person? *Please* Father — you've no idea the sacrifice my family has just made…." Margaret trailed off, her voice pleading from her soul.

There was a pause, followed by semi-apprehensive throat clearing. "I am here…always. A colleague of mine — Father McKenzie — and I collaborated and were able to correlate some recent events to a legend dating back to at least the 1750s. I believe the sooner you could get here, the better."

Margaret took a deep breath before continuing. "Give me a little bit of time to get ready. I'll start that way very soon," she answered, knowing that Henry would not approve of her leaving the house alone for such a thing, especially with her son's body laying upstairs and the weather conditions outside. God only knew what could possibly happen next out there.

"One of the sisters should be around when you arrive. Let them know to summon me and we'll talk," Father Talbert said, his tone of voice warm and genuine, but nervous.

Margaret thought to herself, *Who could blame him for being nervous*? but kept that opinion to herself.

"All right. I'll see you as soon as I can," Margaret agreed, and hung up the phone. She dreaded telling Henry what was about to happen, but when she turned around to speak to her husband, she found he had returned to the deceased boy's bedroom to be with Ann. Due to the importance of the situation, Margaret took this as her chance to act without being caught in an argument about it. She felt this was the best way to possibly save her family from whatever this force was upon Earth.

Quickly she grabbed a pen and a sheet of paper, and jotted a note letting Henry know where she was going. She spared great detail due to the lack of time. While it was already dark outside, she wanted to get there before it got much later. Margaret stuffed the chest into the large bag she'd been using to carry the thing around in, put on her thick, black woolen hooded cloak, and headed out. She had no idea what she was going to do when she got back, but figured things couldn't get much worse than they already were.

Her eyes began to tear as she ran from the house and across the yard to the barn in the freezing air. The family's black stallion was their best horse, and the only one capable of making the journey to the church. Margaret tore open the barn doors and raced inside to saddle up the horse. As if sensing danger, the livestock inside began to bellow and stomp at the ground.

"Hush!" Margaret cried out in frustration.

Her cold fingers worked as quickly as they could to strap the saddle onto the powerful young horse. Her fleshy fingers raked across the horse's black hide as she struggled only briefly to grab hold of the last buckle. With the grace of a practiced equestrian, Margaret swung her leg up over the massive horse and locked her heels into place.

"Get'yup!" she commanded with a hearty snap of the reins. Her heels pushed the spurs into the horse's sides and they were off, flying out of the barn like a bat out of hell.

***

Many minutes later Henry found her note, but as exasperated as he was, he was more worried about his wife setting out after dark in such terrible weather. Apparently, Margaret had felt strongly enough about whatever was going on to pursue the matter further; perhaps it was a way for her mind to cope with the tragedy that had afflicted their family.

Henry stepped outside the farmhouse, curious to see how Margaret had gotten to the church in the first place. He noticed immediately the barn doors were wide open and could tell from a distance that the wagon was still there. He set out across the yard to the barn, where he would have to ignore the freezing air biting at his hands. Until he got the wagon hitched up, his flesh would just have to endure. His young son dead and his equally young daughter dazed out of her mind, Henry wanted desperately to wake up from the nightmare he unfortunately knew he was not having.

As he worked in the barn, he looked up and saw Ann standing inside the house, just beside the front door, looking out a living room window. The events of the evening had all but shut her down mentally, in his opinion. Out in the blustery cold, Henry struggled to hook up the wagon. His mind raced, but his frozen fingers could not keep up. After a few precious minutes had ticked by, Henry was able to get the pin in place and their buggy was finally ready to go. With Margaret having wrecked their automobile and taken their best horse, Henry's only option to go after her was the wagon. In the terrible weather that had come upon them so suddenly this evening, Henry knew Margaret's trip would be a harrowing one in such bitter cold.

Henry jogged back to the house and grabbed Ann by the shoulder. He knew he could not possibly leave Ann alone in the old farmhouse, especially with her dead brother's body lying upstairs. His thoughts in utter chaos, he wrapped Ann up as tightly as he could before bundling himself up in preparation for one cold and windy wagon ride.

"Come on, sweetie, we're ready to go," he prompted his daughter.

Ann stayed silent and continued to stare blankly out in the same direction. The child finally began to shuffle to the door, but paused before exiting the house. Ann turned and looked down the hallway; she had expected to turn and see Henry Junior standing there.

"Henry says he thinks he'll just stay here," Ann said to her father.

A chill ran down his spine. Despite an overwhelming curiosity, Henry could not bring himself to look down the hall for fear of what might meet his eyes.

Ignoring the possibility that something supernatural was happening in their house, Henry returned his attention to the matter at hand. Going after Margaret had to be a priority now that their family was falling apart. In the Glover family's hour of need, the last thing they needed was to lose somebody else. After Margaret's spell of having acted so strangely throughout the summer, he didn't want to allow anything else bad to happen.

However cold the chill that had just crawled down Henry's spine was, the winter outside was much, much worse. Still shivering from the time he'd spent hitching up the wagon, Henry braced his skin for the biting chill that he knew would pummel them as soon as they exited through the front door.

"Daddy, why did Momma leave?" Ann asked quietly as she turned her young eyes to his wiser ones.

"Well, honey, your momma went to go to a…she went to church," he answered, trying to choose his words carefully as the two walked quickly to the wagon.

"Church?" Ann questioned, confused.

"Yes, and we're just going to go catch up with her, that's all." Henry tried to answer her question the best he could, but found his patience dwindling in the wake of the events that had transpired.

***

As Henry prepared to leave with Ann, Margaret rode into the dark night, driving the family horse as fast as she knew it could handle. Breath from both her own chest and the equine beast underneath her poured forth into the night like smoke from the nostrils of a fire-breathing dragon. Blinking back tears that insisted on welling up from the frigid air, Margaret focused on the rocky road ahead. One wrong step and her horse would be useless to her, and she would find herself stranded in the dead of night. With anxious hands she clung to the leather reins as she urged the quarter horse on. Margaret's own black hooded cloak seemed to flow directly into the midnight hide of her stallion as their bodies moved quickly through the darkness.

Margaret was not sure if Henry would follow her; surely he would not leave Ann home alone or bring her out into the dreadfully cold night air. In any case, Margaret's mind did not dwell upon this possibility, and her thoughts turned to her current quest. A potpourri of sadness, guilt, and anger brewed from deep within her heart. Things had felt they were on the brink of turning around for their family just earlier that day, and now their family had been shattered into a million fragments. It was moments like this, and like the horrific events of the entire last summer, that made Margaret question her own unstable faith. With a lifetime of grief and strife, was it any wonder that Margaret could not blindly and fully believe in an almighty higher power like God?

As the wind ripped through her clothing, Margaret shuddered and leaned into the body of her quarter horse. The heat that rose from his muscly body helped Margaret feel just a little less cold, and she closed her eyes for only a moment as she gathered her scattered, heart-wrenching thoughts.

***

Ann didn't feel it necessary to continue talking and went back to being silent. Henry and his daughter climbed up into the wagon, and with a tug of the reins they pulled away from the barn, leaving their farm behind them. A million thoughts coursed through Henry's mind as the freezing air whipping around them, cutting clear through to the bone. He worried about keeping Ann warm, though he'd wrapped her up in as many things as he could grab in a hurry. He supposed it could have been because Ann was already mentally numb over her brother's death, but the young girl never complained about being cold. With the whole world spiraling into anarchy around them, Henry and Ann were off with the hopes of catching up to Margaret. Henry hoped she was not too far ahead of them, but in the worst-case scenario, at least he knew where she was headed.

At least a half an hour behind his wife, Henry did his best to shield his daughter from the cold. He could feel the wagon wheels tremble as they rolled over the frozen, stony ground. He silently prayed the wheels would at least see them safely to the church where Margaret was headed. Though his mind still had trouble grasping the fact that his son was dead, and his wife and daughter were dancing upon the edge of insanity, he wished with all of his heart that he could change the events of the summer. He wished he could stop his wife from ever having gone to her aunt's damned funeral.

CHAPTER 16

Approximately two hours and thirty minutes later, through the rural area to the city, and on roads that were frosted nicely with a thin layer of ice and snow, the black stallion carrying Margaret wearily entered the city limits of Joplin. Street lamps sent light scattering across the precipitation on the ground in all directions, and splinters of light sparkled like fireworks on the Fourth of July. The sparse street signs were frosted over, but Margaret was familiar enough with the area where the cathedral was located to find her way there without delay. The hour was late; she was cold and just wished she could go home. She'd driven the horse as fast as possible, and felt she'd reached the city limits in a decent amount of time, considering the weather.

The church was only a couple of streets away, but her faithful animal companion could simply not go on. Margaret had no choice but to climb down from the stallion and let it go. Having no lamp or fence posts on which to tether the exhausted quarter horse, Margaret let the horse go free and hoped it could find some kind of shelter from the cold.

"Rest my friend, rest," Margaret said, patting the horse on the side. She pulled her cloak tightly about her, adjusted the strap of the large bag that contained the chest, and started to run down the city streets toward the church. It took only a few minutes to run the remaining distance to the cathedral, but she felt a small sense of accomplishment when she finally arrived. She looked over the great building with hope that this would be the end of all her troubles.

The cathedral itself was constructed of large, gray stones Margaret was sure had been harvested from one of the local quarries, like the one her husband worked in. A high tower and bell sat atop the roof's center, and large, stone angel statues guarded the four corners of the building's roof. Several large stained-glass windows lined the outer walls of the church, but it was far too dark to see what wonders had been depicted in them. The closest streetlights cast strange shadows across the cathedral's courtyard, and to the east of the building laid a cemetery that looked to contain ancient looking graves that, though weather-beaten, still stood solemn and still.

In the center of this courtyard stood a tall statue — the figure of a woman bathed in a hooded cloak that covered most of her face. Her arms were outstretched in an eerie welcome into the interment lot, and angelic wings spread out gracefully behind her. The statue seemed strangely inviting, yet as spine-chilling as seeing the Grim Reaper himself. Margaret shuddered, but was not sure if it was from the cold or the creepiness of being there. She just wanted to get inside and find Father Talbert to try and get some answers.

At the top of the stairs was a giant wooden door. Iron crossbars had been built into the old wood long ago to help maintain its sturdiness. The door appeared quite weathered, bearing the look of a cathedral that had been standing for ages. The door had been split into two halves, and each half had large iron hoops attached by iron lion heads to serve as knockers. She wondered just how old the church was; to her, it appeared downright medieval.

Margaret did not bother with the knockers since she was

expected at the cathedral by Father Talbert. Margaret had to push quite hard in order to budge the heavy door, but found it swung open easily once it got started. She had to pull it back with a little muscle before it slammed into the stone wall behind it, and she was also very careful not to slam it when she went in and closed the door behind her.

A large, open area glowed with soft light before her. The inside looked the way Margaret had imagined a typical cathedral would look. Stained glass windows lined the outer walls, though not much light from outside shone in. In the nave rows and rows of pews were split into two sides by an aisle that led up to the pulpit, much like the church had at Lucille's funeral, though on a much larger scale. A wooden table graced the foot of the tall altar behind it, and to one side stood a baptismal pool. Several tapestries, depicting religious events and likenesses of the pope, lined the walls, along with the occasional wooden crucifix. Like the corners of the rooftop, four angel statues guarded the four corners of the main room of the cathedral. Margaret guessed they held symbolic importance, but she herself was not Catholic, and would not know of such a meaning if there was one. Small floor lamps stood at either side of an open archway, apparently leading back past the altar area and down some unknown hall.

As Margaret tried to peer through the darkness past the reaches of the lamp light, the shuffle of footsteps became audible. From the darkened doorway emerged one of the nuns Father Talbert must have been speaking about. She wore a gray habit, and the soft light seemed to give the white portion of the fabric a warm, yellowish glow. A rather thick book was cradled in the sister's arms, but it did not stop the nun from motioning for Margaret to follow her.

Wasting no time, the small-town housewife accepted the silent invitation and followed, cradling the chest in her own arms. The nun led Margaret down what seemed like a *very* long hall.

203

They passed several closed wooden doors on either side of the wide hall. Though too dark to see, Margaret imagined the ceiling was quite high with a rounded ceiling and fancy architecture; she wondered if it had paintings like the cathedrals of old Rome used to in Renaissance times.

At the end of the hallway was an over-sized stained-glass window, illuminated by one of the floor lamps. The brilliant blue in the robes—of what Margaret guessed to be some saint or person important to the church—reminded her very much of the window at her aunt's house. The nun stopped just a couple of doors away from the end of the hall. To her right, the nun raised a hand to knock on the plain, wooden door after shifting the weight of the large tome in her arms; the sound did not echo nearly as loudly as Margaret had thought it would.

The sound of a chair sliding across a wooden floor filled the room beyond the heavy door, followed by footsteps that grew louder as they neared. In a brief moment, the door opened, and an average-built man stood in the doorway. The sister nodded to him but remained silent and nodded at Margaret. Margaret smiled at her. The man looked at Margaret, then at the chest she held. Margaret watched as the nun finished the walk to the end of the hall, where she disappeared around the corner to her right.

"Well, Mrs. Glover, is it?" the same warm voice from the telephone conversation earlier inquired after a brief silence. Margaret had been so focused on where the nun disappeared that his words startled her. "Rough day, my child?" he continued, raising an eyebrow at her reaction.

"Father, you have *no* idea," Margaret answered, shaking her head.

"Please, come in," he beckoned to the woman.

Father Talbert closed the door behind them, but for some reason, the echo seemed louder to Margaret on this side of the door. The priest walked ahead and went straight to his desk. His chamber was pretty plain, just as the rest of the chapel Margaret had seen had been thus far. The room was medium-sized, lit by one floor lamp like the others guarding the entrance to the long hall, and decorated only with a crucifix and two small tapestries, again depicting likenesses of the pope.

The windowless room was not carpeted, and the chair behind a beaten desk was not cushioned. Margaret knew enough about the church to know that this religion demanded the absence of the comforts of luxury as a lesson to be thankful for what you *do* have. A ledger was spread open and lay atop the desk. A fine writing pen and ink blotter lay untouched by the ledger's side for the moment. To Margaret it appeared to be a personal journal; however, she was not the least bit interested in its contents. The priest stood in front of his chair and welcomed Margaret to sit in the un-cushioned chair at the front of the desk. It wasn't until Margaret took a seat that he did. Through folded hands bracing his chin, the priest eyed the woman a moment before speaking. The candle to his right—lit only for his enjoyment—burned steady, but cast a warm, inviting glow across the otherwise nearly empty room.

"Well tell me, what tragedy graces your brow?" the priest inquired gently.

"Father Talbert, I'd like to speak about the—," she began, but stopped. He was right. She needed someone to vent to, if only for a brief moment. "My son. He…." She began to choke up. "Died today. Windows all over my house shattered with the severe drop in the temperature. One exploded and a shard slit his throat." Her throat tightened up again, but her eyes were too dry to well up once more.

"A sure sign the devil is among us," the priest interjected, though he didn't seem to be speaking directly to her at that moment. It was more like voiced contemplation.

"Father Talbert, this chest…and its contents. I…it was

205

bequeathed to me earlier this year by my aunt. Actually, it belonged to my mother, but she died when I was very young. It has brought me nothing but trouble, but I cannot get rid of it," Margaret began to explain, becoming nervous about speaking to a priest in person. Such unearthly things were an awkward topic, even though he seemed genuinely willing to help her out.

"The scrolls you wrote about, they were inside?" Father Talbert inquired, looking at the chest.

"Yes. And a list of family members dating back to the 1700s," she answered. She didn't know how much of this would mean anything to the priest—if any at all—but wanted him to know everything.

"May I see the scrolls?" the older man asked, his eyes seeming somehow tired through the candlelight, though it may simply have been the priest's naturally dry personality.

"Of course," Margaret answered, setting the chest upon the desk facing her. She opened the lid, which she had not bothered to lock this time. The lid creaked open as it had done so many times before, and Margaret gently lifted out the scrolls. "I know it sounds stupid, but I cannot rid myself of these wretched scrolls. I have tried burning them, cutting them, tearing them with my own hands, but they simply resist being destroyed. I have tried soaking them in kerosene, but when I lift the parchment out it is dry—liquid had never touched them. I have tried abandoning them, but they keep finding their way back to me. I do not believe they are of this earth," Margaret explained, getting frazzled just talking about them.

Margaret passed the scrolls across the desk to Father Talbert, and as the rolled parchment passed by the candle, the flame shrank down to nearly nothing, flickered a moment, then grew tall and very bright. Like gunpowder had been sprinkled on top of the flame, sparks popped and then fizzled out for a brief second before settling down to its former size and brilliance.

During this time the floor beneath their feet seemed to vibrate with the motion of an earthquake hitting, and the tapestries that hung upon the wall seemed to flutter wildly, as if caught in some unseen wind storm.

"Ever since I was handed this chest, I have had these terrible visions…and nightmares too. It doesn't seem to matter whether I am awake or not," Margaret added, trying to think of any detail that might be important.

"I believe, as you seem to, that these are from another place… another plane of existence—something neither you nor I could truly comprehend without witnessing it firsthand for ourselves. I can tell you for sure from just what *I* have witnessed that there is some force at work that should not be here," the priest told her. The priest took the scrolls in hands that trembled ever so slightly.

"And what of this legend? You say it dates back quite a way?" Margaret inquired, curious.

"Yes, but for years those of the church who have studied it— though not many—have failed in deciphering its entirety. Over the years of the legend being told, written and re-written, some pieces to the puzzle were missing, and some had just never been found. Supposedly, a human bloodline was chosen by a force not of this Earth. Exactly *what*, no one knows. The point was to choose someone who possessed great inner, mental strength. This person would have to be someone with the ability to create life— therefore, only females are chosen for the task of completing the judgment," Father Talbert began, though details were still pretty vague.

"*Judgment*?" Margaret asked, not understanding what the priest meant.

"As I have heard, a being of two halves—one good, one evil—are each their own separate being, and yet merge into one more powerful one. Caught between survival and living in chaos with each other's opposite half, Fate has suggested that someone

207

choose for them which one will ultimately rule…a judgment, if you will."

"I don't understand. Supposedly my family line is supposed to be this something *special*. But terrible thoughts have passed through my mind, Father. Some things have happened that never should have, and I did nothing to try and stop them. I'm afraid that I am about to do something very terrible. I—"

"The only terrible thing you can do right now is not have faith, my child. This church has seen its fair share of trouble, but we are here, standing as strong as ever," Father Talbert said, unfolding the list of the family names Margaret had handed him. "And it would be a shame not to see you fulfill the fate of your family lineage, that the others have resisted before."

"Resisted? What on earth do you mean by that?" Margaret asked, confused.

The priest looked up over the parchment and scrutinized the housewife for a moment. "All of this in its own time…and it is nearly time," he answered cryptically.

With that, Father Talbert examined the scrolls before unrolling them. He chose the white ribbon first, revealing the same reaction as Margaret had encountered when the parchment stood rigid of its own accord in his hand. The drawing of the figures, perfectly blended, met the priest's eyes, which seemed to have shifted from compassionate to intellectual. At first Father Talbert seemingly did not notice anything extraordinarily strange about the scroll, until the wording hidden within the confines of the pentagram began to grow visible. The older man turned the parchment as he read the inscription, muttering to himself as he figured out the wording. After a moment he rolled up the scroll, replaced the white ribbon around it, and reached for the other one.

Margaret had a thousand questions suddenly sift through her mind like a flood, but left the priest alone for the moment so he could look things over. Upon seeing the second scroll, he cleared his throat in a way that suggested he was terribly uncomfortable.

"What's wrong?" Margaret asked, looking the older man in the eyes. His brow furrowed as he looked back at her; deep intrigue and contemplation etched themselves deep within his skin.

"It's you," he said breathlessly.

"What? Let me see that! When I looked at this before…," Margaret began to explain, but let her words disappear as she took the scroll from the man's hand. Her jaw dropped wide open as she gazed at the image on the once blank parchment. Somehow her features had been reproduced in an ink drawing that looked as old as the parchment it was sketched on. She peered over it, then looked up at him. "What does this mean? All of the times before when I looked at this scroll, all I saw was…."

"Was what; nothing?" he began, but stopped. He paused, rolled up the scroll, and set them both down on the desk in front of him. He sat back in his chair and folded his hands against his chin. Margaret was confused, but only looked at the priest in question.

"So tell me what you've seen. What sort of visions?" Father Talbert asked, suddenly changing the subject, leaving Margaret to wonder why he knew the scroll had been blank before. She felt there were many details he was not yet divulging. Margaret was dying to know what the priest had come across that made him so uneasy he couldn't even speak of it for the moment. But for as much as she wanted desperately to ask, she proceeded to explain in detail, starting from the first encounter at the wake. With each gruesome detail, Father Talbert's eyes grew wider and wider.

"Most interesting," he said quietly as his mind processed the information.

"What?" Margaret asked, confused. His response was far from what she felt was appropriate for a man of the cloth.

"Well, typically, when dealing with any sort of evil…how do

I put this? You have seen its true form. But that wouldn't surprise me, given what you are," he explained.

"So...what does *that* mean?" Margaret asked, tired.

"Usually, a creature of this sort will try to lead you into darkness by showing you a much more pleasant side. Typically, it will appear as a very nice looking person, or as a physical place or situation that would be appealing to you. Monsters will only reveal themselves in a pure form when threatened, angered, or... desperate. Or perhaps, when it is someone they once knew." The priest looked out at the housewife over the top of his spectacles. The middle-aged woman blinked mentally feeling like she'd been hit by a ton of bricks. The two locked eyes a long moment before anyone spoke again.

"Why would something like that be threatened by me? If it indeed knows I possess this information, then it would *have* to know I don't understand what I'm supposed to do with it! I don't understand any of the damned mess!" Margaret was nearly at her limit for tolerating frustration for a while.

"My child, you still do not fully understand. But there are rules that must be followed, even in such an ethereal state," Father Talbert tried to explain. It was a difficult task if one was not well versed in the ways of the theories of Heaven and Hell. And though Margaret had quite an interest in the occult, there was much yet unknown to her, and answers would not be as readily available as other aspects of a similar nature.

"Rules? What rules? Why do you keep referring to me like I am someone — something — You know what I am?" Margaret asked, beginning to question the priest's motives.

"If you consider this, your question will be answered. *God* is the only true all-knowing." His answer was brief, but quite clear. "Though some of the others come close, they are not completely omnipotent, and therefore prone to misjudge."

Margaret, who'd risen from her seat across from Father

Talbert, sat back down and grew silent in contemplation. "Why won't you tell me who I am...or what I am?" Margaret pried, desperate to get some answers.

"I believe we can resolve this little matter using the scrolls you brought. The key has been eluding us for centuries," the priest told her, looking at the weary housewife.

"What do they say? Read them to me," she requested suddenly, catching the priest off guard.

"What, in Latin?"

"No, in English. I want to hear for myself what it is," Margaret replied, her tone almost surly.

Father Talbert looked once more at the scrolls that lie before him, then back up at Margaret. "I can't," the priest answered with a shake of his head.

"Why not? I thought you said you could read them?" Margaret asked, confused. She was beginning to wonder if this wasn't another ruse, like so many before it, though she admitted it was quite elaborate if so.

"Yes, I can, my child. But if I read it, I might actually be casting the spell that is written. Supposing something will actually come of it, we don't want to do that here. We need to go to the sacred chamber and do the ceremony properly," the priest said.

"Where is this 'chamber'? If there is something we can do to stop this, well then, let's go!" Margaret urged.

As the housewife stood and started for the door, the priest laid the scrolls on his desk and gave them a pat as he stood. A wry smile turned the corners of Father Talbert's mouth upward ever so slightly, but Margaret did not notice.

In mere minutes, as the creatures they would be summoning soon remained in their free roam, Father Talbert led Margaret by torchlight down a narrow hallway toward the very back of the cathedral. It branched off from the wider one Margaret had travelled down previously with the nun. The bricks were damp, and it smelled of years of mildew, moss, and gloom.

Though Margaret could not see very well around the point of soft firelight ahead of her, she sensed the hallway starting to descend. The priest stopped at an archway that seemed blocked by a locked gate toward the end of the long hallway. He withdrew a skeleton key from around his neck, and Margaret watched as the older man's fingers fumbled to fit the small key into the rusty lock. She sensed that it was not the older age that made his fingers tremble, but fear of what was to come.

The sound of metal on metal grated on Margaret's ears as the rusty lock fought to be opened. With a loud click the lock snapped free, and the gate swung open with a shrill creaking sound. Margaret supposed this door hadn't been opened in years, and once they entered the new passageway, her theory was confirmed. Ancient looking cobwebs hung about, brushing the two across the face as they entered. Margaret, possessing an incredible fear of spiders, gasped, but managed not to scream.

"What is this passage for?" Margaret asked Father Talbert in a hoarse whisper. Though the two were alone, she feared her voice would stir ghosts of the past somehow.

"Let's just say it's a good thing you can't see off to the left or right," he said, leaving Margaret to wonder what that meant.

"I know I'm going to regret this, but I have to know *why*," the housewife asked, cursing her never-ending sense of curiosity.

The priest shook his head and sighed. "Years ago, before we acquired the grounds in the northwest of the church yard, our tombs were all down here," he began to explain.

"Oh...well...the bodies have been moved up for proper burial since then though, right?" Margaret continued. But Father Talbert's silence answered her question. She suddenly felt very claustrophobic and nauseated at the thought that there were God knew how many corpses long since decayed lying about the walls as they passed them by. Margaret tried to regain her focus, and thought of nothing but following the soft light from the torch fire as Father Talbert led her through.

Minutes later, after what seemed like an eternity, the priest stopped at what appeared to be a blank brick wall. Several stones were disheveled, and Father Talbert reached up for one. The stone slid partially out of the wall, and by doing so, allowed a section of the bricks to open up together, revealing a secret room in the catacombs.

"Ah, here we are," he said, satisfied with finding what he was looking for.

"How long has it been since anyone's been down here?" Margaret asked, hoping for an end to the cobwebs in her face.

"Thirty-eight years," he said coolly.

"Such a long...time," Margaret whispered, almost sorrowfully.

Father Talbert entered and walked about the circular chamber, lighting the torches that lined the walls. Upon light flooding the room, Margaret's eyes adjusted, and she was surprised at the sight that opened up before her.

"You said this was a *sacred* chamber?" she asked.

"Indeed, my child. Long ago, exorcisms were performed here. But the room was built to harness the goodness and light of the holy, and to trap and cast out evil spirits and the wicked," the priest explained, and he shivered as if he felt a cold chill.

The chamber contained lighter colored brick, and was not as ominous with the torches lit. The chamber was in perfect condition—no damp stones, no strange odors, no rotted corpses or cob webs. The chamber was protected from the same decaying fate as the rest of the cathedral's tunnel by some unseen force field. In the center of the room was an altar, adorned with religious symbols and pictures. A pentagram lined the center of both the floor and the ceiling. For what little Margaret had read, that was to ensure the entrapment of spirits. Two candles—one black, one white—stood at equal distance to each other on the altar. The wicks were already burnt, and the wax had melted some on each from obvious use sometime in the past. Upon the altar lay a ledger; its black leather binding was withered and cracked with age. The cover, though written in Latin, seemed familiar to Margaret, and she was able to read the words with ease.

"*Ascension of the Nephilim...*," Margaret uttered under her breath. She was still puzzled by the whole thing, and had no idea what the book was for. Her slender fingers silently pried the cover open, revealing long worn pages within. The writing upon its parchment pages was, without doubt, ancient—at least in part. Margaret scanned the top of the altar, but saw no pen or ink by the book. The only other item atop the altar was a small curved-blade dagger, its blade stained with what appeared to be dried blood.

Father Talbert explored the chamber, conducting a survey of the area. As he inspected the room, Margaret thumbed gingerly through the fragile pages of the book. The priest thought a moment about the previous time the chamber had been used, then began to tell Margaret about it.

"Yes, I am remembering more of the story now...," he began, his voice merely a mutter. Margaret, entranced by the ledger, did not ignore him, but made a noise to assure him she was listening. "A young woman supposedly attempted to summon both halves at a time when both beings were not upon the earth. Her failure was the result. As I recall, that was back in 1873," he began, telling more of the details he'd not mentioned earlier.

"Hmmm...strange. That's the year my mother died...," Margaret began, but her voice trailed off as she read the scribbled writing upon the pages in the book.

"I believe her name was Mary. Yes, that's it...Mary Margaret." Just as Father Talbert managed to speak the words "Mary Margaret," Margaret had finished reading the inscription, and found it to be a signature.

"...Draves," Margaret said, finishing the name where the priest left off. "She was my mother. She died when I was very young." Margaret's voice was trancelike as her fingertips hovered over the ledger, almost feeling a tingle of energy emanating from the pages. "What is this ascension of the nephilim?" Margaret asked the priest. Silence met her ears for what seemed like an eternity before an attempt at an answer was given.

"The nephilim...a creature born of a human mother and fathered by a fallen angel. Female in appearance, and carriers of great supernatural ability; a creature of great intrigue to other unseen forces, wouldn't you agree?" Father Talbot answered the woman.

Margaret stood silent, listening to the priest's words, but entranced by the tome.

CHAPTER 17

Nearly forty-five minutes after Margaret had arrived at the church, Henry pulled up at the edge of town with Ann. As they passed by the wooden sign that welcomed them, Henry noticed horse tracks in the snow that was beginning to blanket the ground. Henry's heart pounded in his chest as he noticed the tracks had stopped not too far out in front of where he stood. He glanced around quickly, and there in what little moonlight shown through the wintery clouds above, Henry spotted the abandoned stallion stomping at the ground to his left.

Plumes of warm breath fogged up the air in front of the black quarter horse as its dark eyes met Henry's; as if waiting for anyone to come along to witness its collapse, the poor horse's knobby knees buckled and the heavy four-legged beast sank down hard upon the ground. Henry knew their horse would be fine, but had no time to spare to go comfort the creature. Henry just nodded and gave the stallion a gentle pat as they walked on by. He knew Margaret had to be nearby, and noticed that after the horse's tracks ended, human footprints continued. Based on how the tracks appeared in the snow, Henry guessed Margaret had been running, and urged Ann on in the same direction.

"Come on, Ann. I believe your ma went this way," he

instructed, taking her by the hand. Henry and his daughter ran beside the semi-fresh footprints that Margaret had made not even an hour before.

"Momma!" Ann yelled out into the night.

"Quiet, Ann, she won't be able to hear you," Henry said.

"We're coming, Momma!" Ann's child sized voice called out, disturbing the sounds of the wind blowing through the city. Henry did not scold her this time; how hard could he really be on his daughter for something so petty after the day they had just lived through?

"Come on, Ann, just a little farther," Henry encouraged the young girl.

Within just a few more minutes the two finally arrived at the church. As Margaret had done, Henry pushed his way through the threshold of the heavy wooden door of the church and looked around. As the doors closed the air inside the church grew instantly warmer than the temperature outside, and Henry found himself relieved to be there, though he had to admit that churches made him unnaturally nervous. Henry found the same atmosphere inside the back of the congregation area; the stoic rows of pews inside the nave seemed somehow cold and void of offering any hope of salvation. The echo of the large heavy doors nearly sent chills down his spine as the sound resonated around the deserted room.

After the sound of the doors closing had ceased, Henry listened for sounds that could possibly indicate where his wife was inside the church. In only a few moments of silence, the sound of hurried footsteps drew Henry's attention toward the far back corner of the pulpit to his left. Candle flames danced sporadically as their warm soft glow continued to illuminate the area around them. Though quite dim, Henry noticed small wet footprints on the wooden floor leading back toward that same corner where he'd just heard the footsteps. Though the footprints were not fresh and had already begun to dry, they were good enough for Henry to follow, as he'd done outside with the tracks in the snow.

"Where's Momma? I though you said she would be here?" Ann asked, peeling off a couple of the outer layers of clothing that she wore.

"Hush now, Ann. We've got to find your ma. I'm thinkin' those footprints must be hers. Let's go," Henry instructed.

"Henry would like it here. I want him to have a beautiful funeral," Ann continued as she looked around.

"Enough with goddamned funerals! That's what started all of this goddamned bullshit in the first place!" Henry yelled. He stopped and glared at Ann. Her face already tear-streaked, the young girl's brow furrowed, and her lip began to quiver.

"But Daddy...don't you care about Henry?" Ann began.

Her father paused. The day had been far too difficult on everyone, and his tone softened. "Sweetie, it's not that I don't care, but right now there's something else a little more important that we've got to tend to first, okay?" They walked through the dark, deserted nave. "Let's go this way," he said, interrupting his own train of thought. "I see candlelight up ahead to our left, but off to our right is nothing but darkness," he motioned, leading his daughter toward the illuminated hallway.

Henry and Ann followed the candle trail just as Margaret and the priest had done minutes earlier. Walking the same path, Henry noticed that the walls looked to be composed of mostly mineral deposits, and felt a shift in the ground level like he was walking down a slope. It occurred to Henry as he walked with his daughter that whatever this passageway led to, there was a very good chance it was an old mining tunnel at one time. With cobwebs already pushed back out of their way and dust disturbed all around, Henry ignored the claustrophobic sensation that panged at his gut. He pushed aside the fear of the unknown that welled inside his spine and the terror of the rotted corpses that did in fact line the recessed walls of the catacomb passages. He silently hoped that in the dim light Ann would not see any of the bodies; he knew she would understand they were dead, and was sure to ask questions as to whether or not that was how her brother Henry would look as well. For as grim and eerie as the passageways were, Henry and Ann continued their trek.

As Henry and Ann continued down the dreary tunnel, Henry stopped short as a burst of warm air and the scent of flowers wafted through the passageway; it was a feeling of purity and enlightenment that flowed through them without any explanation. Henry looked at Ann, who hadn't particularly noticed anything. Whatever had just happened, it felt wonderful, though it was apparent that the sensation was going to be fleeting.

"There up ahead, the passage continues. It looks like they must have gone this way." Henry directed Ann's attention, though the girl was too preoccupied inside her own head to care much about anything else. Henry led the girl by the hand further down the tunnel, and as they reached a slight bend in the passageway, he noticed light coming from another opening just up ahead.

***

"My poor child…," Father Talbert began, but could find no words that would make a difference. "So, your first name is the middle name of your mother?" he inquired, thinking aloud.

"Yes. That was always the way. The mother gave their offspring — always a daughter — the same middle name as their first name. Sort of a tradition, for some reason. I myself followed the same path. My middle name is my daughter's first name." While she had always been interested in knowing the reason behind this, it appeared that no such reason existed. Not that anyone would admit to, anyway.

"Divine intervention. In my studies of darker theology and

219

Father McKenzie's added knowledge, there is a theory that a guardian is assigned to each and every person. Some people are chosen for greater fates than others, and thereby need some indicator to make it known throughout the universe that the bloodline is protected. Perhaps it is the order of names which signifies this for *your* bloodline. I know all of this sounds farfetched, but I am telling this in terms you will understand rather than how it's written in the legend; no offense," Father Talbert assured her.

"That is why I sought help...there is much I did not know and could not find out on my own," Margaret assured the priest. "So, what do we do? Light the candles and read what the scroll says?" she asked, looking at the candles on the altar.

"First, you must *prove* your bloodline. A name alone would not do the trick. It must be something tangible—something... very personal. The dagger's purpose is to make a single slice across the palm of either hand. You must then take your blood and sign your name upon the parchment. This ledger will know that you are nephilim, and the ritual will begin," Father Talbert explained.

"I am one of them...," Margaret sighed as she picked up the dagger.

The blade had been quite the polished sight at one time, Margaret thought, but it had since been tainted with sins and stains from the past. An eerie wave of emotion washed over the woman, and she quivered with nervousness knowing that the scarlet stain upon the blade she faced was her own mother's from days long past.

The housewife took the thin, curvy blade and drew it slowly but firmly across her right palm. There was no way, after having come this far, that she would back out now. At the moment the silver sliced through her tender flesh, a vibration seemed to shoot out from the dagger, startling Margaret. She lost her grip and the dagger dropped to the floor with a metallic clank. Spatters of her blood hit the floor, spattering lightly in all directions on a microscopic level. Margaret was nauseated at the thought of how many more drops of blood lay upon the floor as hers now did.

The rumble lasted only a brief moment, and Margaret returned her attention to her now bloody palm. She took her left index finger and dipped it in the blood, with the intent to use her finger as a pen. She quickly signed her full name: Margaret Ann Draves-Glover. The ancient parchment seemed to drink in the fresh sacrifice quickly, locking the life fluid in for all eternity. Margaret looked back at her palm and found it to be healed over—it looked as if she'd never taken the blade to it. Shocked, she shifted her gaze to the priest. He simply shook his head.

"Exactly like I remember," he said quietly.

"I don't understand...like you remember?" Margaret inquired.

"Now, light the candles...white first, then black," Father Talbert instructed, ignoring her question. The priest's demeanor had slowly been changing since she first met him, and it was slowly becoming clear to Margaret that the priest might know exactly what was going to happen next. Margaret took one candle in each hand and walked over to one of the lit torches hanging upon the wall. She used the live flame to light them in the order the priest had instructed. Once lit, she returned to the altar and placed the candles just as she'd found them. She could feel the priest's eyes upon her, and her insides began to quiver.

The priest withdrew the scroll with the white ribbon and unrolled it. As always, it became rigid and glowed slightly in the dim torch and candlelight in the chamber. He cleared his throat and began to read off the first of two incantations.

"*Ego voco filia uel pacis quod lux lucis...,*" he began in Latin. His voice was shaky and hoarse, as if his throat had suddenly run dry. "*Dimidium uel Legna, nomen uel Divum. Patronus uel vir, tamen dimidium uel alius….*" He flicked his eyes up to Margaret, who felt very confused for some reason, but he continued to read. "*Par pondora uel atrum is frater….*"

He paused, waiting for something to happen, as he'd finished reading the first half to summon the angel. A strong wind began to pick up outside that seemed to rock the entire cathedral. The sound carried through the grounds of the church and down to the chamber to where Father Talbert and Margaret listened for what was going to happen next.

***

Out in the cemetery the few dead leaves that clung to the tree limbs, clutching to the last little bits of life high in the tree tops surrounding the cemetery, rustled among themselves as the bitter cold wind whipped them about. The angel statue that guarded the entrance to the graveyard began to glow faintly, and the hooded figured shuddered. By some trick of the eye, the previously lifeless marble body became soft as flesh, and the arms broke free of their once eternal stone pose. The angelic wings that stretched out across the figure's back broke free of the stone as well, sending crumbling fragments of the marble to the ground.

Sky suddenly found herself taking the place of a statue that had been in silent watch over the dead for so many years. She looked around in confusion for a moment before heading to the steps of the cathedral where Margaret, Henry, and Ann had been just minutes earlier. The angel was not sure why she was pulled to this building, but stopped to marvel at its beauty. Sky felt a feeling of utter warmth and peace from the grounds of the church, though the cemetery at the east corner of the churchyard was gloomy and gothic in appearance at this hour. The site of the cathedral was physically quite dreary, but Sky could sense past the outward appearance and bathed in the residual feeling left from the many weddings and christenings that had taken place inside the walls of the magnificent building.

Being half Heavenly essence, Sky did not mind the arctic cold that chilled her porcelain skin as she stood and marveled, and for the moment she forgot about her goal to perform as many good deeds as possible as her time on Earth neared an end. The angel passed herself through the walls of the cathedral and still felt the sensation of being pulled toward something. She was met with an overwhelming sensation that was calling out to her, and felt compelled to search for something, but the reason eluded her completely. Sky's form sent vibrations through the walls of the passageways as she made her way through the underground chambers of the cathedral.

***

Back inside the chamber, Father Talbert noticed that the white candle had blown out, and that the scent of roses had filled the room.

"She's here," the priest said breathlessly.

"What of the other one?" Margaret inquired, having no idea what part he'd already read, if not the entire thing.

"*Ego voco filius uel chaos quod atrum…,*" Father Talbert began, his voice more nervous as he summoned the dark one. He swallowed hard before continuing. "*Dimidium uel Nomed, nomen uel Thymum….*" He paused to lick his drying lips. "*Addo uel formido quod frater uel Divum, Vultus iam una Gemini,*" he finished. He was so anxious now that he dropped the scroll. It floated to the floor and landed without a sound.

***

Henry could hear voices coming from the opening, and his pace quickened in order to reach it faster. He just knew Margaret was in there. He led his daughter to just outside the opening to what appeared to be the last chamber. Henry crept into the chamber as stealthily as he could manage. He looked back at his daughter, who had not moved from the darkened open doorway. He found a place behind a stone pillar and waited, listening

223

intently to gain better insight as to what was happening. He motioned for Ann, and was about to whisper for her to join him, but before he could say another word, Henry felt a frigidity in the air that had not been there a moment ago.

"What the...?" Henry said, his wonder stumbling out of his mouth as two words.

***

At the moment Father Talbert finished the first spell, a chilling cold crept into the chamber and the scent of decay filled the air. The priest noticed Henry entering the chamber, but said nothing. An expression of suspicion crossed Father Talbert's face, alerting Margaret also of another's presence. Margaret looked at the priest, the look of wonder also written upon her face, and with both untrusting of the other, neither said a word, and continued, ignoring the intruder for the moment. A low whirring noise began within the room, and steadily grew as a wind began to blow inside. The force of the air was so strong it rattled through the chamber like the howl of lost spirits seeking attention. The very walls of the chamber shook, sending the vibration through the floor and adjoining walls of the tunnel as well.

***

As Henry stood hidden inside the chamber, he could feel the vibration under his feet and thought it best Ann stay where she currently stood. While he did not want to leave Ann's side, Henry knew whatever he was about to witness was nothing for a child's eyes.

"Ann, darlin', you need to stay right there," Henry called out softly, surprised he'd not called attention to himself so far. "I'm gonna go get your momma. You don't move from that spot, you hear?" Henry said, looking into Ann's tear-red eyes. Without a word, Ann nodded that she understood and sat down upon the cold, damp ground inside the tunnel.

***

The black opal that Margaret had hung around her neck grew tight, and it felt like an invisible hand were tugging upon it. As the necklace dropped to the floor, the stone shattered but did not send splinters of broken opal scattering across the floor. Instead, black fragments oozed out of the broken stone as it lay there, wounded and bleeding. Margaret watched as the inky fluid began to flow into a small pool, which seemed to be growing in size. She looked at the priest and suddenly realized the truth.

The black fabric of the priest's suit began to swirl about and change. She immediately grew aware of what had been happening to Father Talbert since she'd walked into his office. The hands of Thyme were upon the priest as well. Just as her dream had indicated, a shadow was forming out of the darkness of the priest's clothing. Father Talbert's possessor had become aware that Margaret suspected him, and he laughed insidiously.

"What's going on?!" Margaret exclaimed as the wind in the chamber began to blow wildly. She had to raise her voice a little bit to be heard.

"My child...you should have guessed by now who I am!" the man answered, a devilish grin dripping from one ear to the other. Margaret gasped in disbelief. "Oh, what's the matter? Don't recognize your own blood? Don't you recognize your own *brother*?!" Thyme snapped as he questioned her.

"Adam? No...it can't be. It said, 'Thyme was against me.' *What* is happening here?!" the woman yelled, her mind beginning to swirl amongst the chaos in the room.

"Oh, come now, Margaret. I do not speak of your Earth brother. Do you not remember who you are? You must have known this was the way it was meant to be! I refuse to believe you are *that* stupid! You can't tell me you never understood *why* you were so attracted to the occult all your life. You can't tell me you couldn't see through my 'Father Talbert' disguise."

"B-but h-how can you—?" Margaret began, stammering in

disbelief.

"Every so often, I bind myself to a new body—partly out of boredom, mostly out of stability. *I* am not against you...unless you resist. This is a race to complete a quest that was started eons ago. I am tired of this cruel fate—being bound to roam half completed until the turn of each century. And thanks to the physical bloodline you chose when you incarnated last time, I have been able to remain this way for quite some time. No one can quite catch on to what needs to be done. They have... resisted. But this is not just about them...it's not just about you, either. This is about taking my place as the ultimate power in the universe...overthrowing God and ruling all kingdoms. I am taking what is rightfully mine! And you...YOU are my ticket to that freedom, dear sister," Thyme explained, though his words were coated with insanity and told of things Margaret could not yet understand.

"Why me? What's so special about me?" Margaret asked, taking a step back.

"Because, my dear, your mindset is flexible. You understand there's so much more to things than just black and white. Without that trait, this would be a failure, like it was with your Earth mother! As a nephilim, you are the perfect vessel to see this to the end."

Thyme pointed at the ledger on the altar. His face began to appear distorted, as his true form started to take shape. Margaret was not too sure at first what she was witnessing, but as his metamorphosis continued, it would be impossible for her deny.

"So what happened—why didn't it work before?" Margaret wondered aloud. Thyme shook his head. Thick handfuls of hair fell from their perch on his scalp, while jutting locks of new coal-colored hair took its place.

"They refused to comply with the rules and the spell was not cast correctly. I am going to merge, just as I have for centuries now. Once we are Gemini, you will decide that evil prevails, and you will cast in your soul to our cause. This is for you." The demon, having completely shed Father Talbert's form, stood before her with glowing emerald eyes and jet black hair. His nearly white flesh looked somehow human, despite its absence of pigmentation. He reached down and picked up the shattered necklace.

Thyme's stark white hand held the chain of the necklace that Lucille had been wearing at her funeral. Margaret felt anxious taking anything from the demon, but took the item gently from his outstretched hand. As she looked it over, she noticed that the opal felt somehow empty; it was like looking through hollow black glass.

"It was you trying to take this from her before, wasn't it?" Margaret asked, finally putting everything together. The foreboding figure of Thyme nodded. "It was you who was taking Lucille away from her body at the funeral!" Margaret added, looking into the demon's eyes. For a moment she found herself dazzled by their enchanting emerald glint. Thyme laughed and stepped closer.

"Take it. The spirits collected from ancestors past will complete you, and you will then possess the ability to give yourself to us, completely," Thyme explained. "Any questions?" the demon asked, giving Margaret one chance to ask anything she liked.

"What did the spell say?" Margaret asked, curious. Though she found it odd that she was not astounded by the discovery that Father Talbert had been Thyme all along, she could not resist the sensations that crawled through her body. To her surprise, however, she found herself placing the black opal back around her neck, though Thyme had just told her it was the key to completing Margaret's conversion to the shadows. She had not given the pendant any thought, but felt compelled to put it on.

"It says, 'I summon the daughter of peace and light, the half of Legna, name of Sky. Protector of man, but half of another; equal balance of the dark of her brother," the demon answered hastily as the light drew nearer.

"Wait…I am beginning to remember…," Margaret muttered quietly over the now howling wind. Thyme nodded his head, encouraging her to remember everything. As her memories returned, so would her power.

"I summon the son of chaos and dark, the half of Nomed, name of Thyme; bringer of dread and brother of Sky; form now together Gemini," he recited, translating the words from the Latin version.

"Well, if that's the case…where is she?! I don't see her anywhere," Margaret called at the top of her lungs to be heard over the high-powered gusts of wind blowing around them. Thyme said nothing. He seemed fixated upon the glow that had begun behind Margaret.

The chamber filled with a brilliant flash of bluish-gold light; the sound of wings beating overpowered the howling wind for a moment as Sky entered. The angel looked about her; it had been awhile since she'd seen the chamber. As her eyes met Margaret's, the lighter being turned her attention to the human woman.

"You are Sky. You were by the boy at the hospital," Margaret said, astonished at how well the angel could assume such a close resemblance to a human.

"Yes," the angel replied, her answer but a solitary word.

"How long have you existed?" Margaret asked, curious.

"Before your concept of time was recorded," the angel answered. Sky remained still as she locked eyes with Margaret. Among the beginnings of chaos around them in the sacred chamber, something else was happening.

The charm that Margaret now wore around her neck was indeed hollow. An eerie red glow seemed to leak forth from the parchment pages of the ledger that still lay open upon the altar. The signatures collected over the centuries had begun to bleed out of the pages one by one, forming an unearthly figure that represented each person who'd previously lent their signature. The shadow forms spilled onto the floor of the chamber, fusing together with the unseen droplets from days past. Like liquid ash, the specters flowed across the floor, boiling upward at Margaret's feet. Mystified, Margaret could only watch as the figures of Eva, then Ruth, then Agatha, then Mary morphed from mere shadow figures into more recognizable states. Still dark as night, the figures took on more distinct faces, and each person's essence seemed to look Margaret in the eye briefly, prior to pulling themselves up into the opal charm. With each person entering the amulet, its black color grew deeper, darker, and more sinister.

Once Mary's essence had disappeared into the necklace, the black opal seemed solid once more, and Margaret could feel herself gaining the collective knowledge from the past souls. With a trembling hand, she reached up and pressed the talisman into the pit between her clavicles, breathing in deeply, using her lungs to suck in the power.

"You have the completed Amulet of Souls!" Sky exclaimed in disbelief.

"Is that what this *thing* is?" Margaret asked, rubbing a finger nervously over the face of the black opal. She found herself enjoying the sensations the necklace sent slithering through her skin, slowly making her forget her place as she neared ecstasy.

"Margaret...you must remain here with us! Do not let the power of this trinket *rule* you!" Sky warned, urgently attempting to regain Margaret's attention.

"Shhh...," Margaret hissed, placing an index finger over dry, pursed lips.

As the two spoke, a shadowy feeling began to wash over Margaret. She felt so cold inside, and her thinking became almost animalistic. She looked back at Thyme, who only smiled devilishly. She could feel her heart beating in her chest, but ceased to feel human. All thoughts of recent events faded until they reached a spot in her mind that felt muddled, like she was trying to remember a vague dream. Margaret looked back at Sky, but quickly averted her eyes from the bright light, and with doing so, saw the pentagram drawn upon the ceiling. Confused, Margaret looked down at the floor and found the second one. She knew it was a trap, and remembered seeing it when she first entered the chamber, but now this thing had control over her, and she felt betrayed by her human side.

Sky gazed at the activated black opal hanging around Margaret's neck and frowned. The luminescent being opened her mouth to speak, and in Margaret's current state of mind, the angel's true voice was heard.

The high-pitched sound that Margaret had heard before in her dreams was the angel attempting to speak, but it came out in a barely tolerable sound to the unaccustomed human ear. Margaret's head began to spin, and like the effect of the Tea of Understanding she'd drank back in Louisiana, it suddenly became clear to her what the angelic half was saying.

"My brother, you are here yet again to wreak your havoc upon this innocent land…." The flash of light grew humanoid in form once more, and Sky looked at Thyme.

"*Innocent?!*" Thyme hissed as he spun toward Sky. "This wretched planet is full of death and war. You *must* know this, or you would not bother to linger as I do. You know full well where there is good, there is evil. Where there is evil, there is good. We were doomed to be forever at war, my sister, but not *this* time!" Thyme sneered at the angel.

"Look what you have done to this poor creature! She has no idea what that opal can do!" Sky exclaimed, pointing to the ebony stone that lay across the woman's neck; the chain bounced lightly with each passing heartbeat through Margaret's carotid artery.

"Enough of this!" Margaret exclaimed as she covered her ears. She was unsure what her next move should be at this point.

"Is there anything you would like to ask?" Sky asked, questioning the mortal, her angelic voice returning to a tone Margaret could bear to listen to and understand.

"Do you know of my great grandmother Eva?" Margaret asked, eyeing the celestial creature.

"Eva Ruth Worley, born 1748, died 1841; Ruth Agatha Postman born 1816, died 1884; Agatha Mary Gruenwold, born 1832, died 1909; Mary Margaret Ordiki, born 1849, died 1873; Margaret Ann Draves, born 1870; Ann Marie Glover, born 1901," the ethereal voice answered rapidly.

"I guess you *do* know of it...and you know about Ann?" Margaret said breathlessly. Sky just stared at her, awaiting the next question.

"Of course. It was unfortunate she was a twin...but it was a necessary evil," Sky answered mournfully.

"Hah! *ALL* evil is necessary!" Thyme sneered.

Margaret's eyes welled up as thoughts of her family returned to the front of her mind.

"Junior...Henry...," Margaret sobbed though her eyes were dry. Her thought was so strong her mental message was received by her husband Henry, who under ordinary circumstances possessed no psychic ability.

"Did you know Eva before she died?" the woman asked, shaking the thoughts of home from her mind; her ears were ready for any answer besides the one she was about to be given.

"Of course. She is our sister," Thyme answered with a sneer.

Margaret had to stop for a moment; this was nearly too much to take in. The young woman thought for a moment, mulling everything over.

"What do you mean, your *sister*?" Margaret asked; the look

231

of confusion spread itself thickly across her brown eyes.

"Her name is Ah'lara," Sky answered.

"What do you mean…her name *is*? You make it sound as though she still exists," Margaret asked nervously.

"She does. You must understand, energy can neither be created nor destroyed. Not, at least, in the sense that your human mind would comprehend," Sky answered. "You were asking the correct questions — I assumed that you would know," the angel's melodious voice answered.

"Know — *what*?" Margaret asked, stepping closer. The being didn't move.

"That *you* are Ah'lara, of course."

"But…that's impossible!" Margaret exclaimed in surprise.

"Not impossible. If it were impossible, it would not be so. Over the many deaths she has suffered, each offspring has been left with a part of her. Each of you possessed or possess some portion of Ah'lara's energy, and therefore possess abilities beyond human concepts — to a degree."

"But — but I have a birthdate…a mother and father. I-I'm *human*," Margaret said, rejecting the angel's suggestion as she'd done with the hoodoo witch's suggestion.

"Are you, sister?" Sky questioned, eyeing the dark-haired woman before her. "You may appear as a natural human, and perhaps human characteristics have begun to present themselves as part of your physical vessel. But your soul is marked with a divine imprint that cannot be erased or removed no matter how many times you choose to manifest yourself."

"What are you suggesting? That I make myself reincarnate? That I control who I become?"

"Possibly, yes. It's never been fully interpreted."

"Then why don't I know who I am? Except Margaret, from a small town in Missouri?"

"Perhaps because the tattered past you currently know is

far better than returning to those memories of your true self, which tend to be too incomprehensible for a human mind," Sky answered.

"How is that even possible?" Margaret questioned further, probing for information.

"In the universe there are many things that seem impossible but are not. When you are born into unearthly bonds, more becomes possible rather than impossible, if you are willing to acknowledge it as possible."

"So if all this is true, then where was I between this life and the last?" Margaret wondered aloud.

"Neither dead nor alive; in a place that is neither dark nor light. A level of consciousness that exists between the blurred edges of good and evil, of human or not, of solid matter and nothingness. We call it…Future. It is a city, for lack of better wording—a holding area for souls awaiting placement. Yours is one of the elder souls. It lay dormant there waiting for the right circumstances. It is a city in the sky of darkness and light, from which all of us fall at one point or another into the physical bodies we have chosen."

"Future…I remember Future," Margaret muttered to herself in a trance-like tone as she thought back.

"Beyond there. That is merely a pit-stop, my dear sister. You truly do not remember?" Sky asked, her crystal blue eyes so pure.

"That's what I've been saying all along. Please, tell me. I want—no, I NEED to know everything!" Margaret pleaded.

"Very well. In the beginning of time—" Sky began.

"No. Not this story again. I've heard this part."

"I doubt it. Our mother and father created many of us. I am half angel, half demon. Thyme is half demon, half angel. You were always more of a neutral being, neither stronger in the light nor the dark.

"Our dear brother Thyme, always the bringer of doom and

233

tormenter, hounded you, constantly tempting you with promises of great power. One day, you had a fight with us." Sky explained patiently while Margaret's eyes grew wider and wider. Thyme remained silent for the moment, listening to the story his sister Sky was telling.

"Let me get this straight. I am your sister Ah'lara. I am a nephilim, and at the beginning of time I was in a fight with you two?" Margaret scoffed, baffled.

"I know how this must sound. Just listen—you may begin to remember," Sky suggested quietly. "Our fight was actually over your remaining neutral—you never made any moves to side with anyone but yourself. You grew angry, something neither of us had seen out of you before."

"Yes, and it tasted so wonderful," Thyme remembered, licking his lips.

"To spite us, you said you were going to show us there was more to just balancing good and evil, light and dark. And you wrote the spell that created Gemini."

"I what? You're insane. I couldn't possibly...," Margaret began, but stopped herself. An image came to mind which played out the scene Sky described, and slowly she began to remember. "I was so angry. I had never felt that before," Margaret said in a trance-like tone.

"No! You can't remember, you mustn't!" Thyme said, shaking his head. "If she remembers it all, it could be our undoing!" he growled.

"So be it," Sky answered calmly.

"I wanted to banish you both for never thinking I was as good as you. I had to find a way to make you both suffer. Gemini forced you to get along as an equal force until you could both just agree on one side or another," Margaret explained, ignoring them both.

"But it created a nightmare, Ah'lara. Your spell caused a great imbalance just by tinkering with the natural way of things in the universe. Why do you think Thyme was always after you?" Sky asked her sister.

"Hah! Because she's weak, that's why! I tried to tell her that I could lead her to a greatness she could not imagine. But she was a fool!" Thyme scoffed, his words full of resentment.

"No, Thyme, you're wrong too. Yes, she was weak, but you only wanted to fuel your own desires. And with her negative emotions toward us both, of course that would attract her to you more. This has nothing to do with—" Sky was interrupted.

"I might have been weak, but I was never stupid. I reincarnated myself in the only form I knew that would stand a better chance to silence you both. But as I learned slowly century after century, some of the information did not carry over with me with each incarnation. But now I know that *I* created the spell. *I* created the scrolls and planted them in the jewelry chest. And *I* intend to finish what I was unable to all those times before!" Margaret promised.

"Enough! I am at an end with living in an existence stifled by your insolence! You have no idea what it's like to survive on scraps, being forced into a meager existence, only to battle perpetually every century for nothing!" Thyme bellowed. A growing rage boiled inside his worm-ridden gullet until he could no longer contain himself. Margaret stood between Sky and himself, and he would wait no longer to become Gemini for this century. With Margaret's added energy leaning toward his side, he was sure this would be the final century. He would take the extra power and seduce Sky, leaving her no choice but to accept her dark fate.

CHAPTER 18

Thyme's head snapped toward Margaret, then back at Sky. The demon leapt with a grunt toward the angelic half, and Margaret watched as every fiber of his being disappeared right into the ethereal woman. A rumble grew louder and louder and shook the entire chamber harder than before. Sky rose into the air. Watching the two people morph together, Margaret could see Sky grow semi-transparent as Thyme writhed around inside her. Their figures merged and grew three times as big as either had been previously. A brand new being created itself right before Margaret, and it remained floating in the air. The body was neither male nor female, just a humanoid body which remained levitated mid-air in the chamber. The entire body glowed a silver color, and golden light sparked within the eyes of the creature that were illuminated with a fierce intensity. Streams of energy radiated out from the new being, and wind continued to blow as the body sustained itself in midair. The being had to have been nine feet tall and appeared quite foreboding. Mixed among the sounds of the wind blowing were both shrieks and wails of the damned, and the sound of angelic harps; to human ears, it was a train wreck.

Margaret held steady, keeping her eyes on Gemini. As their

eyes locked, Margaret found herself feeling strange again, caught inside their conflict and able to sense what each half was feeling at that moment.

Shaking her head to break free of the hypnotizing sensation, Margaret heard the being speak for the first time, after gaining knowledge of how to speak in a language that Margaret's bloodline would understand.

"Are you a *god?*" the giant, glowing creature asked the tiny corporeal body standing before it. The living mandala cocked its head to one side as it looked at her, awaiting a response. The language the creature spoke sounded a lot like several words being spoken in whispers at the same time. Whatever it was that made Margaret's bloodline so special included an ability to focus on the core of the voice, so she was thereby able to make out what was being said.

"No," Margaret answered, puzzled. The creature's eyes grew wide, then narrowed into tiny slits; a scowl furrowed the brow as a result.

"Then you have *no* right to stand before the universe... before Gemini!" the merged being screeched. It raised its hands, ready to strike; Thyme had not mentioned anything about being considered a deity.

"*I* am of the Worley bloodline," she stated, placing her hands boldly upon her hips. Even this very human gesture seemed somehow foreign to her. As the woman continued to battle with the alter ego that sought to remove her humanity, she slipped in and out between the two, each time becoming increasingly difficult for her to recover from. The creature seemed confused but did not react otherwise. "Do you hear me?! I am of *the* bloodline!" Margaret stated again firmly as she stared the creature directly in the eyes. This new statement caught the being's attention, and it reared back in surprise.

"Soooo, you *are* a god! We have waited a hundred years for

you." The voice quivered and seemed to sound more angelic, relieved that Margaret was there. "To meet your destruction!" the being screeched suddenly, as the chaotic half bled through.

Margaret loathed the idea that this creature was as unstable as she, but was doing her best to figure out how to handle this. She was utterly bewildered when the being said she was a "god." As she stood, the same sensation she had been fighting since Lucille's funeral began to take over once again. She could feel every shred of decency slip away from her as the more animalistic streak began to swell within her body and claw at her mind to be freed.

From nowhere, a soft voice called to her, trying to get her attention. The housewife's eyes scanned the shadows while Gemini stood silent, but puzzled. Seeing nothing at first, Margaret started to ignore the voice and turned her attention to Gemini.

"Margaret…the incantation…you must speak the words…," the voice said in the same hushed whisper. The voice knew Gemini would eventually hear, but was willing to take the risk.

"What?" Margaret asked, turning her attention quickly to the voice.

A slender hand tossed a scroll to the woman, and light gray fabric on the sleeve of a habit became visible. For a moment Margaret remembered back to the nun that had showed her the way to Father Talbert. She wondered if it was the very same person she'd met earlier, or one of the other sisters that took refuge in the cathedral.

Margaret hastily untied the white ribbon, but did not flinch when the scroll stood rigid or sent the electric sensation through her fingers. Margaret could see wording on the parchment from the light in the chamber, and though it was in Latin, Margaret tried her best to read it.

"*Suo Houd magis vosmet una…*," Margaret began. Gemini's attention snapped to the human woman, as it had been several decades since those words had been spoken. "*Vos oportet subsisto unus in perpetuum….*" Margaret struggled with the words.

"Ignorant girl! Know you not the language?!" Gemini mocked.

Margaret looked back toward the nun's direction in panic.

"Your Latin was perfect," the voice said, offering an encouraging word. "Perhaps you need to finish it?"

"*Effrego seorsum vestry,*" Margaret said, returning to the scroll to read the spell.

"Hah!! Is that the *best* you can do?!" Gemini taunted with a smirk.

"Why isn't it working?!" Margaret gasped in panic.

"Pity you didn't figure out the key…it must be spoken by way of *Geminus Lingua*." Gemini said, laughing. "If you had remembered your own spell in time, you would have brought a friend," the creature said, erupting into insidious laughter.

"What are you going to do?" Margaret asked, fearing something terrible was on the horizon. As Margaret and Gemini had spoken back and forth, the aura around Gemini began to glow so immensely that heat radiated outward, and it was not long before the light was almost too bright for human eyes to withstand. Margaret wondered if this was the light which Madamé Hanté had warned her about.

"You should know! You must be the most obtuse being spawned from the bloodline! You are the one to judge us? I think not!" Gemini howled, its color beginning to shift into a softer glow with a more azure hue.

***

As Gemini stood before Margaret, the being noticed that woman's appearance had begun to change considerably. While Sky sensed the goodness in the mortal, she felt she had to try to contact her from within Gemini, but do so cautiously before her conversion was complete. There was simply not much time left

239

before midnight struck, and the opportune moment to banish or judge Gemini would pass for yet another century. The angelic half battled her way to the face of Gemini, using all of her energy to push Thyme away. The form of Gemini began to shrink down and take on the appearance that Sky possessed. The radiating light became long flowing locks of blonde hair, and the silver eyes turned back to blue. A soft halo floated about the body, and a soft voice spoke to Margaret.

"Come hither, goddess," she beckoned. Margaret had all but lost her humanity, but enough remained in the bowels of her soul to call out to Sky. The human woman's once chestnut hair now seemed greasy and straggly. The rich reddish-brown hue had been dulled to a deep gray that seemed to be bleeding an ebony color as time passed. Margaret's eyes had dulled as well, her pupils enlarged to the point that her entire iris looked solid black. Sky shuddered at the thought of what was about to happen, but she had been planning all the while and banking on a miracle. The angel was well aware that the souls locked into the black opal had already begun to leak through Margaret's pores and contaminate her further.

***

Margaret said nothing as she stepped closer to Gemini. She realized that Sky was only borrowing a window of weakness on Thyme's half in order to call out from the powerful twin being. The human woman hissed and unearthly sounds growled upward from her throat, and she stopped directly in front of Gemini.

"Touch me," Sky instructed. Leery, Margaret took a half step back. "*Touch me,*" Sky instructed again, her voice more urgent.

Margaret was on the verge of completing her crossing to the shadows when a streak of demonic thoughts burned through her brain. Margaret grabbed Gemini by the locks of blonde hair that flowed from Sky, and the angel's eyes grew wide as she caught the intent whirling through Margaret's mind.

Sky's blushed, pink lips pressed against those of Margaret, and the once human woman shot a spike of ebony malevolence to Sky's core. Like wicked lightning coursing through to her soul, Sky went numb, and her will was broken. After centuries of remaining separated from her brother Thyme, the angelic half had made her decision. Sky's eyes welled up in what a human would describe as fear. Distraction was the only way Margaret was going to have a chance to destroy Gemini—albeit a minimal one. Saddened by a wave of guilt that began to seep through her soul, Sky raised her azure eyes toward the heavens. With heaven-wise eyes, she could see through the building.

"Forgive me…," the angel uttered breathlessly.

"You can't!" Margaret exclaimed, realizing what Sky was about to do. "You're an *angel!*"

"Not all angels are good, but *you* can be," Sky answered without looking at Margaret; her eyes seemed fixed toward the ceiling.

It was too late. Thyme had sensed Sky's decision to agree with the evil half and snickered. With a consciousness wholly in agreement, the concentration and purity of the choice was so strong it began to take over almost immediately. A sinister blackness washed over Sky's once brilliant blue eyes, making them appear soulless and empty of love. Her fine alabaster skin began to glow a fiery orange, like molten lava, and thick black smoke began to rise up off of her, threatening to burst into flames. The tips of Sky's long golden hair began to grow dark, and the black color ran through all of her long tresses before turning into ash.

The wind that blew inside the chamber where they all stood scattered the ashes, and as a vortex began to swirl around Gemini, it drew the ashes inward. As the ash consumed Sky completely, what used to be her body seemed to simply dissolve into the now dark, spinning mass around Gemini. Holding its humanoid shape, Gemini laughed wickedly at its success in domination after so many centuries of battling for its own existence.

"AT LAST!" Gemini yelled out victoriously over the sound of the wind inside the underground chamber.

"What the *hell* is going on in here!?" Henry exclaimed as he burst into the flickering light of the chamber from somewhere in the shadows.

"Exactly," Gemini answered, its voice echoing down over them as it loomed ominously above. A charcoal fog lifted from the floor of the chamber, bathing Henry in total darkness. "You are insignificant, human. I watched your presence enter my chamber, but I let you be. You have nothing to do with this, and will suffer greatly at the hands of Thyme!"

"What are you? Margaret, who the—?" Henry began, his voice angry and confused.

"So many more questions!" Gemini said, sarcasm painting the words.

"Damn right I've got questions! This is nonsense! Utter nonsense!"

"Henry…stop—" Margaret interjected, her voice shaky and tired.

"I don't know what *you* are," Henry said, pointing to Gemini, "and I don't know what *you* are doing here…," Henry said, pointing to Margaret. "But we're getting out of here *right* now!"

Stepping forward toward his wife, he swatted at the dark mist that began to sting his eyes. Without moving, Gemini was able to manipulate the very space around it, and Henry found himself suspended in midair toward the highest part of the chamber's ceiling, a trail of the darkness following behind him.

"I do not believe I gave you permission to move," Gemini said, looking at Henry. "Now be a good mortal and stay!"

Margaret looked at Henry with sorrowful eyes. Something in her gut told her that her son wasn't the only one who was going to perish tonight.

"Release him!" Margaret ordered Gemini; her words were meant to be strong, but they quaked with fear. "I am your sister, Ah'lara! I have equal say in this. Do as I say, or I will destroy you!" Margaret exclaimed, her voice heavy with impending hysteria.

"You foolish, pathetic woman. Your heart trembles with desire to watch me unleash my power upon your universe. Even now your curiosity is taking over your human judgment. Do you know what I love most about this?" Gemini asked, looking first at Margaret, then to Henry, and finally back at Margaret.

There was no reply.

"It's that there is no equivalent to my power now!" Gemini stated arrogantly.

"You're a coward!" Margaret retorted, running toward Henry and stopping on the floor underneath him. Henry remained motionless in the air. Her eyes returned to normal as her conscious beckoned to her from a distance.

"Be brave, Margaret…," Gemini encouraged. With a quick wave of a clawed demon's hand, Gemini released Henry from his suspended height but did nothing to slow or stop his fall.

Henry crashed down onto the hard floor and screamed out in pain at the moment of impact. Margaret screamed out as Henry fell, but she was powerless to stop his fall. She rushed over to his side and found her husband alive, but broken.

"Hmmm. Your pain is delightful," Gemini said, breathing in deeply. "Even now your bones bleed inside you and your blood is crawling toward your brain. Why…I don't think he's going to live much longer," Gemini taunted as Henry grimaced in pain.

Henry's eyes turned black as darkness overcame him and he lay there tainted, but breathing…for the moment.

"Stop this madness!" Margaret demanded, tears of worry clouding her amber-flecked eyes as she rose from Henry's side. She knew there was nothing she could do for him, and a hatred for Gemini now brewed within her. In that moment she was sad that the angel had sacrificed herself for no reason.

"Sister dear, why not release yourself from this *hell* and add your energy to mine? Ultimately, we can rule together," Gemini invited, ignoring her request.

"Maggie...get out of here! Ann is waiting just outside this room...," Henry muttered, struggling to stay alert as his body began to go into shock.

"Ann? Here?!" Margaret exclaimed, panic overtaking her voice.

"Ah yes...Ann Marie. Yes, I know about your precious daughter," Gemini taunted. "If you don't assist me, I'll simply turn to her. Oh...such innocence yet to be corrupted," Gemini continued, drawing pleasure from the sickening proposal.

Somehow Margaret knew it was Sky's hope that she would use her acceptance that she was no mere mortal to destroy Gemini, rather than judge in his favor and make Thyme ruler of the universe. Thoughts raced inside Margaret's mind as she attempted to think up something quick, but found her grief too powerful, and she allowed herself to shut down.

A whirring noise had begun inside the chamber. As the time turned over to midnight, the bell on the nearby courthouse began to toll the hour. The wind inside the room grew fierce and began to circulate as a full-sized cyclone now, engulfing the dark mist summoned by Thyme.

"My child...read the passage once more!" the voice from the shadows instructed. While barely a shred of humanity remained within Margaret, a new outlook formed in the center of the woman's mind.

"Yessss! With Gemini destroyed, *I* shall reign!!" Margaret snarled, her eyes turning to black again and snapping back and forth between the voice in the shadows and Gemini.

Gemini reared back, preparing to do battle for survival with the human, but the woman cared not, for she knew she held the key to their destruction in her hands. Margaret began to read the scroll again.

"*Suo Haud magis vosmet una...Vos oportet subsisto unus in perpetuum...,*" Margaret began once more, but as she opened her mouth to speak, she found her voice ethereal, and sounding like she spoke from inside a cavern, it echoed loudly.

"Join no more yourselves together.... You must remain alone forever...," the nun's voice began loudly, from the shadows at first before she stepped closer.

"NO! You cannot *do* this!" Gemini screeched, covering its ears.

The atmosphere in the chamber began to quake. The pages in the ledger that lay open upon the altar began to flip wildly in the breeze, until the cyclone grew so strong that the book flew up into the air and circulated about the chamber along with the other loose items atop the altar. Small flickers of lightning began to crawl out of the midst of the bright aura emanating from Gemini. Static charges made Margaret's hair stand on end, and she could feel the intense tingling from the little bolts of lightning. At the final stroke of midnight, the reign of Gemini began to pass over once more for the century, but this time Gemini would remain under Thyme's domination. Since Sky had rescinded her half, Gemini was now complete, and free to rule in the most sinister way imaginable.

Chapter 19

Terrible times were upon the unsuspecting people of the earth, and the atmosphere outside began to reflect the coming change. Massive black clouds swirled overhead, and wild lightning reached out from all corners of Hell. All of nature began to quiver as it sensed the imminent changes, and the earth began to weep. Waves of sleet began to pour downward from the heavens, as the rain met the freezing air and turned the liquid into tiny crystalline shards.

"*Effrego seorsum vestry in prognatus vinculum…Declino Ex quod vos es cupidum…*," Margaret continued, despite the chaos that swirled about the chamber beneath the church.

"Break apart your in-born bond…. Turn away from which you are fond…." The voice became louder, simultaneously rephrasing the lines in English. Though Margaret was curious to learn the identity of who—or what—was behind her, she dared not turn her attention away from Gemini. What had started as a brilliant silver light now burst into an array of deep amethyst, silver, gold, and blue.

The ground below their feet cracked and began to shift about, while swarms of maggots rose up out of the ground. The sound of flies buzzing and wailing shrieks filled the stale, sulfuric air around them. The ground began to vibrate violently now, momentarily throwing Margaret off balance. She knelt briefly to the ground to get her bearings, and noticed her ears had begun to bleed from the piercing, hellish sounds.

"So, you're the one causing problems this time," Thyme said, his voice cold and emotionless.

"You will regret this! You will suffer at the hands of Thyme!" Gemini growled, its shadowy form beginning to solidify; it was apparent that Thyme had become the dominate personality, since Sky had cast away her angelic half and joined her brother in the darkness. "For the suffering we endured so shall mankind!" Gemini bellowed, the aura around it growing as brilliant as the sun.

Gemini began to speak again; its words would be the fate of Margaret and the unknown helper. As they spoke, Margaret knew what was happening, but felt she was powerless to stop it. She only knew that no matter what happened around her, she needed to finish the incantation.

***

"*Abicio vestry bus mens…Existo solutus ut vicis nemoque dissolvit…*," Margaret continued, her voice increasingly unearthly in sound.

"Cast aside your merging minds…. Be unbound as time unwinds…," the voice chanted along with Margaret.

Gemini grew enraged, and advanced on Margaret quickly. Without trepidation, Thyme was determined to destroy the woman, since it was obvious she was going to defy him and not succumb to his cause. Nearly complete, the demon Gemini was under Thyme's full command, and struck out at the human with razor sharp claws, sending the woman to her knees.

The edges of the clawed fingers raked across Margaret's chest, putting diagonal slashes through both delicate fabric and soft flesh. At first, white hot pain ripped through the wounds like

247

lightning as blood began to trickle outward, but Margaret tried hard to push past the sharp cries of the wound, and shrieked like a banshee in anger. Gemini paused only a moment, and the second attack would prove to be much worse, but in a completely unthinkable way. The illusions that Thyme could conjure up would cause no physical damage, but he thrived on the thrill that mental anguish alone could provide. Part of his evil soul, the sorrow and angst of others, was just one way he continued his malevolence and kept his roots deep within the bowels of the underworld.

***

Gemini stood before Margaret, a body limp and beaten held in one clawed hand. As Margaret looked closer, she could plainly see the body of her young son held in the grip of the foul creature. The boy's small body dangled like a rag doll as Gemini held him by the throat. A horrifying gurgle and choking sound came from the mouth of Henry Jr., and Margaret screamed as blood began to spray outward as it had when the glass shard sliced his throat in her house.

"Henry!! NOOOO!" Margaret's voice ran dry and her scream was hoarse; she threw out her arms to beg Gemini for anything if it would only stop. It was this single illusion that brought Margaret momentarily out of her altered mental status. But as hard as she tried to remember the swamp witch's words that magic was only what you wanted to see, the horrifying vision before her did not change. Did she long to see her son Henry unharmed, running into her arms from play out in their front yard? Of course. And even as he hung in the clutches of her enemy, her instinct was only to protect her offspring. But it angered her deeply that she was not able to do so.

Thyme's terrible demonic voice simply laughed as the grip tightened on the boy's thin throat. Margaret could not bear to watch as her son was taken from her yet again, even if it was nothing but an illusion. She looked back toward the nun, who'd been all but silent for what seemed like the longest time now, but could not see anyone standing in the shadows. As she looked back at Gemini, she could see that the creature's grasp had snapped the poor boy's neck, and he now slumped lifelessly in the massive hand that held him up.

The intense torment that ripped through Margaret's mind fueled an untapped portion of her brain, and she suddenly began to understand things a little better. Margaret regained her composure as best as she could, and rose once more to her trembling feet. Though the raging winds had not died down around her and debris had begun to cloud the air, she was able to break through the physical effects of her pain, and channeled her own energy forward toward Gemini.

Mimicking Gemini's levitation, Margaret's trim body began to rise off the ground. An aura of gold and ruby light formed all around her, dancing off the grey, stone walls of the chamber, and illuminating the otherwise dim lighting as it spread outward. While the housewife was painfully unaware at first that she was no longer standing on the floor of the chamber, it became quite clear to her in no time that she had just accessed unearthly powers that held a completely unknown range of use. In a brief moment, Margaret surveyed the damage from her new eagle's eye perspective. The crevices in the floor glowed hot with the flow of brilliant ginger red lava; fluffy light gray and white smoke puffs ascended out of the cracks with each cycle as the cyclone spun wildly about. She looked up at Gemini, who appeared quite stunned to see the woman use her powers so quickly. While Margaret had been able to amass a large quantity of energy and suspend herself above the floor, she had not yet discovered the ability to do anything else with her innate power that seemed to be guided by the black opal charged with ancestral spirits.

A ball of garish yellow lightning began to form and crackle

ominously between Gemini's hands, and the being hurled it toward Margaret, but her senses were far too keen at this point, and she easily dodged the energy blast. She whirled quickly around to the back of the being, determined to finish the spell and take her place as a superior to the would-be fallen Gemini.

The missed shot caused the ball of energy to catch the far wall of the chamber on fire. Flames licked longingly at the inner walls and spread outward, looking for anything in its path to consume. The ground began to shake again, this time causing the cracks to quiver violently and split even wider in several places in the floor of the chamber. Splits began to form along the walls and ceiling as well, sending shafts of dust from the floor of the church above raining down upon them.

Margaret began to think about what her next move should be, but before she could complete that thought, Gemini's yellow eyes seemed to glow even brighter, and a wave of energy pushed forward away from the united being's body as it turned with impossible speed toward Margaret's new position. The woman screeched and fell to the floor, covering her head with her hands. Debris flew up with the force of the energy wave as it swept over the ground and rose up several feet. Bits of dust and small pieces of wall and ceiling began to chip off and fall about, scattering over Margaret and the unseen assistant. Even from her position on the floor, she began, for the last time, the final words to the spell.

"*Alieno vestry via verto a caecus oculus…*," she began, but was interrupted.

"Forget your way, turn a blind eye…." The voice stopped.

"See no evil…," Gemini said, suddenly seeming to ignore everything that was going on in the chamber. The aura brightened.

"No…," Margaret said breathlessly, trying her best to shield her eyes from the light.

"Hear no evil…," Gemini continued, reaching out its arms to

250

gather all the energy of the universe to intensify their power. But Thyme and Sky had already merged for all time, and time was running out to banish the demon forever.

"NO!" Margaret cried, frightened of the sight before her. Her eyes began to burn from the intensity of the aura. Deep crevices opened up right by Margaret, and scalding steam rose up from out of the cracks; the sound of wailing and shrieking seemed to come from within.

"God no!" the nun muttered from behind.

"*Infinito profugus Gemini!*" Margaret said, finishing the words on the scroll.

"Eternity banishes Gemini!" the nun's voice echoed.

"Speak no evil!" Gemini finished. The once silver aura of Gemini had completely changed into a swirling mass of shadow. The eyes that once glowed a brilliant yellow now burned with the raging fires of hell. The idea that Sky was still present was now gone, and only the purest form of evil remained. With Gemini's words, Margaret's heart sank. She was not sure who had finished their spell first. The cracks in the ground stopped just underneath where Gemini hovered. A brilliant orange glow illuminated the wispy form of Gemini's shadow as it continued to grow more and more solid in form.

"No longer will I be doomed to a life of limited existence. The Earth will bend to my will! Oh, the nightmarish intentions I have planned for you all…" Gemini trailed off with arrogance.

Margaret and the nun both thought that they had failed, and that Sky had surrendered her life to darkness in vain. Insanity trickled within the laughter of Thyme, but Margaret's new outlook and lust for power took over, further enraging her. The woman noticed that Gemini's form had grown ashy along the outer edges, seeming to break apart at a molecular level. Suddenly the air was still, despite the cyclone still raging through the atmosphere inside the sacred chamber. A howl began in the throat of Gemini, and it was hard to distinguish between that and the wind whipping about. Steam poured upward just as the condemned's hands flailed outward from the lava, reaching, reaching into the night for freedom that would never come. Seconds after the final words of the incantation to banish Gemini were spoken, the figure of Gemini burst into what looked like a giant black dust cloud of flies. The individual particles whirled around in a tempest, the tail of which was being pulled downward into the lava filled chasm.

As the remains of Gemini swirled like water going down the drain in a tub, Margaret and the source of the voice realized both spells had been finished at the same time and perhaps had cancelled each other out. The energy was so pure, it took away three of the most precious gifts humans possess, and Margaret and the nun fell to the ground. Both human's eyes had gone blind from the light, their hearing had been deafened permanently from the incredibly loud explosion of Gemini, and their minds had been warped so badly from the events that had just transpired, they were both no longer able to speak.

Though her senses had been removed from the damage, Margaret wondered if her husband was still alive. She had no way to call out for him or see him, Once Gemini had been banished, the cyclone burned itself out and sent the debris it carried crashing to the floor. The ground in the chamber sealed over, leaving no trace that Hell had come to visit the church. The bright light was gone, and the room was plunged into utter darkness; the torches and candles had long since blown out from the cyclone that stormed the air. The chamber was still as the grave.

***

Amid the darkness and the rubble from the collapsing tunnel walls, a distant voice called out somewhere deep in Henry's mind. Like a slave being instructed to obey, Henry clawed his way through the debris and worked his way through the opening to the chamber, his goal only to find his daughter Ann.

***

The force of the cave-in inside the chamber sent shockwaves quaking through the already unstable passageway where Ann had been anxiously awaiting the return of her parents.

Petrified and alone, Ann rose from her seat on the cold, damp floor of the tunnel's doorway and looked toward the chamber that had just collapsed. Having just watched her parents crushed in falling debris, tears streamed from her already sorrow-reddened eyes. With a sniffle, the young girl took a step toward the sunken chamber doorway, but an enormous blast of pressure and dust hit the girl like an invisible hammer, slamming her back and down onto the tunnel floor. As she tried to recollect the breath that had been knocked out of her lungs, Ann unsteadily rose again to her feet. As the shaking inside the passageway continued beyond the confines of the chamber where Margaret had just died, pieces of the wall began to break apart from somewhere in the darkness above the girl.

The tunnel was nearly pitch black, save for a very faint glow behind her, and Ann quickly began to run toward it as the tunnel itself began to close in around her. As the girl ran, she stumbled upon chunks of the tunnel walls where it had already begun to fall from places ahead of her. Terrified, the newly orphaned girl began to cry even harder, the warm, salty tears blinding her more than the darkness.

Fearing she would not live to see the light of day, she could feel her small body begin to grow tired; her day had not been the best in her short life thus far. As her sides began to ache from spasms in the muscles between her ribs, she began to gasp for air. Suffocation inside the empty, dark tunnel seemed a likely end to Ann Marie Glover at that moment. Ann took a deep breath in and stopped running.

A cold mist, darker than the ebony that surrounded her,

engulfed her. Ann fought breathing in the gritty, putrid air, but was already out of breath and was forced to inhale deeply. The tunnel drew darker as her eyes failed to adjust to the environment around her, and the feeling of oppression sat heavily upon her meek chest. The ground shook violently, making it difficult for the girl to stand, and forced her to continue walking toward the faint glow that seemed so distant despite her advances toward it.

A thunderous boom sounded behind her; something had fallen from the ceiling of the passageway and crashed to the floor. Startled, Ann screamed and did her best to run again. As the girl struggled to catch her breath, a dark figure appeared ahead of her, momentarily blocking what little light there had been inside the tunnel. At first a feeling of familiarity crossed her mind, the image of one of the dancers in a black satin dress from her nightmare twirled around and around. The wet of what felt like ink enveloped her body, and for the moment she felt the ooze of liquid filling her lungs. Barely breathing through the muck, Ann no longer felt apprehensive. Her mind burned with a strange new desire, something she didn't fully understand.

As she neared, the figure of a person took shape, and Ann was not sure if she should be frightened of them or happy to see someone there. An arm stretched out, reaching toward the girl, and Ann instinctively knew they were trying to help her.

***

Another of the elder nuns that lived on the premises had been awakened by the rumbling inside the church's catacombs and had come to investigate. Despite the promise of salvation, as the tunnel finished its collapse just at Ann's heels, the girl screamed as her hand made contact with the warm, soft hand of the older woman who'd come to help. That final moment of the day proved to be far too much for Ann's young mind to process, and the girl fainted dead away in the arms of the nun. Feeling for the child, the old nun scooped the girl into her arthritic arms despite a worn and aching back. Whatever had caused the damage, and however massive the damage was at the end of the catacomb's demise, the nun knew that caring for the girl was her first priority. While the nun had no idea what had actually transpired that night, history had taught her that it could be nothing good.

After a little while, the quaking throughout the cathedral ceased, leaving the rest of the night in a hollow, uneasy veil of silence. With the raging winter winds outside finally having drawn to a close, the nun breathed a sigh of relief. Whatever had been the cause of the unrest inside this house of God had slipped away, perhaps having gone with the bitter winter winds outside.

As brilliant rays of the sun lit the inside of the knave, the elder nun who had rescued the young girl from certain doom had done all she could with the child, and was now seeking the assistance of someone with higher authority to decide what was to be done with her. Ann was resting peacefully stretched out across one of the pews in the front row near the pulpit. The nun had covered the child with a shawl and left the girl to her dreams.

***

Ann stirred when she heard voices nearby but lay still, knowing she wasn't at home in her own bed. As much as the girl wanted to believe all of the events of the night before had only been a terrible nightmare, she knew all too well that it had actually happened. In the course of one day she had lost her entire family.

Whispers floated Ann's way as a man and a woman talked back and forth a moment before footsteps began to come toward her. Startled, Ann sat up quickly and rubbed her eyes. The frightened girl lowered her eyes to the floor and remained silent. The events of the horrible night she'd just survived fresh in her mind, the girl questioned why she was the only one in her family left alive.

The footsteps stopped right in front of Ann, bringing the tops of two sets of shoes into the girl's view as she stared at the floor. Appearing to be in a catatonic state, Ann's pale face, grief-leaden eyes, and strong silence broke the nun's heart to see.

"I'll take it from here," a man's gentle voice said, and he waved the nun off. The nun looked at the girl with sympathetic eyes before nodding to the man and walking away. A tall man loomed over her, and he knelt down beside Ann, looking her over a moment before speaking. "I know you have been through a lot. I don't expect you to talk to me right away, but I'm sure you can hear me," he began softly.

Ann stared blankly at the floor; she could feel herself shutting down to reality, and did not respond to the man in any way.

"I know you lost a great deal last night, but you need not blame yourself. Whatever sins of the past clouded the lives of those you lost were not your fault, and in no way could have been prevented. In time your sorrow and feeling of loss will fade away, and you will understand when the time is right." The man's voice was gentle and soothing. His words were complex for the girl's age, but something about them made Ann look up from the floor and at the man's face.

A look of understanding spread across Ann's face as she realized who was speaking to her. Seeming like a dream, somehow, she understood the truth beyond his spoken words and beyond her years. He reached out his hand toward Ann, and with only a short moment of hesitation she slipped her small hand into his. She had to be sure he wasn't going to hurt her. He rose from his kneeling position in front of her and helped the girl up off of her seat. He led her away from the knave, past the pulpit, toward the back of the cathedral, and looked down at the girl with an awkward smile as they walked. Ann's rattled insides made her feel she'd somehow forgotten to speak, but soon found the courage to try.

"What's going to happen now?" Ann asked, her voice quiet.

"You have a lot to learn. We'd best get started," he answered flatly as he looked her over with corpse-like eyes.

"Are you dead?" Ann inquired, curious.

"You beckoned me back," he replied with a tainted smile.

"Daddy? You won't try to stop me like Momma did, will you?" she questioned.

"Of course not. I will serve as your guardian until you have regained your strength."

"And then?" Ann asked, an unnatural eagerness brewing behind her words.

"All hell's gonna break loose," Henry answered with an insidious laugh.

"Where do we go from here?" the girl asked, looking up at him.

"Home," he answered.

"Home, Daddy?" she asked, her child-like voice so innocent.

"Yes, Thyme, home."

About the Author

H.D. Huddle was born and raised in rural Missouri near the Kansas border. She is the second oldest of five children and comes from a long line of writers and creative minds. As a daydreamer with a curious mind, she began writing in the sixth grade in school and has been writing ever since. By her side is her husband Jim and son Bruce, who are ever-supportive and curious to see what she will come up with next.

A life-long fan of horror and science-fiction, she uses her creativity and experience thinking outside the normal lines to imagine worlds beyond her own. Also a fan of fantasy sword and spell-casting games, monsters, magic, angels, languages and the occult, she weaves the "what-ifs" of life into spell-binding stories that fully engulf the reader's imagination. With emerald eyes that look toward the sky every night and wonders what is out there at the end of the day, she dreams up the next adventure her characters can begin and what enchantment they might find to share with the reader. Fascinated with time, space and alternate possibilities, her mind set is on a wide track to encompass the universe and beyond. Convinced there is no such thing as "coincidence", she always tries to reach past the obvious and look deeper into the meaning of life's little quirks.

www.ingramcontent.com/pod-product-compliance
Lightning Source LLC
Chambersburg PA
CBHW050727180626
46814CB00002B/636